❧ ❧ ❧

Catherine stepped between them. Whatever Janet might still feel towards her, Catherine realized she would not have come to Seal Rock in a police helicopter to express it. This had to be official business. Catherine toyed with a strand of hair, her fingers automatically working it into a braid. She noticed what she was doing and stopped. She knew it reflected her fear.

"Nic Cavanaugh, this is Janet Schilling," she said briskly, then turned slightly, away from Nic, and continued, "Janet, what is it? Why are you here?"

"I need to talk to you."

"Yes," she snapped, exasperated, "so you said. So get on with it."

Janet moved a step closer to Catherine. "The *Valkyrie's* been found."

"What?" Catherine exclaimed. "The *Valkyrie?* How? Where? When?" She felt stunned, the blood draining from her face. To find the boat, after all these years....

❧ ❧ ❧

ROUGH
JUSTICE

CLAIRE YOUMANS

RISING
TIDE
PRESS

Rising Tide Press
5 Kivy Street
Huntington Station, NY 11746
(516) 427-1289

Printed in the United States on acid-free paper.

Publisher's note:
All characters, places and situations in this book are fictitious and any resemblance to persons (living or dead) is purely coincidental.

Publisher's Acknowledgments:
The publisher is grateful for all the support and expertise offered by the members of its editorial board: Bobbi Bauer, Beth Heyn, Hat Edwards, Pat G. and Candy T. Special thanks to Edna G. for believing in us, and to the feminist and gay bookstores for being there.

First printing August, 1996
10 9 8 7 6 5 4 3 2 1

Edited by Beth Heyn
Book cover art: Peggy Mocine

Youmans, Claire 1952-
        Rough Justice/Claire Youmans
                p.cm
ISBN 1-883061-10-5
Library of Congress Catalog Card Number 96-67602

DEDICATION

This book is for everyone who
contributed to its making — you know who you are.

~ 1 ~

Foaming green water tugged at Nic's boots. Her hands, stiff with cold, stung where the salt bit the cracks in her skin, but she couldn't lose her grip on the rail protecting the sailboat's mast. *Wayward* smashed into the sea and another wall of water crashed onto the deck, splashing into Nic's eyes and blinding her.

The seas lifted the stern and rolled beneath the keel. The wind howled in the rigging. Nic scanned the eastern horizon, searching the endless grey for the darker line of land. She breathed a sigh of relief: she saw nothing but endless waves and white foam merging into the stormy sky. Land, hard and unforgiving, on which a boat could smash to bits, was a danger far greater than the storm.

Wayward poised on the top of the swell, then began her giddy slide into the trough. Nic hung on to the mast guard and waited for the next wave to bring her up for another look. *It's getting dark fast,* she thought. *I won't get another look until sunrise.*

Nic had long since lost track of days or dates, but she knew she'd been about five hundred miles out when the storm began to move south. She had been sailing on a roughly northeast course, headed for the Strait of Juan de Fuca and the inside passage from Washington through Canada to Alaska.

When she changed course to get out of the path of the storm, she made what seemed like a prudent decision. She thought she had plenty of sea room. A summer storm, even an early one, shouldn't last long, she'd assured herself— a day, at most, two. But it had lasted longer than that by a full day. Now, Nic admitted to herself, she was frightened. Her safety margin of open water had to be just about gone. If the storm did not abate soon she was going to have to sail right into it.

As she turned to make her way back to the cockpit, a rag of blown foam slapped her across the face. As she reached to wipe it off, she lost her balance and slipped, barking her elbow on a stanchion base. "Damn," she muttered as she gritted her teeth and waited for the pain to subside. Head down against the wind, she began to crawl.

She concentrated on her hands — grip and wait, move and grip. The crawl seemed endless, her path riddled with obstacles. Finally, awkwardly, Nic slid down from the cabin top into the cockpit, switched her safety harness to its cockpit tether, and gave the cockpit a last once-over before going below.

The wheel held secure, lashed amidships. The heavy Manila ropes dragging off the stern might be old-fashioned, but they were still attached and still working. Then, without warning, one of the ties holding the boom secure came undone as she watched. Lunging for it, Nic caught it just as it blew free, re-tied it, then checked the rest of the ties. Finally, she decided, the deck and cockpit were as secure as she could make them.

It seemed to take her hours to lift out the hatchboards, tumble down the companionway, slip out of her safety harness, snap the harness tether to a pad-eye, and replace the hatchboards. She leaned against the hatch, exhausted. *It's just a storm,"* she reminded herself. *"It can't last forever. The point is to survive until it's over.*

Nic lurched forward, grabbing handholds, to the head, where she hung her red foul-weather jacket and pulled off her knee-high blue waterproof boots. She kept on the bib-topped pants that matched the jacket and her heavy wool socks. If she had to go on deck again, she would need to get ready quickly.

Wayward trembled and shook from the force of the seas, and the noise, that peculiar combination of rushing, crashing water and the whistling and roaring of the wind in the rigging, called up visions of disaster. The boots refused to stand up. Nic finally let them fall and clambered aft to the navigation table.

It was now fully dark. She was in 47 degrees of latitude. The June night would be short, about 8 hours between sunset and sunrise, 7 hours or less from last light to first. Though Nic had already decided to wait until daylight to turn into the storm, she leaned over the chart, as if it could somehow reassure her.

Nic's only light came from a waterproof torch, impossible to hold steady in *Wayward's* tumbling. There was no other electricity. Two days before, a wave had broken over the stern, soaking the cabin and shorting out the batteries. The radar, the satellite-activated Global Positioning System and depth-sounder were all useless, as were the lights and engine. The mechanical speed log had torn loose. She couldn't find a position from the sun or the stars if she couldn't see them. *Shit,* she thought. *I might as well pick a position by closing my eyes and pointing.* She was in the Pacific Ocean, somewhere off the state of Washington, about in the middle of the state's coast. But how far off? A hundred miles? Fifty? Five? Forty if all her guesses about boat speed were correct. Forty was enough. At five knots, she'd still be at least ten miles offshore when the first glimmerings of daylight appeared. If the winds had not died down, she'd turn back out to sea and the safety of open water.

"No storm beats me," she barked as she clambered over the leeboard into her sea-berth. A way of life could crumble in your hands, people changed before your very eyes, but a storm — a storm could be endured.

Suddenly the warps' drag vanished. Nic's eyes snapped open. *Wayward* took flight, catapulting Nic over the leeboard. "Holy shit, we're rolling," she screamed into the night, as she tucked her chin and tried to grab the mast. Her body bounced off the lockers like a ball in a pinball machine.

Then *Wayward* crashed into something solid. *Oh, no,* Nic thought, horrified, her heart sinking as she saw water pouring in from a rent in the boat's port quarter bow. The flow diminished as *Wayward* crashed again to starboard. Nic held her breath and watched, but on that side the hull held. Nic gripped the mast while the sea rushed overhead, roaring with the power of the entire Pacific Ocean. "How in the hell am I going to survive this?" she said to herself, her brain racing ahead with plans to do just that.

It felt like it went on for hours, but it could only have lasted minutes. Then the ocean's thunder receded. Nic knew she could not trust her inner ear, her sense of balance inured to continual motion after weeks at sea. *But,* she thought, *I think we've...stopped.*

❧ 2 ❧

Janet Schilling poured Glenfiddich into a heavy crystal glass. She settled into her favorite chair and prepared to enjoy her view of the storm raging outside.

Except for the gas fire flickering in the fireplace, the living room of her first-floor condominium was dark. The whole north wall was glass, its view encompassing the south jetty protecting the Salkum River harbor, the wide slice of ocean forming the harbor mouth, the north jetty, shooting far out into the sea, and the rural shorelands of the state park directly across the harbor. Janet could sometimes see the lights of the city of Charbonneau, across the harbor and upriver from her condominium, which was in the county seat of Salmon Bay. But not tonight.

The storm hid everything except the wild water which dashed against the breakwater not a hundred feet from Janet's chair. She rose and walked over to peer out the sliding glass door. The storm-driven wind roared in from the southwest with such violence that it seemed to assault the glass, peppering it with grapeshot rain. Janet Schilling sighed, content.

The endless rains and violent storms of the western Washington coast never ceased to thrill her. Summer and winter, she loved exploring the lush Olympic Mountains rising in the east, and took a kind of comfort from the inexorable battle between the sea and the land taking place on the ocean beach just steps from her door.

Janet had fallen in love with Sacajawea County when she'd taken a summer job as a clerk in the County Prosecutor's office at the end of her first year in law school. The combination of unspoiled wilderness, high mountains and untamed sea attracted her as nothing had before or since. She felt at home here, as she never had in the parched California foothills where she was born.

A flash of anxiety marred her contentment. She'd just bought a new boat, a Grady-White sportfisher, now moored in the Salmon Bay Boat Basin, just east of her apartment building. White waves crashed against the breakwater, slopping over the top, adding salt water to the puddles left by the rain. Maybe she could see her boat from the lanai, make sure it was riding well. Janet pulled open the sliding glass door, just as a fresh fusillade of water spattered against the glass.

Stepping through the door, she rewrapped her worn plaid wool robe, pulling the belt tight. The ancient wool felt soft against her hands.

Janet pushed her black hair out of her face and looked over the edge of the lanai to the boat basin, but she couldn't see the boat through the driving rain. *Damn,* she thought. Ignoring the rain from which the lanai roof only partly protected her, she turned toward the harbor.

Though the waves breaking against the rocks sent spume and spray flying nearly to her slippered feet, the storm's power was deceptive, she decided. The sea within the breakwater was relatively calm. For a second, she thought about pulling on some clothes and heading over to check the boat anyway, but decided against it. It was already late, and she had to be in court in the morning. As Chief Deputy Prosecuting Attorney for Sacajawea County, she was in court nearly every morning. Shivering, she stepped back from the rail.

This was not the time to get sick, or let her performance slip from too much whiskey or lack of sleep. It was almost time to announce her candidacy for the top job, the elective office of County Prosecuting Attorney, and nothing was as important as that, not even the boat.

Suddenly, she came to attention. To her left, far out between the jetty walls, well outside the roiling bar that stretched across the harbor directly in front of her, something moved. She stepped forward, gripped the rail and stared.

It was at least a mile away — maybe more, huge, white, and racing forward at an incredible speed. It looked, she thought with growing astonishment, like a wave, but it had a rectangular shape unlike that of any sea phenomenon she'd ever seen. It was a moving wall of tumbling water, pushing, not rolling, across the surface of the sea. Spectacular, even awesome, the sight sent a cold finger of fear up the back of her neck. Her breath caught in her throat. The wave shoved something before it.

At first, she saw only a dark patch on the front of the rushing wall of white, but as it raced closer and closer, she saw that the hapless object was a boat. A sudden picture of her own small craft so totally overpowered sent her stomach sinking with fear. From the comparative size of the wave against the jetties, it became clear that the wave's prisoner was not a boat but a ship, scooped up and carried by this terrific force as if it were a bathtub toy. *Not possible,* she thought, as her mind raced ahead to deny the evidence before her eyes. Although the wave surged on at the speed of a running horse, it seemed slow because of the fantastic scale. The detail Janet could make out grew until there could be no more denying what she saw.

The wave came so fast that it wasn't until it was almost upon her that Janet realized this monstrous wall of water was so huge it could overrun the breakwater and carry her building away with the same ease with which it carried the ship. Her mind raced, trying to piece her inadequate knowledge into some kind of rational plan. She should have gone inside, should have closed the door, should have retreated to an inside room away from breaking glass, but she didn't. Whatever was going to happen, she wanted to be a part of it.

As the wave passed the inland end of the north jetty, it reached out into the flat intertidal wetlands of the park, spreading out and diminishing even as it rushed past the last hundred yards of the south jetty.

Gallons of salt water rushed over the jetty, covering the public path with black water and white foam. Waves broke over the seawall, overflowing the condominium's swimming pool. Water poured over the breakwater into the Boat Basin, floats and boats bouncing with the unexpected surge.

Then it was over, and the storm was just a storm again. The wave was gone, and it seemed to Janet that it might never have existed except in her imagination.

But it had left incontrovertible evidence of its passage. Half a mile away, directly in Janet's line of sight, the ship the wave had carried lay awkwardly on its side, stuck on the Salkum River mouth's churning bar.

~ 3 ~

Once the ocean stopped roaring overhead, it took several seconds for Nic to realize that *Wayward* really had come to a stop. Soaked and bruised, she pulled herself up from the puddle of icy water that surrounded her and hauled herself up the companionway ladder. She felt battered and weary, too chilled and exhausted to face more dangers. *If you freeze, you die,* she reminded herself sternly and pulled out the hatchboards.

Climbing out into the cockpit, she saw what had happened and began to laugh. *Wayward* stood high and dry on her full keel, leaning upright against a cliff that rose higher than her masthead. The rain had stopped, but the rocks high above Nic's head still dripped. Miraculously, *Wayward* still carried her mast and boom. Nic reached out and gently stroked the boom to reassure herself it was still there.

It had been a rogue wave, a deadly, unpredictable storm wave that looked like Niagara Falls on the hoof, thundering across the ocean with the speed of a running horse. Nothing else could pick up a boat and deposit her on shore like this. Nic uncleated the remainder of the trysail sheet, rubbing her thumb absently across the abraded end, awed at the force that she'd survived.

Seaward, rocks sheltered the cove where *Wayward* rested. The wave had picked the boat up and carried her right over the top of them. Nic looked over the side. The tide was high. The wave had hurled the boat almost beyond its reach. Even so, Nic wore an incredulous grin as she scrambled over the side of the boat and down to the beach.

No lights, Nic thought. *Doesn't look like anybody lives here.* The sea seemed to crash in all directions. Odds were *Wayward* had crash-landed on an offshore island, Nic decided. That meant she was entirely dependent on her own resources, just like she'd been ever since she'd left Auckland two years before.

Well, she had tools, materials, food, and a supply of fresh water, which, though limited, could be replenished through rainfall. It wasn't a serious problem, if there was nothing wrong with the boat she couldn't fix herself. Danger, self-reliance and hard work were integral parts of ocean sailing.

Nic went forward to examine the hole in *Wayward's* bow. The edge of the surf lapped at her boots as she approached it. Whistling softly, she ran her fingers across the ragged edges. It was bad, but she could fix it...if this was all the damage that had been done to the hull. If the rig would hold up. If she could get the boat floating again.

Nic crossed the beach to perch on a flat rock. Fingers of wind toyed with her cropped blonde-streaked hair. The wind seemed softer on land, gentler, giving no hint of the ferocity it generated out at sea. She lifted her face to it, allowing a sense of reckless exhilaration to sweep through her. She had survived a rogue!

After a few minutes, exhaustion overcame her, but she was still smiling faintly as she climbed back on board. After taking a dry sleeping bag from its waterproof wrappings, she stripped to the skin and fell into the driest berth on board to sleep, dreamlessly, for twelve heavenly hours.

※

High winds and seas persisted even after the storm broke in the early hours of that Tuesday morning, but stars showed through the rents in the clouds tearing across the sky. By noon, the storm was nearly spent. The wind lost its virulence; the chill air warmed in the sun. On *Wayward,* Nic returned to consciousness slowly, increasing in awareness gradually until the absence of motion and the noise of the surf — so unlike that of the open sea — brought her completely awake. She decided to figure her position first, then start working out the repairs. She rolled out of the berth, grimacing at her aches, and pulled on her salt-crusted clothes.

Firing up the propane stove which, thankfully, still worked, and setting coffee on to perk, Nic went searching for her sextant, tidying as she went. Normal sea conditions were rough, but nothing like the night before. Locker latches had failed, books had jumped over rails, and water had splashed everywhere.

Nic finally found her sextant nestled into the curve of her small guitar case. Setting the sextant aside, she picked up the case to examine the guitar.

Her ex's daughters, whom she called her stepchildren, had presented it to her a couple of Christmases ago. Because they'd given it to her after she and Rita had split, Nic treasured it as a sign of their continuing love for her. She loved both girls as much as if she'd borne them, and missed them dreadfully. She stroked the wood, strummed softly, adjusted the tuning, then strummed again. Carefully, she returned the guitar to its case. Things couldn't be all bad when she still had her guitar and she could smell coffee perking.

Nic hurried to turn off the stove. She took her coffee and navigation equipment on deck. Her jaw dropped. A stark white column rose high above her on the headland opposite *Wayward.* A lighthouse! A grin spread across her handsome face. Half her problems were solved right there.

She'd seen no light the night before, so there wasn't a current keeper, but someone might come to the island regularly to maintain the building. There might be a radio, and something — a name over the door, a painted number — to give her an exact position she could find on her charts.

She gulped her coffee, jumped over the side of the boat, and strode across the beach. In the cleft between two grassy banks, she spotted a path. It was barely visible, a slender line obscured by the untrammeled grasses waving above it. She jogged up it. All of a sudden, she realized she wanted company desperately.

A row of stunted evergreens guarded the brow of the hill, protecting a small garden from the prevailing southwest winds. Nic heaved a sigh of relief. Someone lived on the island.

The lighthouse stood on the northwest promontory of the island, all but its base exposed to the winds. Beyond the garden, the land fell off steeply. A circle of subsidiary islets dotted the eastern sea. Gulls circled above them, screeching. Far beyond, clouds stretched north to south, caught by the top of a mountain range. It was all Nic could see of the mainland.

The base of the lighthouse tower was a small, rectangular building. Its white stucco walls gleamed in the sunlight. On the south side, under a little overhang, was a door. Nic made for it. The red trim around the windows looked fresh and clean. Snowy curtains hung at the windows. She knocked briskly on the plank door.

For several minutes, there was no response. She knocked again, louder. Then, from the corner of her eye, Nic saw a curtain twitch. She waited, shifting impatiently. Then she heard the rattle of a chain. The door opened to the six-inch crack the chain allowed. Nic turned on one of her better smiles and opened her mouth.

"What are you doing here?" the woman said before Nic could speak. "This is a private island, a wildlife refuge. It's posted. There's no trespassing."

"I'm not here by choice," Nic retorted, stung. "My boat's grounded on the beach down there."

The woman cocked her head, giving Nic a glimpse of a heart-shaped face and a narrow mouth. She pursed her lips and regarded Nic with a pair of huge brown eyes. Hair so dark a brown it was almost black flowed past her shoulders. A single streak of grey sprang back from her forehead. Her tanned skin was smooth except for tiny sun-wrinkles around the eyes. *Somewhere around forty, give or take,* Nic thought. Close to Nic's own age.

"How long will you need to be here?" The woman's tone was still guarded, but no longer sharp.

"There's a fair amount of damage to the boat, including a hole in the hull. I can fix that. The biggest problem's going to be floating her. There will be big high tides near the summer solstice, and that'll be the best chance."

The woman nodded. "A week, then, more or less." She looked Nic up and down, her nose wrinkling slightly. "I suppose you need things."

"I could use fresh water," Nic said, matching the woman's businesslike tone, "if there's any to spare. Wood to build a cradle. I'd gladly pay for what I use."

"That's not necessary," the woman said, the corners of her mouth softening. "There's a freshwater tap by the garden." She pointed to it with her chin. "Water's scarce here. Don't waste it. There's a woodpile behind the house. If you don't need to take the wood with you, put it back."

"All right," Nic said. "Thank you."

But the woman had already shut the door.

She must be alone here, Nic thought as she sorted through the woodpile. She set aside some boards which looked like they'd once been part of a house. The woman couldn't live on this island year round, Nic decided. In winter, the island would be cut off by storms for weeks at a stretch. She shifted a two-by-four to the growing pile. The house had been systematically disassembled, Nic noted. It had probably stood where the garden now grew, its water system now reduced to a tap for the garden hose. It was more interesting to speculate about the woman. Why was she living on this island? Why didn't she run the lighthouse?

People who lived alone with nature intrigued Nic. All the ones she'd met before were solitary cruisers like herself, almost all of them men. But this was a woman living on an offshore island. Nic wanted to know more. But that would come later. Now she had to begin the arduous task of hauling the wood down to the beach.

It took several hours. By the time she finished, the tendons in her arms and legs burned like red-hot wires. Sweat dripped from her lank hair despite the cool breeze. Shoving her hair back out of her eyes, she wrinkled her nose, realizing she smelled. Weeks of water-sparing added up, as did the days of the storm. She wanted, no, she *coveted* a bath. With access to fresh water, she could have a really good one. She made a final trip up to the plateau to fill the Sunshower. Setting the heavy vinyl bag on a flat beach rock to heat, she started to work.

First she hauled her tools out of their locker near the quarter-cabin's engine room access. Then she strapped on a canvas tool belt and started loading it up. And when she caught sight of herself in the vanity mirror, she snorted with laughter.

Her short, brown-streaked-blonde hair hung in filthy strings. It looked like she'd hacked it off with a rigging knife. Salt foam had dried in the outside corners of her hazel eyes. Normally slender and wiry, with well-defined muscles, after the four-week ocean passage she was gaunt. Her cheeks had shrunk, making her face look like a naked skull. The jeans and T-shirt she wore were so encrusted with salt, not to mention dirt, that they could probably walk on their own. To her own eyes, she looked like an escapee from an asylum.

Grinning ruefully at her own appearance she thought, *It's surprising the woman opened her door at all to a stranger looking like me.*

≈ 4 ≈

Through a crack in the bedroom curtain, Catherine Adams watched the stranger sort through the wood-pile. *People don't just come to Seal Rock*, she thought. *Not without an invitation. I had a right to be startled. I was shocked — scared.* But on reflection, the woman looked OK. Catherine was sorry she'd been rude, but at least it bought her some time to size up the situation.

Though ragged and none too clean, the stranger had seemed to radiate an inner strength and self-reliance which Catherine found attractive. Once she'd nearly been destroyed through other people's selfishness and arrogance. She'd never fully recovered. Life had taught her that strength was not necessarily arrogance. Self-reliance was not necessarily selfishness. "At least I know the difference," Catherine thought aloud. "It's taken me long enough to learn." In recent years, she'd been trying to cultivate both those qualities in herself, and admired them in others.

Catherine watched as the stranger sorted through the woodpile. She was not as tall as Catherine herself — slender, fair, with fine-drawn features. Her soft contralto voice held a vaguely British accent. She had spoken only of herself, in the singular, so apparently this stranger had set off alone to cross the open ocean. To want to do that, Catherine figured, you'd have to have a yen for adventure and change. To succeed at it,

you'd have to be confident — both of your skills and of your
ability to live life on your own terms, by your own rules.

If I could, Catherine thought, *that would be the kind of
woman I would choose.*

Catherine flashed back to the night before the stranger's
arrival. The rogue wave had wakened her when it crashed against
the lighthouse tower sometime during the middle of the night.
Big seas didn't frighten her. She felt secure in this lighthouse
built to resist whatever the sea could hurl against it.

She'd huddled in her bed, feeling snug and protected.
She was safe on the island. No one could hurt her there.

Catherine had come to the island several years earlier,
and ended up staying, of her own choice. She relished its beauty
and accepted its limitations as well. Having decided that close
personal relationships of any kind were to be avoided, she accepted the fact that a solitary life was her only alternative.

Catherine watched as the stranger filled a Sunshower,
which she hauled back down the hill with an ease that belied
its weight. The woman didn't return.

She turned back to her computer and tried to concentrate on the paper she was writing. It didn't work. *She's going to
be here for a while,* Catherine thought. *Guess I need to know more
about her.* Turning off her computer, she slipped out of the
lighthouse, crept up the slope of the plateau, and lay in the tall
grass to watch the woman work.

The boat was a sailboat, well up on the beach, leaning
against the cliff. Catherine saw a gash in the forward quarter,
about a foot above the waterline. She saw a scar on the mast
where something had torn away, and one of the wires that held
the mast down was broken, springing away into invisibility from
the crosspiece. A heavy rope, still tethered to the stern, wound
round the mast like ticker tape. On the stern, block letters read
" *Wayward, Auckland.*" That explained the stranger's accent.

Catherine scanned the high-water mark on the cliff and
compared it with the waterline of the boat. *It will be touch and*

go getting the boat off the beach, she thought, *even at the extra-high tides that will come with next week's summer solstice.*

The woman finished working the brace she'd built under the sailboat's bow. Catherine smiled at the stranger's obvious satisfaction as she stood back to admire her work. Then she glanced at her watch, grabbed the Sunshower, slung it onto the foredeck, and climbed up after it. She rigged the Sunshower from a halyard, and went below decks.

Catherine knew she ought to leave. She had seen enough to form an impression of the stranger, enough to verify her story. Then the woman reappeared through the forward hatch. She tossed her towel on the deck and pulled the shower nozzle open. Water gushed forth to wash the dirt, salt and sweat away.

Catherine's stomach clenched. She yanked at the neck of her T-shirt as she found it hard to breathe. Her hands ached with a sudden need to touch. Someone, anyone, but particularly the slender woman with the all-over tan and rawhide muscles. It was out of the question, Catherine told herself. She tightened her fists until her nails bit into her palms.

But I can't lock myself in the lighthouse until she leaves, Catherine thought desperately as she tried to clamp a lid on this sudden surge of long-repressed feeling. *I've got to be friendly, but I can't let her get too close. No matter how much I want her to. There's no point in thinking about what I can't have.*

Nonetheless, she stayed and watched.

~ 5 ~

"Ben wants you, Janet," Maud Fleming said when Janet returned to her office from court that Tuesday morning. "It's about the ship on the bar."

Janet Schilling, looking and feeling magnificent in a navy Chanel suit, paused while grabbing her messages from the corner of her secretary's desk.

"On my way," Janet said. Quickly, she scribbled notes on most of the messages. Maud could handle those. The ship she'd seen catapulted onto the harbor bar the night before was the prime topic of courthouse conversation this morning. It was a pretty good guess it would be the County Prosecuting Attorney's, too. But why would he want to talk to her about it? She paused in her writing and thought about the bar.

The Salkum River flowed into the Pacific Ocean between the communities of Charbonneau and Salmon Bay. The delta formed a wide, deep natural harbor. The forces of the inflowing tide and the outflowing river resulted in a wide bar of silt and sand building up near the harbor mouth. Even though there was a deeper channel partially protected by the jetties and scoured by the river's continuing flow in the center, the bar — and it was always called just that, "the bar," in reverential tones — was relatively shallow even there.

Because it was so shallow, and the inflow and outflow met there so abruptly, the bar was always rough and dangerous, the seas steep, with breaking crests. Only the most experienced or foolish skippers crossed the bar at any time other than the high-tide slack, and that included captains of ships. Proofs of its danger were the many sunken vessels that littered the bar every year. Though the Coast Guard made many miraculous recoveries, people died on the bar every year.

Janet shrugged as her thoughts shifted to Ben. Anything that happened in the harbor interested virtually everybody in the county. Ben knew where she lived; he probably just wanted a firsthand report of last night's events.

She pocketed a few of her messages, and handed the rest to Maud. "Here," she said. "These are your department." Heels clicking on the linoleum, she headed down the hall. The easiest way to find out what Ben wanted was to ask.

County Prosecutor Ben Davidson looked up in greeting as Janet tapped on the open door of his corner office. "Morning, Janet. I've been waiting for you to get out of court. I wanted to talk to you about the ship."

"I thought so," Janet replied as she came in and sat down. "I saw the whole thing from my front window."

Ben nodded. "I hoped you had. The Coast Guard rescued the crew last night, of course. Now the owners are taking the cargo off, then they're going to use tugs to haul the ship off the bar."

Janet waited. Ben was nearer seventy than sixty, small and physically tough. He had strong, distinguished features, topped by thick white hair, a little long, worn combed back. His courtroom manner was oratorical. Not much had changed about him since he had first hired her as a summer law clerk sixteen years ago. He had been her mentor and friend ever since.

"One of the boats taking off the cargo had engine trouble around nine this morning," Ben said. "When the crew anchored to fix it, the anchor snagged something. The divers had a look. They found a sunken purse seiner. They don't know which one, yet. You know we lose a fishing boat or two almost every year, but here's the weird thing — the divers found most of a skeleton in the cabin."

"Just the one?" Janet leaned forward in her chair, feeling her muscles tense with excitement as the adrenaline started to flow. Her mind raced ahead. Only a single skeleton, when those large fishing boats normally carried crews? That could mean a homicide.

Homicides of any kind were uncommon in this quiet coastal county. Most were solved immediately, many even reported by the shocked and tearful perpetrator, and disposed of through a guilty plea. And murder trials, with their life-and-death issues, were even more rare. But when they came, they were the peaks in a prosecutor's career, showcasing the lawyer's abilities in front of the public.

Janet loved all the big cases. Anything to do with the elaborate game of litigation law excited her. As Chief Deputy Prosecuting Attorney, she assigned all trial work. But she kept the big ones, especially the homicide trials, for herself. She hoped this skeleton would turn out to be another peak for her, before she left litigation for the largely administrative and political role of the elective office of County Prosecutor.

"There's only one set of bones so far," Ben told her, smiling at Janet's reaction. "Homicide and Marine are out there now." He gestured at the office's wraparound windows. Janet could see the police boats circling the salvage operations. "You'll want to get involved in the investigation," he went on. "Pretend you're a cop, not a prosecutor. Do more than take formal statements, answer legal questions, and file warrant applications."

"I could change and run out there in my boat, or radio out and have them pick me up the next time they come in," Janet suggested eagerly.

"Do it. I already asked Wallace if she could cover your afternoon Omnibus calendar. She can."

Senior Criminal Deputy Tamara Wallace was Janet's immediate subordinate in the Criminal Law Division. Janet nodded but didn't get up. Ben had raised his index finger, so he had more to say.

"Remember, you announce for Prosecutor a week from Friday," Ben said. "A body recovered on the bar is newsworthy. A homicide is newsworthy. You need all the publicity you can get." It was no surprise to anyone that Ben wanted Janet to succeed him when he retired. What was surprising was that she had serious opposition.

"Ed Halliday's been in the papers a lot, lately," Janet responded thoughtfully, naming the state legislator who planned to run against her in the fall elections. "You think I can use this to get the press to pay attention to me."

Ben nodded and looked at Janet, allowing concern to cross his expressive face. "Janet, you're an excellent prosecutor, a fine administrator. The right person for the job. But you don't have Halliday's kind of popular base. You don't have kids in the schools, you don't belong to a church, you don't have a wife to take an active role in community affairs, and when you're not up in the mountains or out fishing, you run off to Seattle to do God knows what. Lawyers know you and like you, and law enforcement likes you — except for Chief Daniels — but the average person around here doesn't know who you are. Not the way they know Halliday."

"My record's no secret. What else do they need to know?" Janet couldn't help sounding defensive. Chief Daniels puzzled her. He seemed to think he could tell her how to do her job and control the Prosecutor's office from the office of the Chief of Police. That wasn't how the system worked and Daniels ought to know it. The independence of the Prosecutor was an essential check, guaranteeing fair and impartial law enforcement. She brushed consideration of Daniels away. He was a never-ending annoyance. However, name recognition among the general public did worry her. Prosecutors didn't get the kind of press legislators could command. "Halliday's been in the Legislature so long, I doubt if he remembers how to practice law," she added dryly.

"Halliday's practical experience may not matter to the average voter," Ben countered. Lacing his hands behind his head, he leaned back in the custom-built brown leather chair. "At least they've heard his name recently. At least they know where he stands on issues, and don't tell me issues are irrelevant."

"The law's the law. If Halliday doesn't like it, he can do a lot more to change it from the Legislature than he can from this office." Janet was firm on that point.

"I agree. But that's not as important to him as getting where he wants to go."

At least I'm out of the closet, Janet thought, staring at the wrecked ship. *Even if I was kicked out.*

Several years before, when Gloria had left her so spectacularly and tried to blackmail her into a one-sided property settlement, Janet, following Ben's guidance, had stood firm and let her sue. With a shiver of distaste, Janet remembered how awful it was when the suit was filed. She'd hated to go out in public, even to go to work. Finally, after she'd spent several uncomfortable months of feeling herself the object of gossip and speculation, the lawsuit was settled. By then, Janet's lifestyle was an accepted fact of life in the community. Ben had been right, and Janet was grateful.

While she still had to endure what she called the five-minute double-take every once in a while, she no longer had to worry about living a double life. Her confidence — and her ambitions — had soared after that. With a sigh, she thought, *At least, that's not going to give me any political trouble. Unless it's the only thing anybody remembers.*

Janet nodded, slowly, as she tapped a well-polished nail on the desk. She thought she knew what Ben was talking about. "I've got the track record, but he's got the name value," she ventured.

"That's the idea," Ben said. "Run with it."

"I can get the name value, while there's no way he can build up his track record," she said thoughtfully.

"That's right. To get publicity, you need a vehicle, a reason to get your name in the papers." Ben used the rich voice and theatrical gestures that formed part of his courtroom arsenal. "They'll tell their grandchildren and their great-grandchildren about the Giant Wave and the Great June Storm."

"Finding this body plays right into that," Janet said, smiling. "The repercussions from the wave will carry through all summer and right up to the election. That part of it is news, and it's going to stay news. But the investigation could stall out."

Ben raised his eyebrows. "What if it does? Remember the Santos case?"

"The one in Seattle? When the U.S. Attorney did that big investigation into 'organized crime ties to crack,' and threatened to RICO everybody in sight?" Janet asked. She drew circles on the desk with her fingertip.

"That's the one," Ben said, smiling. "Remember the outcome?"

"There wasn't one. It fizzled out. They finally charged some small-timer from Chicago with possession. I think he got probation." She sneered.

"But while it was happening, the media couldn't get enough, right?"

"The Assistant U.S. Attorney handling it quit right in the middle of it." Janet remembered. She began tapping the desk again. Her nail polish was a bluish red that went well with her pale skin. She was careful about sun protection, but her skin neither burned nor tanned. "Didn't he go to some plum job in the Justice Department?"

"He did. And that investigation played a major part in getting him that job."

"You're saying it doesn't matter if the investigation doesn't get results." Janet frowned. She liked results.

"It doesn't. Not in this context. It's not your fault if the cops screw up the evidence or the court turns the bastards loose. But you can use the investigation to get your name out in front of the people who've never heard of you. Use it to make your speeches to the voter in the street. Anything connected with the Wave is news, and not just in Sacajawea County. Everybody in western Washington loves storms, so it's a great filler when there isn't a hell of a lot else going on."

"Halliday won't have any way to counteract it," she went on, excitement building as she realized how useful this potential homicide could be to her election bid. "How much I can do with it depends on how far the investigation goes." That still worried her. What if it wasn't a homicide at all? Or if cause of death were inconclusive? But then she looked at Ben, and detected a narrowing in the older man's left eye. "There's more, isn't there, Ben? What are you holding back?"

The Prosecuting Attorney nodded, and a wintry smile formed at the corners of his mouth. "You can play this one right up to the election in November, Janet. I got a call from Chief Daniels not long before you came in. The Marine division radioed in for assistance. Homicide's not just out there as a precaution. Every through-hull they've found on that seiner was deliberately broken open."

Janet echoed Ben's grim smile. Through-hull fittings allowed sea water to come into a boat for engine cooling and domestic use, and then flow out again. If they were broken, the water would come in freely...until the boat finally sank. One broken through-hull could be an accident. If they were all broken, someone had deliberately scuttled that seiner.

Rising swiftly, Janet reached across the desk for the file Ben held out to her and said, "I'll tell Wallace I'm going, then I'll get out there immediately."

~ 6 ~

It feels so good to be clean, Nic Cavanaugh thought as she settled gratefully on a rock in the late-afternoon sun, leaned against the cliff which sheltered *Wayward,* and ran her fingers through hair still damp from her shower. She picked up the running letter she was writing to her stepdaughters. Emily was twelve; Anne had just turned ten. Nic wrote to them often, sending the cumulative letter off at the end of passages or once a week when she was in port. Though she never gave up hope of having one or both of them join her for a passage, until now she'd only been able to have them visit when she was safely in port. Rita, their mother, hated the ocean, got sick and frightened in the swells of the open sea. That was part of the reason for their split, though not the only one.

Nic clicked her pen and began with a bare, factual recital of the storm, leaving out the worst bits, and ending with a description of the rogue wave and the crash into the island. She maximized the adventure while minimizing the danger, and emphasized that she had everything she needed and repairs were well in hand.

That sounds tame enough, she thought with satisfaction. She didn't want to add to Rita's collection of fears. After all, Nic's contact with the girls was totally at Rita's discretion. She felt a wave of resentment at the law that denied her enforceable legal rights. And since they had two living parents, Nic couldn't even legally adopt the girls until they were adults and it became a

matter solely between her and them, in which no one else had
a say. "Now," she wrote, "I'm going to see if I can't make a
friend of the woman who lives in the lighthouse."

                            ☀

"Want to come in to shore with me?" Janet Schilling
shouted above the roar of her Grady-White's engines as she
prepared to cast off from the Harbor Patrol boat to which her
boat was rafted. "It's getting close to five."

"Not yet," Homicide Detective Ed Nuñez hollered back
from the deck of the Harbor Patrol boat, which was anchored
over the wrecked seiner. "I'll come in with Marine. But I'll
stop by the Oyster Bar later, if you want to have a drink."

"OK," Janet yelled. "I'll see you there. Want to get that
stern line?"

Ed nodded. Janet went forward to collect the bow line,
reaching across to take it from a Marine officer and lead it aft
so it wouldn't foul in the props. In the cockpit once more, she
took the stern line from Ed, then she sat behind the wheel.

Janet had never known anything to match the thrill of
speeding across an open stretch of water, hull bashing the waves
where it touched down, the engine's thunder left behind, as
though she traveled faster than sound.

Sun glinted off the rippled surface of the water. It would
have been a perfect day to stay out on the boat, she thought,
maybe even cross the bar to brave the swells of the open ocean,
turn off the engines to drift and fish and enjoy an entirely different, bone-deep kind of thrill. Not this afternoon, though.
In a notebook on the table inside the small cabin she had written the numbers which would be the first break in her possible
homicide case. She had to get to a phone as quickly as possible,
a secure land-line, not a cellular or a radio link.

Throttling down to the required no-wake speed as she
approached the breakwater, Janet slid the boat perfectly into

its slip. She switched off the engines, pleased at her growing expertise, then jumped to the dock to secure the mooring lines.

She glanced at her watch. No time to change her jeans and polo shirt for a suit. No need, either. Everyone would be gone by the time she reached her office. But in Alaska, the time was two hours earlier, so she could make the call today. The sooner the better.

We need to move fast, she thought. This was hardly a fresh kill, but even in an older case, the first few days were crucial. If this was a murder, someone, somewhere was culpable. Someone, somewhere was assuming safety. When the seiner's identity was publicized, that someone would hear about it, and begin to worry, perhaps take steps to cover long-forgotten traces. *If we move quickly,* she thought, *we might get them before they can destroy the evidence we need to make a case.*

Janet grabbed the notebook from the cabin, locked the boat and headed for the courthouse.

☀

Tuesday evening, Nic rooted through a locker in *Wayward's* aft cabin, searching for a bottle of wine among her dwindling stores. There was one bottle of a good white left. She set it aside.

Nic had dressed up — well, sort of — in tan chinos, a bright Hawaiian shirt, and tan sandals with deck soles. She dug through her small collection of jewelry to find a pair of Polynesian shell earrings and a matching necklace, which she put on. *I almost look respectable,* she thought with a grin as she straightened her collar. If she could manage it, she wanted to make a friend of the lighthouse woman. Nic didn't like to admit it, even to herself, but she was lonely.

☀

Catherine twisted her long hair into a French braid, tying the end off with a covered band that matched her dark blue T-shirt. She'd stuck a salmon in the oven to bake; now she stepped back into the kitchen and opened the oven door to check it. It looked good and smelled better. She planned to get some salad greens from the garden, then walk down to the grounded boat and ask the stranger to dinner. *I owe her an apology,* she thought as she picked up the colander. *I had no business being so rude.*

☀

Nic carried her bottle of wine up the path, admiring the wild beauty of the island as she walked. When she came to the crest of the hill, she stopped. The woman had left the lighthouse and was in the garden. She sat back on the heels of her worn Keds among lettuce plants, picking individual leaves. A snatch of melody reached Nic's ears. She didn't seem to notice Nic was there.

"Hello?" Nic said softly.

The woman jumped, startled, nearly tumbling backwards, but regained her footing quickly to come to her feet. Nic extended the bottle of wine.

"I come bearing gifts. I think I owe you an apology."

"That's really not necessary." Catherine walked over to look at the bottle.

"I saw myself in the mirror," Nic said chuckling, "and I scared myself. I don't think I would have opened the door to me at all, the way I looked."

"I *was* startled," Catherine admitted. "Nobody ever just shows up and knocks on my door. But I didn't have to be so rude. I'm sorry." She took the wine from Nic's hands. "Thank you. Come and drink it with me."

"I'd like that. I'm Nic Cavanaugh."

Catherine dusted her free hand on the seat of her jeans and extended it. "Catherine Adams. Welcome to Seal Rock."

Nic fell into step beside her as Catherine led the way to the lighthouse, wine in one hand, colander in the other.

"Where are you from?" Catherine asked tentatively.

"My last stop was Hawaii," Nic answered, "but I'm originally from Auckland. I'm sailing to Alaska, via the inside passage. Normally you'd sail north from Hawaii and take the passage from north to south, but I have friends in Seattle I want to see before they leave for the summer," she elaborated.

"You're doing this by yourself? In a sailboat?"

"By myself," Nic mocked, with a good-humored grin, "in a sailboat." She glanced sidelong at Catherine, to see if she would laugh. Catherine was taller than she was. Her frame was large and square, her face, in profile, flat, though a smile twitched her wide mouth. Nic was pleased to see Catherine had appreciated her humor.

Catherine pushed open the lighthouse door with her hip and motioned Nic inside with a quick jerk of her head.

"You don't run the lighthouse," Nic said, "or I would have been at your door last night, right after I piled up on your island."

Catherine set the wine on a coffee table in front of a massive wood-framed couch. Two matching chairs, end tables, and floor lamps completed the living-room grouping which stood in front of a huge stone fireplace fitted with a convection heater. Catherine stepped through a doorway before replying. Her voice came to Nic over kitchen clatter. "No, it's decommissioned. The Coast Guard decided it was confusing to the ships trying to find the lights on the jetties at Charbonneau." She emerged with a tray holding glasses and a corkscrew. "Please. Sit down." She set the tray on the coffee table next to the wine, indicating the couch with a nod.

Nic sat and looked around. The tower rose on the seaward side of the building. The ground floor, Nic decided, had probably been the lighthouse office and shop when the dismantled keeper's house still stood. The partition walls forming the rooms of Catherine's home were, Nic could see, recent additions. Apparently, she lived alone out here. *Why?* Nic wondered. "What do you do, out here in the middle of the ocean?" she asked curiously.

"Marine biology." Catherine inserted the corkscrew. "Ornithology, too. I follow the breeding and migration patterns of the birds and marine mammals as part of a continuing study for the University." She pulled the cork out and poured.

"Which one?" Nic asked dryly. "Once I found out this island was inhabited, I didn't bother to figure out my exact position. Not when there was someone to ask."

"The University of Washington. You're off the coast of the state of Washington. Welcome to America." She passed Nic a glass, which Nic raised in salute.

"Come look at my charts." Catherine got up, indicating a section of the north wall, where she had pinned up a number of different nautical charts.

"I have this one," Nic said, pointing out the large-scale ocean chart. "Where are we on this?"

"Nowhere," Catherine said, laughing. "The island's too small. Try this one." She ran her finger down the shoreline depicted on a coastal chart, and stopped at a point a third of the way down. "You"— she tapped a speck — "are here."

"My coastal charts start up here, at Cape Flattery. I thought I was further south. I guess I got a bit off course."

"You sure did." Catherine returned to the couch. "How did that happen?"

"Just lucky, I guess."

"Seriously."

She's a little flip for someone who managed to ground her boat on an island within sight of the mainland, Catherine thought. Of course, the Kiwi accent didn't help. Somehow, it lent everything she said an air of lazy amusement.

Nic pointed at a spot on the big ocean chart. "I was out about here when that storm began to move. I was right in the track, so I turned off to run before, then I got pooped getting the main off, and lost all my electronics. I couldn't get a celestial fix, but I knew I was getting close to shore. I didn't know how close."

"You mind telling me what all that means? I've been around boats — fishing boats, mainly — all my life, but it's still going over my head."

Suddenly Nic felt awkward. Sailors talked a different language. She should have remembered that.

"Here's the storm," she touched a point on the wall. "And here was I, heading this way. The storm started moving towards me. If I'd kept on going the way I was, I would have run right into the middle of it, and been in it far too long. So I turned this way," she pointed, "to get out of it as quickly as possible, which put the wind behind me." She turned to look at Catherine. "One of the things you don't want to happen is for waves to break over the stern of the boat. There are things you can do to prevent it, but they don't always work." Nic shrugged. "So a wave broke over the stern and dumped a lot of water on board. That buggered the batteries and with them, the engine and the electronics. I don't need the electronics to know where I am, as long as I can see the sun or the stars, but I couldn't see either because of the clouds, so all I could do was guess." Nic shrugged again and grinned. "I guessed wrong. What are we, fifteen miles or so from the coast?"

"A little less." Catherine leaned over to point out the scale on the chart. Nic might be flip, Catherine thought, but it sounded like she knew what she was doing. Maybe it wasn't the accent that made her seem that way, she thought. Maybe it was the Puckish grin. She couldn't resist smiling back.

Nic rested one elbow against the bare white wall and leaned against it. "If the rogue hadn't dumped me here, I would have been on the mainland beach before morning. Did it hit up here?"

Catherine nodded. "Woke me up. I felt the tower shake. It's hard to believe you survived it." She refilled her own glass, then held out the bottle to Nic in invitation. Nic sat down beside Catherine and let her pour more wine.

"What I think happened, quite seriously," Nic said, "is that I did get lucky. *Wayward* — my boat — bounced back and forth between your cliffs, got a hole in her bow and popped an upper shroud, but that's all the damage I've found so far."

"That doesn't sound too good," Catherine said dubiously.

"It's not," Nic replied. "It's better than it could have been, anyway. I have what I need to fix it on hand."

"But you're grounded. Can you get the boat off the beach?" Catherine knew she sounded worried, and she was. Having Nic on the island too long could be dangerous. She was a very attractive woman.

"I have kedging gear," Nic said confidently. "Most cruising boats carry equipment to haul themselves off coral reefs. There's no reason it shouldn't work just as well getting me off a beach. I hope." She raised her eyebrows and smiled. "But you must have a boat, yourself. Don't you? How do you get to the mainland?"

"Oh, I have a boat," Catherine told her. "But it's a just a small one. A Boston Whaler Outrage. It's designed for ocean sport fishing. I use it around the islands here. And to run into town if I need to, but only when the weather's good. Charbonneau and Salmon Bay are the nearest towns. They're about seventeen miles away, across the bar, on either side of the Salkum River harbor. You can see them on the chart." She pointed in the general direction of the wall.

Nic nodded. She'd seen them. "Where do you moor your boat?"

"There's a little harbor on the other side of the island. It's just a cleft in the rocks with some pilings and a float. It's exposed to the swells, though. So I haul the boat on shore with davits most of the time, and the float takes its chances."

A buzzer sounded in the kitchen. Catherine got up.

"That's dinner," she said. "Want to stay?"

~ 7 ~

As soon as Janet got back to her office late that Tuesday afternoon, she called Directory Assistance. She jotted the number on her pad and quickly punched phone buttons. Once connected, she asked for what she wanted. The clerk put her on hold. She tapped her fingers on her desk impatiently while she waited. Senior Criminal Deputy Tamara Wallace appeared at the door of her office just as the clerk came back on the line. Janet held up a finger as she spoke into the phone.

"Yes," she said, "I'm here. Uh-huh. Got it. That was the last year? No subsequent renewals under that name? Good enough. Thank you." She hung up and grinned at her subordinate, waving her to a chair.

"The fishing boat?" Wallace asked as she sat down. She liked her boss. The intense curiosity and devotion to the game of litigation law they shared gave her more in common with the tall, elegant woman sitting across the desk than she had with almost anybody else in the world.

But Janet Schilling was also tough, controlling and temperamental, and Wallace was glad she seemed to be in a relatively good mood. Janet wasn't going to like what she'd come to say. *Better let her get her news out first,* Wallace thought.

"That was the Alaska Department of Fisheries," Janet told her. "The divers brought up a limited entry salmon-fishing permit." She waved her notes at Wallace as she went on. "It was still stuck to the seiner's windshield. I just called in the number. It belongs to a seiner called *Valkyrie*, owner Glen J. Lowry, Charbonneau."

"So you have a probable ID."

"More than that. Lowry was a pretty important fellow. You wouldn't remember. You hadn't moved here yet. Lowry was president of *Salmon Forever* — the commercial fisheries conservation group. He vanished, with his boat, one spring night about four years ago. He was supposed to be heading up to Alaska, but never picked up his crew." She tapped a nail on the desk. "There was a lot of publicity at the time, but when no trace turned up, it was presumed he was lost at sea."

"But he wasn't."

"Looks like he didn't get out of the bay. And the boat's through-hulls being broken open, well..."

"Do you think you have a murder case?" Murders excited Wallace. Janet had assigned her a few, but she hadn't yet had one that had gone to trial.

"We don't know yet, Wallace. We can suspect all we want, but if we can't prove cause of death, we don't have squat. Richards or no Richards."

Wallace leaned forward in her chair. "Richards. That's the case the Attorney General's office brought after the County refused to prosecute. They got a murder conviction without producing a body, right?"

"That's the one."

"But they found bloodstains all over the defendant's house, right? And there was other physical evidence, even a confession to a third party. And the Supreme Court said the jury could reasonably conclude that the victim was dead, by homicidal violence, at the hands of the defendant."

"You got it," Janet said. "But if we have remains and can't show cause of death, I seriously doubt if we have a murder case, even if we can prove conclusively who scuttled the boat." She shifted her gaze to window, where the police boat was just starting to move towards its dock. "It's still good for some press, though."

Wallace wasn't interested in that aspect of it. It was the legal question that interested her. "You're saying the defendant could tell any old story, and the jury would be forced to accept it. All we could argue would be speculation. But we have to prove a case beyond a reasonable doubt to get a conviction."

"Very good." Janet turned back to Tamara Wallace, smiling her approval. She blew several strands of soft black hair off her face. She wore it medium length, pushed back from her face. Being wavy, it looked professionally styled with virtually no effort on her part beyond getting an expert to cut it, but the right side did have a tendency to fall into her eyes. "That's the kind of judgment call I want you to learn to make. You don't file cases you can't win. So what would you charge?"

"With those facts? It depends on the defendant's story."

"Of course it does." That was a good answer, Janet thought. She wanted to push the younger lawyer. Wallace had a good brain and good trial skills. While she loved the game, she retained her passion for justice. That made her a natural prosecutor. "So," Janet went on, "what do you do?"

"Question a lot. Negotiate with the lawyer. Charge before hearing the story only if I have to. Then cut a deal. Probably for manslaughter."

"Excellent." Tamara caught on fast. If Janet split her Chief Deputy's job into Civil and Criminal Divisions when she became Prosecutor, Tamara could handle the Criminal side with minimal guidance.

"Janet, speaking of deals, the public defender in that auto theft you gave me wants to plead to joyriding." Wallace didn't have the authority to make the deal she wanted to make without her boss's approval.

"In that one, we've got the case," Janet objected. "Dealing when you have an open-and-shut case isn't something we do in this office."

"This time there are reasons," Wallace countered. "The kid's a first-time offender. He's only nineteen and wasn't acting alone. The other two are being tried as juveniles, but one of them has a sheet as long as my arm. I hate to stick this kid with a felony jacket when I'm positive he wasn't the instigator, and the others get off as juvies. The kid with the sheet didn't quite meet the criteria for us to ask that he be tried as an adult, but I'd like to make the motion. You'd have to sign that, too."

Janet reviewed her memory of the file quickly. Wallace was right. It was an appropriate deal, and moving for a decline of juvenile jurisdiction on the ringleader was a good idea. She waved a dismissive hand. "Sounds right. Do what you want."

This potential homicide must be awfully important if she's leaving policy decisions to me, Wallace thought. "OK," she said firmly, "I will. But I want to know something. How does a purse seiner work?"

"That's right," Janet said. "You probably wouldn't know. OK. They're fifty to sixty feet long and carry a small skiff that's maybe twelve to fifteen feet long. There's a house in front, where the crew lives and where you drive. The back deck is open. There's a huge winch there that holds the net. The mother boat lets out the net. The skiff tows the net in a circle around a school of fish, bringing the end back to the seiner. The bottom of the net is cinched closed, forming a bag. Then the whole thing is winched in."

"A bag," Wallace said thoughtfully. "Oh, sure. A bag. A purse. Purse seiner. I get it."

"I don't," Janet said, turning to look out the window at the police boat, which was just pulling into its slip. "Far as I know, the *Valkyrie's* skiff hasn't been found, and that's strange."

⚓

Nic looked around the main room of the lighthouse while Catherine, having refused an offer of assistance, finished preparations for their dinner.

The lighthouse tower rose in the middle of the western wall. A staircase wound upward out of sight. The stairs contin-ued down to some kind of cellar, but the way was blocked by a padlocked plank door at the foot of the tower. The kitchen was partially open to the long main room. Beyond it was a utility room. Nic could hear the rumble of a generator and see the round cylinders of propane tanks. The modern bathroom backed onto the kitchen, with a large bedroom in the northeast corner. The remaining corner held a combination dining area and art studio. A canvas stood on an easel, covered with a sheet. *That's odd,* Nic thought. *She paints, but there isn't a single painting hanging anywhere.* She glanced at the kitchen, but Catherine was out of sight. Feeling slightly guilty, she lifted the sheet off the painting.

This is good, Nic thought. As a painter, Catherine was technically competent, surrealistic in style. A train station sat isolated in a desert landscape. Tracks rose from the station. A tiny train rushed toward a domed city suspended in the sky. In the right foreground, a two-faced, four-armed woman reached longingly for the station, while her other face supervised her remaining arms in binding herself to a stake with lengths of her own black hair. Nic let the sheet fall back over the canvas and went back to the couch. The painting disturbed her. She wondered what it meant to Catherine.

Catherine came out of the kitchen with a tray just as Nic reached the couch. Nic went to help her set the table.

"Do you live out here all year?" Nic asked as they sat down.

"Yes. Let me give you some salmon." Catherine opened the foil wrapping the fish. It smelled of lemon and dill.

"How do you get supplies? Propane for the generator, gas for your boat?" Nic added salad to her plate as Catherine served herself with salmon.

"The University sends a supply boat quarterly. Gas, propane, food, paper, journals, books. Anything I want. I have a grant from them for the studies I do. And when other researchers come out, they bring things, too." She took salad for herself, then pressed her baked potato until it burst. "If there's anything I need, I can go into Charbonneau whenever I want to, as long as the weather's decent. And I think I mentioned, I grew up in commercial fishing. I still know a lot of people who fish. They'll stop by if I radio in and ask them to. They can go out in worse weather than I can. It's not quite as easy as living on shore, but I don't lack for anything. As long as I remember to order it."

Nic regarded the woman across from her thoughtfully. Catherine's explanation had been a little too complete, she thought, as she toyed with her fork. Certainly there was one thing she obviously lacked. "Aren't you lonely?" Nic asked softly.

"Not really." Catherine took a bite of salad. "There's a lot going on out here. The sea lions and birds have their own societies. It's fascinating. There just aren't too many humans. Except in spring and summer quarters. Graduate students come, mostly, learning field work. They follow me around for a week or two, see what I do. Other researchers come out to collect or verify data. Sometimes there are too many people. I think I like it best here when it's just me and the animals and birds." She paused to take a forkful of salad. "What about you? It seems to me you're alone more than I am."

"Maybe I am." Catherine was right. Nic spent a lot of time alone, but she rarely felt lonely. "But it's like what you said," she went on. "There's a lot going on out in the ocean. Birds. Fish. Dolphins. Whales. Just not too many humans." Nic grinned. "I see humans when I'm in port. Or when I crash on somebody's island." She ducked her head and watched Catherine's reaction while she took a bite of salmon.

Catherine laughed. "I doubt if that happens very often."

"This is the first time," Nic admitted. She felt an instant rapport with Catherine's description of her solitary life. Here at last was someone who could understand her own passion for the open sea.

"Have you ever sailed?" Nic asked.

"No," Catherine replied. "I've only been out on power boats."

"At sea?" Nic cocked her head. "Out of sight of land?"

"A few times." Catherine smiled. "On research vessels." She laid down her fork and gazed off into the distance. "I liked it. A lot."

"Gets in your blood, I think," Nic said firmly. "Once I'd been at sea, I couldn't give it up."

"You say that like there was someone trying to make you."

"Well," Nic said, giving Catherine a sidelong glance again. *I might as well get it over with,* she thought. *See how she reacts.*

"There was. I had a partner," Nic said aloud. "She wouldn't go."

"That's sad," Catherine said, keeping her expression appropriately sympathetic. Inwardly, her heart leapt and her stomach fell all at once as she felt a rush of confusing and contradictory emotions.

"It was, really." Nic pushed back her chair and leaned back. "I felt like she wanted me to stay the same as I'd been when we met. She didn't like it when I started studying naval architecture. She liked it even less when I built the boat. She started putting more and more time into her business. Eventually, it consumed her. She didn't even have time for the kids, much less me. When the girls went away to school, it seemed like there was nothing left between us. The boat was ready, so I chucked it all and went sailing."

Nic watched Catherine through narrowed eyes. Over the last few years, she'd just about resigned herself to being alone — at least until she swallowed the anchor and permanently moved back ashore. But Catherine seemed to understand the major forces that drove her: love of new experiences and her love of the sea.

"How many children did you have?" Catherine asked.

"Two. Girls. They're Rita's by birth, but they come to me as often as I can arrange it. She's pretty good about letting their dad and me split their holidays. Unfortunately, she won't let me take them to sea, but they'll be of age soon enough."

"They're not in college?" Catherine was surprised and curious.

"No, not yet. Not for a few years. I know it's not done so much in America, but at home a lot of children go away for school."

"I went away to school," Catherine said with a faraway look on her face. "I couldn't go home, but I lived with a family." She turned to Nic and smiled. "It was a good experience. They were wonderful to me. I dated their son all through high school, until I figured out I'd rather be dating his sister." She laughed. "Jimmy's one of the people who brings me supplies. We're all still friends."

Nic wondered why Catherine couldn't go home. Maybe the school was too far away, or money was a problem. Before she could ask, Catherine spoke again.

"You said you studied naval architecture. What did you do before that?"

"Regular architecture." Nic laughed. She couldn't believe the fortune that had led her to this island, to this woman, who just might be someone with whom she could share the cruising life she loved. A friend, anyway, she amended hastily — her feelings were developing awfully fast — who didn't think her life bizarre.

"If I never see another shopping center or apartment complex again, it will be too soon," Nic continued. "Boats are much more fun." She took a sip of her wine, then asked, "What exactly do you do? How did you come to live on this island?"

"I got it back." Catherine pushed her plate away. Her grin was mischievous. "I went to the University of Washington in Seattle and got my degree in Marine Biology and Fisheries Management. Then I came home and went to work in the Tribal Salmon Hatchery."

"Does that mean you're American Indian?" Nic pushed her empty plate away, and leaned forward. The culture, art and civilization developed by the Coast Salish peoples and the tribes who lived north of Vancouver Island were cited in all the cruising guides as major highlights of cruising in the Pacific Northwest.

"Yes. Can't you see it? No, maybe you can't. You're not from around here. I'm only a quarter-blood, anyway, but I'm a member of the Salkum Indian Nation. That's how I got the island." Catherine smiled, gesturing to encompass the view from the lighthouse windows.

"When the government started developing lights on this part of the coast, they wanted to put a lighthouse here," she went on. "This was tribal land, traditional hunting and fishing grounds. The lease was made out in my great-grandfather's name, as if he owned the island himself, which of course he didn't. The government paid for the lease when it was signed, and the tribe used the money to build a school. When the Coast Guard decommissioned the lighthouse, it came to me." Catherine got up and began clearing the table. Nic rose, too, and picked up the salmon platter and the salad bowl. "It'll go to the tribe when I die, of course," Catherine said. "I've made sure of that."

"Let me wash up," Nic said when they reached the kitchen, "since you cooked."

"OK," Catherine said, passing over the plates. She smiled. She liked having Nic here. She just liked the *company.* "Get a grip, girl," she told herself. "Don't want what you can't have."

"What did getting the island have to do with the University?" Nic asked.

Catherine leaned against the refrigerator, watching Nic's swift, economical movements with pleasure as she rinsed the dishes and put them in the dishwasher. *Must come from living on a boat,* she thought.

"It's a research opportunity like nothing else on the coast," Catherine said aloud. "The lighthouse had been automated for years. No humans lived here, so the birds and animals could live in a virtually natural environment. Yet because of the lighthouse, there was a place for a researcher to live and work."

She loves living out here as much as I love being on a boat, Nic thought as she wiped off the stove. Nic felt a pang of longing. She did love her life, and she wasn't about to change it, but meeting Catherine made her realize how much she wanted to share it with someone who understood.

"I realized I could live here with the birds and the animals," Catherine said, warming to her subject and using her hands to emphasize her words. "I could see how they lived in the wild over a long period of time. I could do studies; write papers and articles for journals. I made grant applications. One of them was to the University of Washington. I got several grants, but the University also offered me a job as a field researcher attached to the Department of Fisheries research laboratory in Charbonneau. I do my own studies, and I gather data for other researchers. All I have to do is live here and do what I want to do."

"You love it here." Nic smiled at the sparkle in Catherine's eyes.

"I do." Catherine could say that honestly. She loved the island and loved her work, but that wasn't the only reason she was here.

Nic stepped forward, and reached out to touch Catherine's cheek with the tips of her fingers. "I'm glad I landed here."

Catherine jumped sideways, knocking Nic's hand away with her own. "Don't do that," she cried.

Nic dropped her hands to her side, confused. Catherine's reaction seemed all out of proportion to her gentle gesture. "I'm sorry," she said. "I didn't mean to upset you. I guess I'd better go. Thank you for dinner."

∾ 8 ∾

Wednesday morning, the day after the wrecked fishing boat and its grisly cargo had been discovered, Janet arrived at her office early.

She'd had a late night Tuesday, her excitement over the Lowry case leading her to stay out well past her normal bedtime. She'd started by meeting Ed Nuñez at the Oyster Bar as they'd arranged. The two friends finished the evening at a poker game over in Charbonneau at the Salkum Tribal Casino, where Janet had won over five hundred dollars and Ed a little more. As poker players, they were pretty well matched, and usually both ended up winners no matter where they played. In other kinds of gambling, Janet had found, they only won consistently when they played together. This was something they'd often discussed while sipping beer and pretending to fish off the stern of Janet's Grady-White, without coming to any definite conclusion.

The exhilaration she felt carried over to the morning. She had awakened at six-thirty, as usual, worked out, showered, and had breakfast at the Main Cafe. Today's suit was silk, woven in a navy and ivory tweed. The jacket was worn buttoned, the waist circled by a slim navy belt. Janet's ivory blouse had French cuffs held closed by platinum cufflinks engraved with her initials. Her earrings were large gold and silver knots. A Paloma Picasso necklace of kisses in gold and silver filled the neckline of the blouse. The pleated trousers flowed down to break over the instep of her navy Farragamo heels. Janet loved feeling elegant.

Most of the attorneys wouldn't be in until nine, but here and there, as she walked down the hall to her office, Janet saw signs of early-bird industry. Her secretary, Maud Fleming, like all the support staff, had been at her desk since eight.

"Just a minute, Doctor," Maud was saying, "here she comes now." Maud hit the hold button. "It's the Medical Examiner, Janet. He's already called twice."

"Put him through. And would you bring me some coffee, please?"

At her desk, Janet picked up the phone. "Yes, Jim?"

"Out on the town again, Janet? There wasn't any answer on your home line."

"I must have turned it off." She didn't apologize. Jim Knighton, the Medical Examiner, frequently worked at night, and thought nothing of calling anyone he wanted to talk to at any hour. Especially, she sometimes thought, her.

"What have you got?" she asked.

"Just a confirmed ID on the seiner skeleton."

"Lowry?"

"It's him. Since we had a probable ID, I called dentists until I found the one he used. She went in last night to check her files, brought the X-rays over to me, and we got a match. She can positively identify her work. All the details are in my report."

"Great. Did you get an address for Lowry?"

"Yep. Want it?"

Jim sounds pleased with himself, Janet thought. She wondered what else he had for her.

"Please." She wrote the address down then asked, "What else have you found?"

Jim Knighton laughed genially. "Janet, I can't keep anything from you."

Janet occasionally wondered if the divorced pathologist's phone games weren't a childish way of attracting her attention. If so, it didn't work. She waited, silently, until the Medical Examiner continued, his tone now brisk and businesslike.

"This is the meat of it," he said. "We have an unusual situation here. When a body is left in the open, whether it's a natural death or a homicide, predator action results in a natural scattering of the bones in a predictable manner. A variation in the pattern is one of the ways we can tell if a body has been disturbed."

Janet knew that. She tapped her silver Tiffany pen impatiently on her pad. Jim Knighton continued.

"This body was in a confined space. Though we had predator action to strip the skeleton, the predators were small ones, mostly crabs. They couldn't scatter the bones, and they didn't pull the skeleton apart. So there's more of it than we'd normally get, and it's in better shape. Ossified cartilage, for example. Cartilage gets hard as a person ages. It's always more fragile than bone, so it's unusual to find it complete and undamaged by predator action. But in this case, because of where the body was, the cricoid cartilage — that's the Adam's apple — is remarkably well preserved."

"Go on," Janet said, doodling triangles on her pad. Jim always liked to lead up to his findings with more background than she needed outside of court, but he wouldn't give her his findings without it, no matter how hard she pushed, so she'd long ago given up and let him do it his own way.

"The markings on the cricoid are unmistakable. Lowry's throat was cut."

Janet winced. That was nasty. "So we have a murder," she said, hardly able to conceal the excitement she felt.

"That's what I'd call it. My report's being typed. I'll send it over when it's complete."

"Do Taylor and Nuñez know this yet?"

"Not yet. I have calls in to them, too, but the homicide team is out at the wreck with the Marine Division divers."

"Hold the identification information, will you please? We need to locate the next of kin, and we don't want them finding out from the papers or the tube. That's why we haven't released the name of the boat yet. Did you get any information on Lowry's family?"

"No. I asked the dentist, but all she knew was that his wife had died a year or so before he did."

"OK. We'll track them down. If Ed or Mick calls you back, ask them to get in touch with me."

"Your wish is my command," the pathologist said.

"Thanks, Jim," Janet said, smiling as she ended the call. She punched the intercom button. "Maud, get Nuñez and Taylor in here as soon as possible."

At the same time that Janet had placed her breakfast order in the Main Cafe that cloudy morning, Nic stepped out of her bunk aboard *Wayward* right into a puddle of water.

"Shit," she muttered, sloshing through the cabin to the manual bilge pump. Where did *this* come from? She bent down and tasted it. It was fresh, not salt.

"Damn it." She leaned over to try the freshwater pump on the galley sink. Nothing. Air. "At least it's not another hull leak," she thought as she reached for the handle of the bilge pump and began pumping.

After repairing the hose that had come loose, Nic dug out two five-gallon collapsible plastic jugs from the cockpit locker. She carried a manual desalinator in her emergency kit, but hauling fresh water would take less time than making it. The tide was coming in, which meant she'd have to carry the jugs up the side of the cliff to get them onto the boat. Nic hated any situation which required action before coffee. She threw the jugs onto the beach and jumped off the boat to begin slogging up the hill to the freshwater tap.

Catherine poured herself a cup of coffee from her automatic drip pot. She took it out the front door of the lighthouse to see how cold it was outside and if the clouds looked like they might burn off later. *I wouldn't bet on it clearing up,* she thought. The low clouds had a dense and permanent look about them. *Better take a jacket to the cliff.* Today she planned to film the behaviors of the juvenile sea lions. She was looking forward to their antics, and didn't want to be distracted or have to come in early. She was just about to turn and go inside to get dressed when Nic's blonde head appeared over the top of the hill.

Nic looked bedraggled, with a cowlick sticking up from the top of her head. The Madras plaid shirt she wore tucked into her jeans had the sleeves rolled up. Catherine instinctively stepped forward to meet her, then quickly ducked back into the house, torn between her need to keep her distance and her desire to make a friend of this woman from the other side of the world.

I've got to get her off the island fast, Catherine told herself. *She'll get her boat fixed sooner and leave faster if I help her do it.* Even as she heard herself say it, she knew she wasn't being completely honest with herself. But here was Nic, carrying plastic jugs, and walking toward the garden water tap, head bowed, muttering words Catherine couldn't hear.

"What are you up to?" Catherine called tentatively.

"Hauling water," Nic answered, envying the steaming cup in Catherine's hand. "My freshwater system sprang a leak."

"Can you fix it?" Catherine asked. *She has to have fresh water,* Catherine thought. *She can't get further than Charbonneau or Salmon Bay without fresh water. She could be around for weeks. I don't think I could take it.*

"Already did," Nic replied.

"Do you want some coffee?" Catherine asked, relieved. If Nic would be gone in a week or so, she could risk being friendly.

"Please." Nic turned off the freshwater tap, leaving one jug only half full, and followed Catherine into the lighthouse, where she gratefully accepted a cup of coffee.

With a second cup of coffee sitting on the round oak table before her, and the smell of soy sausage sizzling under the broiler in the kitchen where Catherine, now wearing jeans and a light blue sweater, cooked, Nic felt content. She could get used to this. Even if all Catherine was interested in was friendship.

"Scrambled or fried?" Catherine stuck her head out of the kitchen.

"Whatever you like." Nic still thought Catherine had overreacted the night before. All she'd done was touch her cheek. She wanted to ask her about it, but Catherine didn't seem willing to give her an opening.

"Scrambled, then," Catherine said as she disappeared. When Nic went for a refill of coffee, Catherine was just spooning the eggs onto plates. Nic picked up one of them, and helped herself to sausage.

"I'll get that," Catherine said.

"Let me help." Nic smiled as she carried a plate into the dining room.

"Do the dishes, then," Catherine suggested as she followed.

All in all, Nic thought, it was a companionable breakfast. But Catherine still wouldn't give her an opening. Nic didn't like forcing issues, but she knew she'd have to. She needed to get this straight between them.

After breakfast, Nic cleared the table. The size of the sink and the abundance of hot water cheered her. She liked any job with a beginning, an end, and a concrete result. She began to whistle as she washed. Catherine put the jam in the refrigerator, and shook her head.

"I should hire you," she said. "I've never seen anybody so happy about doing breakfast dishes."

"Try doing them on a boat sometime. Much harder." She turned from the sink and wiped her hands on her jeans. "Listen, Catherine. I didn't mean to upset you last night."

Catherine shook her head. When she spoke, the words came with great effort. "You weren't out of line. It's me. I'm not comfortable with closeness, and I get jumpy when people touch me. I'm sorry."

Nic cocked her head at Catherine. The taller woman had withdrawn into herself, standing with her head bowed and shoulders slumped as if she expected to endure some kind of violent reaction from Nic.

"You don't have to be sorry," Nic said gently. "You're you and that's the way you are. It's fine with me. All you have to do is say 'no.'"

"I *am* sorry, though," Catherine said softly.

"Nothing to be sorry for." Nic turned back to the dishes. "You want to come down to the boat for lunch?"

"I was going to use up that salmon," Catherine objected in her normal brisk tones. Nic was willing to accept her as she was, and that was something Catherine wanted to think about.

"Bring sandwiches, then. One o'clock?"

"All right."

"As long as I'm here, let's join forces," Nic said. "I'll wash up if you cook, but I'd like to pay for the food, too."

"Half," Catherine rejoined quickly, too quickly, because immediately she realized she'd agreed to see Nic three times a day. That was more contact than she felt she could handle and still keep the relationship at the level of easy friendship that felt safe to her.

"Bargain," Nic said, and grinned. "I'll see you at one, then." She felt very pleased with herself as she dried off the dishes. Nic wanted to stroke Catherine's long, dark hair, and caress her thin, strong hands, yes. But she also simply wanted to tell her sea stories and show off her boat to someone who would understand, and who had sea stories and an island to show off in return. Being a perennial pragmatist, Nic would take what she could get.

Catherine had admitted that there was something in her, in her past, perhaps, that made her resistant to any kind of intimacy, but Nic had managed to create a chance to overcome that resistance — three times a day.

With a wave to Nic, Catherine left quickly, hurrying toward the viewing shelter on the cliff where her equipment was stored. She worried about her tenuous self-control that seemed to be failing her. The more she knew Nic, the more she liked her. And as she twisted her long braid between her fingers, Catherine realized she was afraid. Of Nic, a little, but mostly of herself. There wasn't anything she could think of to do about it except acknowledge her fear and go on as she'd planned. And be careful.

⚓

It was after ten before Maud buzzed Janet to let her know the homicide detectives had arrived.

"Send them right in," Janet said.

Mick Taylor, massive and phlegmatic, his shirt buttons straining to hold across the belly that hung over his trousers, led the way. Ed Nuñez, almost theatrically handsome in a navy blazer and sharply creased grey slacks, followed, bearing a large cardboard carton. He held it out to Janet, who didn't take it. Mick was notorious for practical jokes, and he had a willing co-conspirator in Ed. Either the box would be extremely heavy or it would fall apart at the bottom if not held a certain way, spilling its contents all over her suit. Janet wasn't going to fall for that. With a cagey smile, she indicated the desk top with a nod, and waited until the carton was on her desk and the detectives seated before speaking.

"How's your head?" Ed asked her, winking.

"How's yours?" she retorted with a grin. "Mine's great. I just talked to Knighton. He's got a positive ID on the skeleton. It's Lowry, all right. And Jim says his throat was cut. It's a homicide."

Ed's smile turned grim. Mick sighed heavily. Neither could avoid thinking about the last terrible moments of Lowry's life, the sharp pain and the spurting blood.

"We've been assuming it was him," Mick said after a minute. "He lived out on the bay on the Charbonneau side."

"Is this the address?" Janet turned the pad on which she had written the Medical Examiner's information so that the detectives could see it.

"That's it," Mick said. "Lowry kept the *Valkyrie* there. There's a sixty-foot float at the end of a good-sized dock."

"We looked through the papers to see what was reported when Lowry vanished four years ago," Ed continued. "It wasn't much that's any good to us. Prominent fisherman presumed lost at sea. Lots of testimonials. That kind of stuff. Of course, there wasn't a formal missing-persons report filed. With the boat gone, it was pretty obvious he wasn't missing like somebody who just disappears. But we did get a courtesy copy of the Coast Guard's overdue-vessel report and the results of their investigation."

"What does it say?" Janet asked. She'd read it later. Right now, Ed could fill her in on the important parts faster than she could read.

"Lowry was reported missing by Frank Vincent of Charbonneau on March 29th. Lowry was supposed to have picked Vincent up on the 28th to head out fishing, but he never turned up. Vincent tried to reach Lowry over the phone and the radio, went out to his house and found Lowry's car in the garage, the boat gone and nobody home. Vincent checked with the neighbors. The boat had been gone and Lowry hadn't been seen for about twelve days before Vincent reported the boat overdue." Ed smoothed the lapels of his jacket and crossed his legs. He went on.

"Vincent said Lowry would have taken on fuel before leaving for Alaska. He usually went into Hole in the Wall, that little harbor on the Reservation, to buy untaxed diesel off the truck and in barrels, cheap, rather than buying it in Charbonneau." Ed shrugged. "I guess it's worth the trouble if you're fueling a big boat to go to Alaska."

"It's illegal as hell," Janet said, "if you're not an Indian. But there's not a lot of risk to it. There's no real enforcement. It's not our jurisdiction, and the Coast Guard has better things to do."

"Yeah. The Indians don't sell to just anybody, either. The fuel dock owner liked Lowry because of *Salmon Forever*. So the Salkums asked around and found out nobody had seen him up there, either. There was a cold front moving through when he was last seen. The bar was pretty rough and there were good-sized swells out in the ocean. Since the Coast Guard hadn't gotten any distress calls, it was presumed he headed out to Hole in the Wall by himself, something went wrong and he went down. Lost at sea. That's how the file was closed."

"What did Lowry's family say?" Janet said, not looking up from her notes.

"There wasn't any to speak of," Mick said. "Just a stepdaughter, and she hadn't heard anything from him either."

"Is that who we'll notify now?" she asked Mick.

"Yes," Ed said. "Her name is Catherine Adams."

Suddenly, Janet felt her face contort as a wave of disorientation swept over her. Catherine Adams. There couldn't be two women by that name. Not in a county this size. She caught a strange look passing over Ed Nuñez's face. Ed would remember, too. She pulled herself together quickly.

"What's the address?" she asked, above the sound of her pounding heart.

"1224 Church Street, Apartment 3, Salmon Bay."

Janet copied it down as Ed said it, though she knew it wasn't current. It *was* Catherine. She hadn't forgotten the address. She could still recite Catherine's phone numbers, at work and at home. She wrote them both on the pad, neatly, under the address, even though she knew Ed was watching.

"That's out of date, Janet. We checked, and she doesn't have a phone or electric service in the county. Not in her name, anyway." Mick said. "We'll have to track her down. We've got somebody calling the Department of Licensing."

Janet wanted to tell them nobody was going to talk to Catherine Adams but her. She'd loved that woman, damn it. It was the first chance she'd had at a relationship since Gloria left. Then Catherine had broken it off. No reason, nothing.

"There's more," Ed interjected quickly. Janet realized that some of what she was feeling must show on her face. She steeled herself to listen. Ed nodded to Mick. "You tell her," he said. They both knew Mick had worked on a seiner as a teenager.

"OK. You know how seiners work? There's the big boat, and there's a skiff. The skiffs are double-hulled aluminum inboards."

"Yeah." Janet tapped her silver pen impatiently.

"Sometimes the seiners tow the skiffs, but not real often," Mick continued. "Mostly they hook them onto a boat boom and haul them up on the stern of the big boat. That's how they're designed. It's safer not to tow something in the ocean. They don't sink, but if they fill up, it's a hell of a lot of drag. That's dangerous. Lot of drag even if they're empty. Uses more fuel and you go slower than if you had it on deck."

"And? Spit it out, Mick." Janet started tapping with her pen again.

"The *Valkyrie's* skiff is missing. The divers looked all over down there. It's not hooked up to the boat, and it's nowhere around on the bottom. There's no report of one being found around that time. Since everybody knew a seiner was missing, you'd think anybody who found one would have reported it."

Janet nodded. "I wondered about that, but I forgot to say anything to Ed last night. The killer had to get away from the seiner somehow. That's the obvious way." She felt empty, not even able to get excited about searching for the missing skiff. She kept thinking about Catherine. Janet had kept after her, wanting some kind of explanation. Finally, Catherine had vanished. Moved, left her job. She was simply gone. And Janet had at least found enough pride to keep from illicitly using her official resources to trace someone who would go to those lengths to lose her. If Catherine clearly wanted it over between them, she'd finally had to accept it.

"We're going to start a trace on that skiff," Mick continued. "Sometimes they're marked, sometimes they're not. That kind of boat doesn't have any other use outside of seining, though. We'll turn it up."

Janet nodded. "Go to it. What's in the box?" she asked.

"The broken through-hulls," Ed said. "We're going to take them to the evidence room, then we'll start working on the skiff. We've got people working on tracking down Adams, like I said. We'll let you know what we find."

"Good," Janet said. She swiveled her chair to look out the window before the detectives were out her office door.

Janet's emotions were so overwhelming she didn't know where to start feeling them. She was angry, sad, disappointed, hurt — all over again. She gripped the arms of her high-backed executive chair, her face expressionless. Except for the whiteness of her knuckles where she held the chair, she was motionless. After all this time, she still felt her relationship with Catherine was unfinished business. Now she had a legitimate reason for finding her. If she could locate Catherine, maybe they could finally talk. Maybe they could even have a second chance.

She hoped Catherine hadn't left the county. She might have moved to Seattle, to Aberdeen, or even to Alaska. But Janet doubted it. Catherine had left Sacajawea County once, but she'd come back. Janet remembered how passionate Catherine had been about her love for this place and its people. It was one of the things they had shared.

Abruptly, Janet stood up and hurried across the hall to the County Clerk's office. She wanted to find Catherine before the detectives did. Who broke bad news was decided on a case-by-case basis in Sacajawea County. The population was small. People knew each other. Sometimes it was better to get bad news from a friend than from a stranger, sometimes not. Sometimes someone on the ME's staff seemed most appropriate. Sometimes a police officer or a prosecutor did. It depended on the case. But if Janet found Catherine first, she could make sure she was the one who told her about the recovery of Glen Lowry's body.

Janet checked the computer indices for any court files related to Glen Lowry. There was a probate file, she discovered. It had been established to get him declared dead. Without evidence, it can take years to establish a presumption of death. With the evidence Ed had outlined for her, the court had entered the order quickly. Everybody in the county knew that if a fisherman and his boat both vanished in dubious weather, there was a single, near-certain conclusion.

The insurance companies hadn't contested the determination. Glen Lowry's fate seemed clear. They'd paid off on both Glen Lowry and the *Valkyrie* without a fight. Alice Miller Lowry, Glen Lowry's wife, had been the designated beneficiary, but she had died before he did. The insurance proceeds had passed to Alice's daughter, Catherine Beatrice Adams, under that obscure section of probate law that allows a stepchild to inherit when there are no other near relatives.

The estate had been handled by Henry Charm, a prominent local lawyer with a civil practice. Catherine had used Henry's office address in the file. Henry, Janet knew, wouldn't disclose Catherine's address without knowing exactly why Janet wanted to talk to her. And then the best she'd get from him would be an offer to break the news himself and arrange a meeting if it was necessary. Like most lawyers, Henry guarded his clients like a well-trained Rottweiler. And since legally Catherine wasn't a person of interest, let alone a suspect, there was no way she could be forced to talk to, or even see, anybody.

Janet went downstairs to the Assessor's office. Looking up Catherine's name in the indices, she found that Catherine owned a large chunk of property in Charbonneau, the address for part of which matched Glen Lowry's, and something known as Seal Rock. The legal description made no sense. Quickly, Janet flipped through the map books until she found the page. She knew the place. It was a cluster of offshore islands with a lighthouse on top of one. She often fished nearby. But knowing what Catherine owned didn't get Janet any closer to finding her. All property tax statements were sent care of United Bank and Trust, rather than to Catherine, personally.

She knew the bank wouldn't give out Catherine's address without a court order. The Salkum Tribal Office should know where she was. But Mick and Ed could get the address from the tribe easier than she could. They could call up buddies on the tribal force, handle the whole thing informally. If tribal elders or tribal police officers wanted to accompany them to her house, or break the news themselves, the detectives wouldn't care. Janet would have to call the tribe's lawyers, and they would be just as cooperative as Henry Charm. She'd find Catherine, certainly, but she probably wouldn't find her first.

Janet felt driven. Getting to Catherine first dominated her thoughts. If she could only talk to Catherine first, she'd be the point person of the investigation, Catherine's contact, the person who would call her with developments, whom she would call for updates. It was the best shot she had at getting close to Catherine again.

Janet's fine legal mind was racing; she wasn't about to give up. She knew one more place to look, right in the courthouse. Registering to vote involved establishing residence. A bank or a post office box wouldn't do: it had to be the address of the place where the person really lived. Janet hurried down the stairs to the Elections Department. She thumbed through a computer printout.

Bingo! There she was! Janet had found her at last. Catherine Adams was registered to vote in Sacajawea County. Her residence address was Seal Rock, Washington.

～ 9 ～

The helicopter thundered over the waves. The noon sunlight reflected off the swells where they broke into miniature waterfalls, glinting like scattered diamonds. The sameness of the seascape, for all its endless minute variations and undeniable beauty, gave Janet a strange sense of motionlessness. There were no landmarks to give dimension to the passing scene.

She was enjoying the helicopter ride — in fact, loved to fly. The forward tilt of the police helicopter and the clear, rounded windshield which curved down almost beneath her feet didn't disturb her a bit. And flying was the fastest way to get to Catherine. The detectives had taken her decision without comment. What Ed might think privately about her motives didn't matter.

As she watched the sparkling water fly by beneath them, Janet knew it would hurt to see Catherine again. She remembered the last time they had met. She'd thought they were going for a hike along the beach. She'd hoped Catherine would come home with her. It would have been the first time. She had wine and flowers, dinner waiting in the refrigerator, carefully chosen CDs stacked in the player.

From the beginning, it was obvious to her that Catherine was wary of a relationship. But then, in her own way, so was Janet. They had hiked and skied together, gone out for meals and movies and drinks. They always talked of the present, of what they were doing, of the world around them, of the region they both loved.

The fact that they didn't talk of their pasts or their feelings hadn't seemed important. There was so much else to talk about and experience — the snow on a cedar bough, the sunset over the ocean, the beavers building a dam, examining the way moss grew on the trees, collecting mushrooms, sharing the sheer joy of sticking their tongues out to catch snowflakes.

Though Janet wasn't a person who discussed emotions often or readily, her own feelings toward Catherine grew and deepened through the winter. She had assumed that Catherine was responding in kind. She had slowly, gently begun changing the tenor of their relationship, with the kind of care she'd bring to a major case. A gift here, an unmistakable loving touch there. She thought Catherine had welcomed these affectionate advances, and felt the same.

But then came the warm late-winter day when Catherine had asked Janet to meet her at North Jetty Park. The promise of spring was in the air. It was warm enough to go without jackets, but they both had heavy sweaters slung around their shoulders. In the field by the trail head, Catherine had stopped abruptly, and in an icy tone, said, "Janet, there's something I have to say, and I think I need to say it in person. I don't want to see you any more. I don't think it's good for either of us. I'm sorry, but that's the way it is. There's really nothing else to say." She shrugged. "Except that I'm sorry, and I wish you well."

She had turned away, walking toward the parking lot and her car. Stunned, Janet had finally managed to find her voice. "Wait," she had cried, dashing after Catherine, grabbing her bare arm, hauling her to a stop. She wanted, needed, an explanation. She couldn't believe what she'd heard.

Catherine whirled. She struck Janet across the face. Janet dropped Catherine's arm, and was shocked to see red marks where her hand had gripped.

"I'm sorry," she said. "I shouldn't have grabbed you." Feeling awkward, tongue-tied, she couldn't find the right words.

"I just want to know why," she said hesitantly. "I want to know what went wrong." With a massive effort, she laid her heart bare. "I thought we had a future together, Cathy. I...I love you."

Catherine was implacable. "Don't call me Cathy," she snapped, annoyed. "I've told you that. We're just not right for each other, Janet. Not that way. That's all. I'm not going to make the mistake of rehashing every word either of us ever said. And I'm not going to say 'Let's be friends.' We both know that won't work."

"Why not?" Janet was willing to grasp at straws.

"Because you wouldn't let it alone. It's just not in you to give up on anything you want without a fight. You're too much, Janet." She twisted her braid around her fingers. "It's my fault, too. I should have said this sooner. What *you* wanted just rolled right over what *I* knew was the right thing to do.

"I'm going now," Catherine had said. Then bluntly, "It's over, Janet. I'm sorry, but it's over." So saying, she turned, tossed her braid over her shoulder and strode away. Janet would never forget the sight of her, those set shoulders, that straight back, the braid bouncing cheerfully over the bulk of the Cowichan sweater she wore tied around her shoulders as she hiked up the slope to the parking lot.

The chopper hit an air pocket, dropping her firmly back into the present. After all her years of law practice, Janet's professional demeanor was ingrained enough to enable her to carry off almost any engagement without the loss of composure. But she had no confidence in those abilities now. She stared at the glittering water, wishing she'd had time to prepare for this meeting, knowing it wouldn't have done any good. All she had to do was think about Catherine and she became incapable of coherent thought.

Was it that she still loved Catherine, Janet wondered, or was it that Catherine had rejected her?

The island group hove into sight. The lighthouse tower thrust into the sky; the pilot circled, looking for a landing site.

Janet would have known Catherine at any distance. There was no doubt it was her, standing on the edge of the eastern cliff, dark hair billowing in the ocean breeze, hand shading her eyes as she watched the circling helicopter descend.

Yes, she had found her. Janet's stomach lurched, and not just with the sudden change in altitude as the helicopter hit an updraft.

As the chopper banked into its final turn, Janet spotted something else, then lost it as the helicopter turned and she found herself looking at the empty sky. She'd seen a second figure. Another woman.

Within seconds, the helicopter touched down.

Janet noted that the woman next to Catherine was short, fair and wiry. Well-defined muscles stood out on her bare arms and legs. She wore a cropped and faded T-shirt, cutoff jeans and boat shoes. Her sun-streaked hair, tossed by the helicopter's tempest, blew back from a tanned, sharp-featured face. The pilot announced their landing. Janet, feeling hollow and unsure of herself, gripped her briefcase like a security blanket and opened the door.

Catherine hadn't changed at all. That fierce independence Janet had admired still showed in her stance. Her quick, intelligent gaze took in the chopper, its pilot, and Janet. Catherine looked Janet over, then stepped out to meet her.

"Janet?" She sounded surprised, puzzled.

"Catherine." She nodded a greeting, keeping her face, she hoped, expressionless, burying her uncertainty under professionalism. "We need to talk."

Catherine nodded, leading Janet a little distance away from the idling helicopter's thunder, so they might be able to speak in close-to-normal tones.

"You said we had to talk." Catherine planted her feet at shoulder width, her right fist on her hip. "About what? I don't think I have anything to say to you that I haven't said a hundred times before."

Janet shook her head. "Cathy, it's business. It's..." She broke off. The other woman had come forward, to stand just behind Catherine and to her side. The woman's stare was guarded. The muscles in her neck and across her shoulders stood out.

"Who's your friend?" Janet heard anger in her own voice. She could feel her body move into an aggressive stance. She was jealous! Something she certainly had no right to be.

"My name's Nic Cavanaugh." The woman's voice was soft, educated; she had an accent that was almost, but not quite, British. So she wasn't as rough as she appeared, and, from the confident tone of her voice, she was clearly not a person to underestimate.

Catherine stepped between them. Whatever Janet might still feel towards her, Catherine realized she would not have come to Seal Rock in a police helicopter to express it. This had to be official business. Catherine toyed with a strand of hair, her fingers automatically working it into a braid. She noticed what she was doing and stopped. She knew it reflected her fear.

"Nic Cavanaugh, Janet Schilling," she said briskly, then turned slightly, away from Nic, and continued, "Janet, what is it? Why are you here?"

"I need to talk to you."

"Yes," she snapped, exasperated, "so you said. So get on with it."

Janet moved a step closer to Catherine. "The *Valkyrie's* been found."

"What?" Catherine exclaimed. "The *Valkyrie*? How? Where? When?" She felt stunned, the blood draining from her face. To find the boat, after all these years.

"The rogue wave carried a coaster onto the bar. They found the *Valkyrie* during salvage."

"On the bar? What was it doing there? What about Glen?" She clenched her hands to avoid fiddling with her hair, a gesture she knew Janet would recognize.

"He was on board. The Medical Examiner's made a positive identification. I'm here because you're the official next of kin. Someone had to notify you, and let you know that it looks like he died of homicidal violence."

Catherine began to sway. For a moment, Janet began to think she might faint; Nic apparently did too, since she stepped to Catherine's side. But Catherine regained control of herself and brushed the other woman away.

"Are you all right?" Nic asked, concern showing on her face.

"I'm fine. Thank you," Catherine said, giving Nic a quick but brittle smile.

"Shall I leave?" Nic asked.

"No," Catherine said. "Stay. Please." Of all things, she didn't want to be left alone with Janet. She waited till Nic nodded, then breathed deeply several times, concentrating on her hands, gripping each other so tightly she could feel nothing else.

"They told me he was lost at sea," Catherine said finally, speaking very quietly, staring at the empty sky. "He belonged at sea; they should never have found him." She looked at Janet, straightened, and spoke decisively. "What's left should go back to the sea. That's right. I suppose I can just call Culpepper's and ask them to arrange it?"

Janet should have expected that reaction. It was like Catherine to be practical, to think of arrangements, to want things as simple as possible. Yet that hadn't even occurred to her in her headlong rush to see Catherine again. Janet felt badly off stride. It was not simply Nic's presence, though that was of course disconcerting; it was finding Catherine again, and coping with the flood of memories that were released.

"I'm sorry, Cathy. That's not possible, not yet, anyway. I should have been clearer. We can't release the remains yet."

"Why not?" Catherine snapped. She looked appalled, Janet thought. She hadn't taken in everything Janet had said.

"There's no easy way to say it. The *Valkyrie* was scuttled; all the through-hulls were opened. According to the Medical

Examiner, your stepfather died because his throat was cut. Deliberately. I'm sorry, Cathy. He was murdered."

"Murdered?" Catherine repeated the word faintly, as though she had never heard it before. "Oh, Janet." Her voice faltered. "It sounds stupid to ask, you wouldn't have come otherwise. But — you're sure?"

"It's normal to ask," Janet said. "Yes. We're sure."

Catherine's face crumpled. *This means an investigation,* she thought. She didn't want to think about what it might uncover. She'd have to pump Janet about it. That was a frightening thought. Catherine clenched and unclenched her hands, finally folding her arms as if chilled, and gripping the sleeves of her cotton sweater.

Nic watched Catherine carefully, her own hands clasped behind her back. Catherine wanted her to stay; and she wanted to stay, but she didn't know how to help. Being on the island alone together was a concentrated experience. *I know her, but I don't know about her,* Nic thought. This tall, well-dressed, well-put-together woman and the news she brought were part of Catherine's other life, the life she had outside the island and the time she and Nic had shared. Nic decided she'd have to watch and take her cue from Catherine.

Catherine continued gripping her sweater, her mind flooding with memories of her time with Janet. What she remembered most clearly was Janet's relentless insistence on her own way, and her own inability to resist. It had almost gotten them lost once, cross-country skiing in the mountains, when Janet led them far off the ski trail in pursuit of mountain goats. As Janet had promised, they'd been back before dark, but just barely, and not before Catherine had become cold and wet and terrified of getting lost; angry that she had allowed herself to be persuaded, against her own better judgment. Janet could do that, with her sneaky lawyer's tricks. Catherine had hated always having to be on guard against them.

Almost triumphantly, Catherine recalled that the only time she'd ever been able to stand up to Janet successfully was when she broke off with her. She hadn't treated Janet very well afterwards, and was sorry for the hurt she had caused. But to this day, she was sure Janet never understood what she did wrong. It was sad, but there was no other way she could keep Janet from overwhelming her. Catherine had felt like she was fighting for her very soul.

Now here was Janet was in her life again, raising questions about her past she'd just as soon never hear. *I'm going to have to fight her off again,* Catherine thought in despair. Then she reminded herself that things were different now. For one thing, they weren't dating; that had been over a long time ago. And she had Nic's support now. Even though they hadn't known each other long, since they were the only two people on the island, Catherine felt like she knew Nic well. *It ought to be easier this time,* Catherine said to herself, but she knew that was just wishful thinking. She felt both Nic and Janet watching her, and knew it was time she spoke.

"Do you know anything else?" Catherine asked. "I mean, about what might have happened to Glen?"

"Not yet. Another reason I'm here is to follow up on the Coast Guard report, see if you know anything else about it," Janet answered kindly. The news had upset Catherine, obviously, just as survivors were always upset. She wanted to reach out to Catherine, but couldn't. Catherine wouldn't want it, and, as a public official, it wasn't her place to give more than official comfort. Janet could find it in herself to be at least a little grateful that Nic was there for Catherine.

Catherine shook her head. "It happened what — four years ago, about? I don't know what I could tell you now that I didn't tell them at the time."

"The report indicates he left the 17th of March. When did you last see him?"

Catherine moved behind a boulder, beckoning Janet and Nic to follow. The boulder sheltered them from the wind generated by the helicopter's idling rotors.

"I was cold out there," Catherine said by way of explanation. "I don't know for sure when I last saw him," she went on. "I think, probably, the day before."

"Where?" Janet wished she had a pad to write on. She felt scattered, and taking notes focused her.

"The house where he lived."

"You'd inherited it from your mother, right? But you didn't live there." Janet tried to keep her demeanor and her questions professional and impersonal. But, she realized, Glen's death must have happened right around the time Catherine had broken off with her. Was there any connection?

"It wasn't mine yet, not really," Catherine said. "It was still in Mom's estate. Glen was going to live there till he left for Alaska for the season, and clear his things out then. I wasn't really sure what I was going to do. There were complications..." Her voice trailed off. She looked up, and saw the flush that spread up Janet's neck. She almost smiled as she said, "Yes, you were one of them. Then this — " she indicated the island — "came up."

Nic looked at Janet with some surprise. She looked to Nic like a confirmed city woman, balancing perfectly on the expensive high-heeled shoes that made her even taller, despite the rough ground. Hardly the kind of woman she'd picture Catherine liking. Yet it appeared they'd had some kind of relationship. Nic wondered what had happened between them.

There didn't seem to be much to say that wouldn't take them onto the forbidden ground of their shared past, but Janet felt she had to ask, "Why here?"

Catherine's face lit up. "It's the most incredible research opportunity. The environment's unique. I have half a dozen long-term projects going — the University jumped at the chance to fund me."

"What did you and Lowry talk about when you saw him on the 16th?" Janet delivered the question in mechanical tones. Seeing Catherine, hearing her happiness as she talked about her work, hurt. In Janet, hurt too often turned to anger.

What she wanted most was to leave before she lost whatever precious shreds of control remained to her, and before she lashed out in a way she would regret.

"Things." Catherine shrugged. She unfolded her arms and started toying with her hair again. "I don't know. There was a ton of stuff in the house that dated back to my grandparents' time, maybe before. I'd been sorting through it off and on for months. I don't remember that we talked about anything in particular."

"Did he tell you when he was leaving?"

"I don't think so." Catherine cocked her head as if in thought. "Not then."

"Or about his moving out?" Janet asked.

"That was settled." She seemed on firm ground here, Janet thought, her voice brisk and clear. "I wasn't in any big hurry or anything," Catherine went on. "I figured he'd go when he went."

"Did it surprise you when you found out he hadn't told you he was going?"

"No. I mean, it was maybe a little early for him to go to Alaska, and I would have thought he'd tell me before he left for good, but he didn't have to. We both knew what was going to happen." Catherine brushed the notion aside. "Maybe he had just gone to get fuel and meant to come back. That's what the Coast Guard thought. He hadn't taken his things from the house."

"What was left?" Janet stuck her hand in her trouser pocket, rucking up her jacket. She found a coin to fiddle with, turning it over and over between her long fingers.

"Nothing special. Just things. Some furniture. Clothes. Books. Old tax records. Papers. Tools. *Things.*"

"What happened to them?" Nic had moved closer to Catherine again, watching, listening. Janet gave her a wary glance. She wondered how long they'd been together.

"I sold some things, gave a bunch of stuff to charity, tossed the rest. I have tenants in the house now. I don't go there very often." Catherine sounded sad. Her head fell forward, her loose hair obscuring her face.

Without deliberate thought, Janet stretched a hand to Catherine. She wanted to walk across the island with her, talk to her, find out how she'd been, how she was. Catch up. Begin again. Then she caught Nic's eye on her. She let her hand drop to her side. There was nothing more to say. She wished for a reason to send Nic away, but there wasn't one. Nic was there by Catherine's choice; Janet was not.

"That's it, then," Janet said. She reached into her briefcase for her pen and a pad. "A couple of detectives might need to ask you some more questions, when we know more about what went on. Is there some way they can call you?"

"Yes. Here —" Catherine held out her hands and Janet handed her the silver Tiffany pen and the legal pad. "I'll write it down. They might have to try a few times, but usually I'm where I can hear the bell." She returned the pad and pen to Janet, who extracted one of her cards from its silver case and handed it over in exchange. She thought of writing her unlisted home number on the back, but decided not to.

"If you can think of anything that might be useful, you can call me at this number. If I'm not in, I'll call you back, or the detectives will. We're looking for anything that might give us a direction. Did anyone have a grudge against him? Did he mention any threats, any prowlers, strange phone calls, anything like that? Did he mention he was going to meet anyone? Did anyone call? You might surprise yourself with what you remember."

"After all this time?" Catherine looked skeptical, but inside she felt her heart sink. Examining the past wouldn't change it. The idea of exposing it to the cold light of a criminal investigation was frightening. Painful. Impossible. But maybe, because so much time had passed, the investigators were just going through the motions. "Janet, do you really think anybody will be able to remember anything new? Do you really think you're going to find out what happened?"

"Honestly?" Janet shrugged. "I can't tell you. Sometimes we get lucky. We're certainly going to give the investigation our best efforts." She'd had to say these things to victims' families before, but that didn't make them unfelt or untrue. "No one should be allowed to get away with murder." She added emphatically, "They won't this time, not if I can help it."

~ 10 ~

The helicopter disappeared into the mist that clung to the mainland, miles away. Nic watched Catherine, who was staring at the tracks the helicopter's skids had left in the dry grass of the plateau.

"I'm sorry about your stepfather," Nic said quietly.

"That's nice of you, but you don't have to be," Catherine said, looking up. "It was a long time ago, and we weren't close." She began walking up the path toward the lighthouse.

Nic fell in step beside her. That woman who had come in the police helicopter had stirred something up in Catherine that went far beyond the news she brought.

"Who is she, Catherine?"

"Here." She flipped the card to Nic. *Chief Deputy Prosecuting Attorney,* Nic read. She'd assumed something of the kind.

"That's not what I meant." Nic passed the card back. Catherine stuck it in the back pocket of her jeans. "What is she to you?"

"Nothing." Catherine sounded surprised. "She's somebody I used to know. That's all."

Nic did not believe it. The prosecutor's emotions had been too close to her flawless surface for that to be entirely true. She'd been more than Catherine's friend, that at least was clear.

They reached the lighthouse door.

"Cathy," Nic began.

"Don't call me that." She whirled on Nic with an astonishing fury.

"But she..."

"Janet knows better. *He* called me that, and I hate it. Nobody's called me that since I left home. I've told her not to do it, but she does it anyway. That's how she is. She does exactly what she wants and doesn't pay any attention to anybody else. She doesn't *think!* She's the kind of person who takes a vegetarian to a steak house!"

Nic raised her hands and backed away, a grin appearing at the corners of her mouth. It was obvious now how the relationship between Janet and Catherine had gone bad. "I'm sorry," she said. "I'll never do that. I promise!"

Catherine shook herself. "Sorry," she said. "She just makes me so mad. Being around her is a constant battle. You aren't like that. You *listen.* I shouldn't take it out on you."

"It's all right," Nic said. "Don't worry about it. I'm not."

They started for the lighthouse again. The news Janet had brought upset Catherine more than she thought, Nic decided. Or maybe it was that Janet had brought it. Janet and Catherine — two strong-willed people, one of whom hadn't a clue about give and take and the other without the patience to teach or cajole. *Must have been a right cat fight,* Nic thought, secretly amused.

"You feel like company?" Nic asked when they reached the lighthouse door.

"Thanks, but no," Catherine said. "I've got work to do, and so do you. And I think I'd like to be alone for a while. I need to digest this."

Nic nodded. If Catherine wanted time to be alone, she was entitled to it. "See you for dinner, then?"

"Sure," Catherine said. She watched Nic until the top of her head sank behind the hill. She went inside and closed the lighthouse door. Catherine sank to the floor, her back against the door, and allowed great wracking sobs to consume her.

"I hate being alone," she sobbed as she pounded her fist on the floor. "I hate it."

✦

Shortly after Janet returned to her office, Wallace stuck her head through her office door. "Janet," she said, "I need to talk to you about the Macklin sentencing. It's on tomorrow morning."

"What about it?" Janet put down her tape recorder and motioned the Senior Criminal Deputy to sit. Wallace saw tension in the way her boss rubbed her thumb against two fingers, and the way she didn't sit back in her chair.

"You've got down a request for an exceptional sentence. How come?" Wallace asked. She knew that to request a sentence outside a predetermined "standard range," the prosecutor had to argue specific circumstances that justified exceptional treatment. She had looked through the file, but saw nothing that warranted that kind of sentence. Had she missed something? She'd sooner ask than make a mistake.

"Read the file." Janet's voice turned harsh, and she jabbed at the file with a polished nail. "Take a look at what Macklin did to that kid."

Wallace sighed. She'd been afraid it would go like this. Janet's rigorous conscience made her see almost everything in clear terms of right and wrong. She didn't understand the meaning of "compromise" under the best of circumstances, but in child-abuse cases she was positively relentless. "I know, Janet," Wallace said. "I've read the file. It's bad. But it's exactly the circumstances described in the statute we convicted him under. That means it fits in the standard range. I've got to have more than that if you want me to argue for an exceptional."

"Do you?" Janet's tone was dangerously mild. When she was seven, just before her mother was killed in the accident and her father retired from the bench, felled by a grief that never healed, there had been a child-abuse case tried in his court. It had been a bad one, with multiple defendants and multiple victims, two of whom came from Janet's school. Though her parents tried to keep the details from their children, Janet was intelligent and curious. She found out enough to give her nightmares, and, she suspected, permanent scars. To this day, she felt every pang of every victim in every case she saw. As always in Janet, hurt turned to anger.

Oh, shit, Wallace thought. *She's furious, and I don't think it's about this. I wonder what happened on that island?* She held her ground by looking directly at Janet, but didn't answer Janet's question.

"You're not the judge," Janet went on, beginning softly, her voice rising to its normal level as her anger burst forth. "Your job is to argue a position, not make the decision. Even an exceptional sentence isn't enough. The kid's a basket case after having to go through a trial, and for what? The jury wasn't out an hour. Argue that." She grabbed the file from the desktop and flipped through it.

"Look here." She shoved the file in Wallace's face and waved at her illegibly scrawled notes. "Here are your arguments. Excessive cruelty; part of a pattern; previous offenses; extreme danger to the community. Want more? Try the precedents. Use that file I started, the one of exceptional sentences from trial courts all over the state on all the sexual offense statutes, with case numbers and digested facts. Analogize. Jesus, Wallace, do I have to tell you your job?"

"No, Janet." Wallace kept her voice calm. She knew how her boss felt about child-abuse cases. Everyone did. Wallace hated them, too — there was nothing worse — but Janet seemed to feel it more deeply than other professionals. Wallace thought she'd have abusers drawn and quartered if she could.

"I'll argue it," she told Janet, "all of it. But don't expect miracles. I was hoping you had something more, maybe a new angle."

Suddenly the anger faded, and Janet fell back into her chair.

"Sorry," she said awkwardly, which Wallace knew meant she was sincere. "It hasn't been a good day. I shouldn't take it out on you. But I would like to see that son of a bitch," she indicated the Macklin file, "do some very hard time. He won't get what he deserves, but we might get some extra time for him if we give the judge a hook to hang it on. Do your best."

"I will." She got up. "Don't worry about that." She brushed her boss's temper away with a wave of her hand. Janet hardly ever meant anything personal by it, and was easy to forgive because she was harder on herself than she was on anybody else. When Wallace got to the door, she winked at Janet. She was rewarded with a quick smile, which she returned. Whatever its cause, the storm was over. For now.

⚓

Thursday afternoon after lunch, Nic Cavanaugh wandered back down the cliff path to *Wayward*. The patching job was drying nicely. Catherine had loaned her a portable generator. It chugged away, charging the boat's batteries. Soon she could leave, if she wanted to. But she didn't. Not yet.

The previous evening, Nic and Catherine had played backgammon until well after dark. Catherine didn't play very well, but didn't want to quit. She seemed distracted. Nic had wondered if she wanted to talk about her stepfather, but Catherine avoided the topic. *If they weren't close,* Nic wondered, *why does it seem to upset her?* Then the thought was lost when Catherine asked her if she wanted to help record the sea lions the next morning.

The next day, she and Catherine had spent most of the morning on the cliffs with video cameras directed at the juvenile sea lions. Though she never interfered, never tried to make pets of them, Catherine had developed a relationship with many of the huge mammals. Nic had never seen anything like it.

Now, as Nic climbed onto *Wayward,* she thought, *I'll take her sailing. If she likes it...* She didn't dare go on, not even to herself. She was hoping for an awful lot, awfully soon, but the more time she spent with Catherine the more time she wanted to. Who knew what could take root between them? "You don't know until you try, "Nic said aloud with characteristic optimism. She gazed out to the lighthouse and then at the long beach exposed by the low afternoon tide. It looked inviting. She decided to bring Catherine a seafood dinner.

After rooting around in a cockpit locker, Nic found a small folding shovel. She grabbed a string bag from the galley and jumped off the boat. Tiny craters pockmarked the smooth, wet sand. She began to dig. Nearly every shovelful yielded a harvest of rectangular razor clams. Nic hadn't checked to see if the clams were in season, but that didn't worry her much. The mainland beaches might need regulation, but her own eyes and common sense told her that overharvesting wasn't a problem out here.

The shingle beach below the lighthouse headland was just barely above the tide line. When she'd filled her bag, she set it in a tide pool, then rounded the headland carefully, discovering a tiny, shallow cove that would have a sand beach only at the lowest tides. Crossing the shingle which skirted the island, she waded ankle-deep through gentle surf to round the northern edge of the headland.

On rocks that were now only just offshore, and even on the boulders nestled up against the island, the sea lions basked, rolled, and barked. Nic stopped, enthralled. She was closer to them than she'd ever been. If they noticed her, they didn't seem to mind her presence. A strange hollow hooting came from somewhere to her right. She turned. The sound came from a fissure in the rocks. A giant bull flipper-flopped its way out of the cave and down onto the shingle. It was ungainly, clumsy, but strangely majestic. Seeing Nic, it stopped and fixed her with an intelligent gaze.

Nic wondered if she should retreat; the thing was several times her size and she was the intruder, but suddenly it rolled over on its side and waved a flipper at her. She nearly doubled over with laughter. Catherine would love this! Nic couldn't wait to tell her.

In the water, the sea lions became sleek torpedoes. Nic watched the juveniles play sliding games until a wavelet lapped her sodden shoe. She glanced at her watch, and was amazed to see most of the afternoon was gone. Not only that, it was time to leave. The tide had turned. As she hurried along the beach to the tide pool where she'd left the clams, Nic realized how great it was to have someone to talk to who liked what she did, and how much she'd missed that. *I hope she likes to sail,* Nic thought.

⚓

That same Thursday afternoon, as cameras flashed and clicked, Janet took a breath, pacing her voice before launching into the final portion of her speech to the assembled reporters. Her burgundy Ultrasuede suit with its pink blouse, her Paloma Picasso "Scribble" pin on the lapel, looked businesslike without being mannish. It was a politician's suit, the color highlighting her skin and hair so she'd look healthy on television without looking overly made-up. There were eight reporters in the conference room, with cameras, microphones and notepads. Some were from the local press, but stringers from the metropolitan papers were there, too.

"The solution of this case is primarily in your hands, ladies and gentlemen," she said in her well-modulated voice. "There will be no easy answers." A flash went off right in Janet's eyes, distracting her. She didn't have a prepared statement, didn't need one, but she did have an outline, which she wanted to use. Taking a measured breath, she allowed a pregnant pause to ensue as her gaze roamed across the room, giving the impression of personal communication with each reporter (and camera lens), while allowing her vision to return to normal.

"Too much time has passed," she went on, "for regular law-enforcement work to result in a quick solution to Mr. Lowry's death, although of course we are pursuing every possible avenue of investigation.

"Connections which might have been obvious at the time of his killing are gone now. Witnesses' memories fade. You are the people who have the power to bring them back, by bringing this case to their attention, and bringing them in to us. Your active participation in this investigation may well be the factor that makes it a success."

Janet turned to the easel to begin running through the short outline of facts she'd prepared. When she finished that, she took a few questions. Then it was over. She could tell from the reporters' reluctance to let her go that they had loved it.

The Prosecuting Attorney agreed when she stopped in his office after the reporters had finally left.

"That was good work, Janet," Ben said. "There's more, too. I got a call from that UHF station wanting a private interview. I sent that to Maud to schedule for you. They'll broker it to the rest of the TV stations, and if one of them shows it they all will. The *Register* wants an exclusive. The Seattle and Tacoma papers and the networks will have their regular people down tomorrow for in-depth follow-up. What do you think?"

Janet crossed her legs, folded her hands on her knee, and assumed a poker face. "Is the *Register* going to endorse me? If they are, I'll give them an exclusive interview and do a follow-up conference with the others. If they don't want to commit, they can take their chances with the same information everybody else gets."

"That's a strong position." Ben frowned, considering it. All publicity requests were funneled through his office. As the elected official, he had the option of utilizing all the promotional opportunities himself or passing them on. Traditionally, he'd been generous, except in election years. Over the previous eight or nine months, he'd been giving almost all press coverage to Janet.

"Too strong?" Janet valued Ben's experience as much as his support.

"Maybe not. What's your rationale?"

"Everybody reads the *Register,* but they take one of the other papers, too. If the *Register* gets some exclusive material, they might be willing to lock into an endorsement. But there should be something different in the other papers, to supplement the *Register's* coverage. Give people a reason to read all the papers."

Ben Davidson, a campaign veteran, leaned back in his chair, lacing his hands over his midsection. "OK," he said. "I think I like it. You'll get more coverage that way. You're taking a tough stance with the *Register* but it'll do for a negotiating position." He swiveled his chair to look out the window, then turned back to Janet. "That was a nice touch about the press helping the investigation," he went on. "They've gotten a lot of static lately about their interference screwing things up. But you might get it back in your face from the *Register.* You're the one asking for press cooperation. If you want good coverage for your homicide, you'll have to give them material. It's a good point. Certainly the Seattle and Tacoma papers won't cover it as thoroughly."

"Detailed coverage of a local homicide will sell a lot of *Registers,* whether or not they get an exclusive." Janet felt confident of her position. The homicide was getting her the press she needed, but the media needed her, too. The homicide was news — as was Janet Schilling.

Ben nodded. "That's your comeback. They'll want to cover it. But it's too early for the *Register* to commit to an endorsement. You'll have to handle it discreetly. You can't just come out and ask for it."

"I'll settle," Janet told him with a grin, "for a solid hint."

～ 11 ～

When she finished with Ben, Janet stopped by the car wash to get her car its weekly bath. Then she headed home, pleased as always with the navy blue BMW's smooth acceleration and neat handling. She was going to have to call Sharon at her home on Orcas Island. It was already Thursday, and there was no way Janet was going to be able to meet her in Seattle for the weekend as they'd planned. These monthly assignations — Janet couldn't think of a better word — were friendly and fun. Sharon's circumstances and the distance prevented the relationship from developing further. Janet had to admit that while the lack of commitment and intimacy sometimes bothered her, most of the time it suited her just fine.

Cutting around a pickup truck, Janet realized she was close to Catherine's old address. She braked suddenly to turn onto Church Street.

Twelve twenty-four was three blocks back from the U-shaped highway bypass that served as Salmon Bay's main commercial street. Janet didn't know it well; Catherine had only moved to this apartment during the bitter ending of their relationship.

It was a pleasant old street, lined with oaks. The stately Victorian houses were gradually being replaced with low-lying modern office buildings as the commercial part of town expanded and the houses that remained were divided into professional offices and apartments.

Twelve twenty-four had been a grand house in its time, and was still lovely. It stood in the middle of four lots. Janet flushed as she remembered driving past this house, or even parking out of sight behind a neighbor's laurel hedge, hoping for a glimpse of Catherine, long after she had given up hope of anything more.

She pulled into the driveway and followed it to a parking area in front of the former carriage house. She took a deep breath and got out of the car.

Gravel paths dotted with weeds wound through the overgrown lawn. Careful of her heels, Janet followed one to the front of the house. Lanky roses sprawled in heaps. Overgrown raspberry canes tangled into a bramble. The house needed paint, but the fragrant climbing roses running wild up trellises in front of the porch provided considerable coverage and at least a superficial charm. At the foot of the somewhat rickety steps Janet paused to count four black mailboxes affixed to the side of the ornate front door.

"Looking for somebody?"

The voice belonged to a massive woman who sat ensconced in an Adirondack chair. Janet decided she must be nearly eighty. Her yellow-grey hair straggled from an untidy bun. Two canes leaned against the dusty arm of her chair. She wore a faded print dress the size and shape of a tent. The heavy support stockings didn't keep her ankles from running over the edges of her white orthopedic sandals.

"Yes, ma'am," Janet responded in her best "public servant" manner. "I'd like to speak to the person who's lived here the longest."

"I guess that'd be me," the woman said. "I own the place. I haven't got any vacancies, and there's nothing I want to buy. If that doesn't tell you what you want to know, come up here and take a seat." She gestured with a cane to the empty chair beside her.

Janet gingerly sank into the chair, resisting the impulse to dust the seat.

"I'm not selling anything," she said. "I work for the county, and I'm looking for information about someone who lived here several years ago."

"Taxes?" The old woman's eyes were bright, her voice sharp.

"Not taxes, either." She extracted her silver card case from an inside pocket and offered the woman a card. The old woman held it at a distance, then brought it slowly closer until she peered at it from a few inches away. Then she laid it on the arm of the chair and from the depths of her lap produced a pair of grimy glasses, which she perched on the top of her nose. She moved the card out, then in again. Finally, she set it down and the glasses disappeared into the folds of her capacious lap.

"Janet Schilling. That you?"

"Yes, ma'am."

"And you're a prosecutor?"

"Just like it says."

"What can I do for you?" she asked with the friendly curiosity Janet recognized as typical of a person with nothing to hide and a powerful interest in her neighbors.

Janet glanced at the mailboxes, spotting a faded label in copperplate script on the box marked "1" that said *Mrs. A. Svensen.*

"Are you Mrs. Svensen?"

This seemed to please her. She cackled, her great bosom jiggling to a point where Janet could hardly keep from staring.

"Smart one, aren't you?" she finally said, gasping for breath. "Yes, I'm Marge Svensen. Now, why don't you tell me what I can do for the Chief Deputy Prosecuting Attorney?"

What could she do for me? Janet wondered suddenly. What had she hoped to accomplish here? She was uncomfortably conscious of Mrs. Svensen's intelligent gaze, and knew she had to produce a credible answer.

On some level she was still chasing Catherine, and that wasn't right. So she either had to give her interest some legitimacy in connection with the Lowry case, or she had to leave.

"I'm sure you heard about the ship that went aground on the bar during the storm," Janet began.

"Of course. Nobody's talking about much else. There's never been a wave like that as long as anybody here can remember."

"Do you know what they found under it?" Janet asked.

"What is this? Twenty questions? Certainly, I know. They found that fisherman who used to run *Salmon Forever* and his boat."

"The fisherman's name was Glen Lowry. His next of kin was a stepdaughter, a woman named Catherine Adams. I understand she lived here."

"I didn't know she was his stepdaughter." Mrs. Svensen made a sympathetic face. Her hands rested on the arms of her chair. "I didn't connect the name, if I ever knew it. Yes, Catherine used to live here. She didn't live here long, though. She moved away shortly after he died, then. July, I think it was. I know where she is, though. She comes to visit sometimes when she's in town. She's living out on an island, off the coast. Seal Island? Seal Reef? Seal something, anyway. You ought to be able to find her from that."

"Can you tell me something about her? What kind of a tenant was she?" Janet saw no need to tell Mrs. Svensen she'd already found Catherine.

"She was a good tenant," Mrs. Svensen said. She gripped her cane and shifted slightly in her chair. "Paid her rent on time. Wasn't noisy. Didn't have a lot of people tramping in and out. Kept to herself. I wish she'd stayed longer, but there you are. She studies things, you know, whales and seals and so on. That's why she went out to that island."

"A quiet person, then? Stayed home a lot?" Janet wasn't sure she liked where she was heading with this. Catherine's way of life was of no relevance, she reminded herself. Or was it?

"She liked to go camping," Mrs. Svensen replied. "And she'd go out on the university boats. Her mother had died and Catherine inherited, so she spent a lot of time out at the island. But she'd always let me know when she was going to be away, not like some of them. No, I take that back. There was one time she went off for the weekend and didn't let me know." Mrs. Svensen's eyes twinkled. "I thought she might have given in to that special friend of hers — and about time, too — but when she came back Sunday, she had a table and some boxes from her mother's house, so she must have stayed there, and just forgot to call. I didn't like to ask. Wasn't any of my business, really, though I was a little put out. Still, it only happened the one time."

"What friend?" It wasn't Janet's business, either, but she didn't think Mrs. Svensen would mind. She seemed to relish having an attentive listener. She raised her eyebrows and smiled a little as she answered.

"It may not be your cup of tea, and it wasn't mine in my younger days, but there's somebody for everybody, I say, and it doesn't make any difference who it is as long as you're happy. Catherine never made any secret of where her interests lay, so I don't have to. It was another girl. I never knew her name, and she never came around that I knew of. Catherine said this girl was bothering her, that she didn't want to see her. She sounded nice enough to me. Sent her flowers off and on, too. You'd think a girl would like that sort of thing, but Catherine would get mad and rip up the cards, and one time she made the florist take the whole thing back."

Janet remembered that incident all too well, and knew it meant that then, at least, there had been no one else in Catherine's life. And wherever she had been that last weekend of Glen Lowry's life, she certainly hadn't been with Janet.

"The records show Mr. Lowry disappeared on St. Patrick's day, March 17th. The holiday makes it easier for people to remember, which is important after all this time. Can you think back and try to remember if you heard anything that might have a bearing on Mr. Lowry's death?"

Mrs. Svensen looked at her quizzically. "Now, how would I hear anything like that?"

People always misunderstood that question and there was no other way to ask it that didn't tend to put words in their mouths. Janet expanded.

"Maybe Catherine saw him before he left, and he told her something about who he was meeting or where he was going that she mentioned to you."

"Wouldn't the Coast Guard have asked her that?"

"Probably not. It was just an overdue vessel, then. Or she might have forgotten something. It's often the things that don't seem important at the time that turn out to be material."

"I don't have to think back," Mrs. Svensen said. "I know she saw him. She had to have. That weekend she didn't come home, and didn't tell me? She was at her mother's, that I do know, because of what she brought back here on Sunday. And that was the day after St. Patrick's Day, because I probably wouldn't have noticed she was gone at all if they hadn't had a county-wide dance at the high school down there on the corner " — she waved a cane — "and the kids were whooping and hollering till all hours so I couldn't get to sleep, and when they finally quieted down, that was when I noticed Catherine hadn't come home, and that was when I started worrying, so I couldn't get to sleep then, either."

"Was she fond of her stepfather?"

Mrs. Svensen sat back in her chair and pursed her lips.

"I don't think it's going to bother her much, if that's what you mean. I don't think she was very close to him. Like I said, I didn't even connect the name, though I remember her saying her stepfather had died. It didn't seem to bother her much even then, but of course he wasn't her real father. You have to remember that she knew he died four years ago. More than that, now. This finding the body, well, it won't be much of a shock for her. She's already buried him in her mind."

Janet knew that for a fact. "I believe you said she moved from here in July of that same year?"

Mrs. Svensen nodded. "That's right. She gave notice for the first, but I let her stay over the fourth. There was a long holiday weekend that year, and she needed the extra days. Oh, that was a time." The old woman shook her head and smiled. "As soon as she found out from the lawyer that the Coast Guard wanted to give her that island back, she was like a whirling dervish, running around, mailing off papers, ordering things. She told me she talked the University into paying her to live out there and look at things, and got a grant from somewhere to fix up the place. She acted like it was the answer to a prayer, but I never could see why she was so excited to go and live in a place like that, with nothing but sea gulls for company."

Then Mrs. Svensen's eyes twinkled, and Janet was again uncomfortably conscious of her intelligence.

"I expect I've told you more about frogs than you want to know, young woman. I told you how to find her right off. I know I tend to ramble on."

Janet dissembled. "It can help to know something about a person when you have to bring them bad news."

"I suppose you may be right." Mrs. Svensen cackled again and thumped her cane on the floor. "Well, when you see her, you tell her I'm thinking of her, and if there's anything I can do to help her out, all she has to do is ask."

Janet assured her she would. But her assurance and farewell were delivered absentmindedly. She hurried to the BMW. She wanted to drive. Something Marge Svensen had said troubled her deeply.

Catherine had said she'd seen her stepfather for the last time on Friday, March 16th. But Marge Svensen placed her at Glen Lowry's house on Saturday, the 17th, and maybe on the 18th as well. It was not a mistake that Catherine, who worked a regular five-day week by that time, would have been likely to make. Catherine's memory was almost as good as Janet's.

Catherine *could* have made a mistake, she told herself. Loose gravel sprayed beneath the tires as Janet roared out onto the bypass. She didn't want to believe that Catherine had deliberately lied, but a sinking feeling in her stomach told her that it was exactly what Catherine had done.

~ 12 ~

Friday morning, after finishing the breakfast dishes, Nic stood at the stove sautéing onions. The leftover clams would make a good chowder for their lunch.

Catherine came in and poured herself a glass of water from the pitcher in the refrigerator. She'd begun a final edit of her latest paper as soon as she'd finished breakfast. "Why are you doing that now?" she asked. "Lunch isn't for hours yet."

"It's better when it has time to rest a bit," Nic replied. "I want to show you I know how to cook, so I want it to be good."

Catherine smiled. "I'm sure it will be fine."

"Listen, Catherine," Nic said, turning from the stove. "In a couple of days, I'm going to be able to pull *Wayward* off the rocks."

Faced with the actual prospect of Nic's departure, Catherine found she didn't want her to go. Her face fell. "I guess you have to, if you're going north."

"What I wanted to ask you was if you wanted to give me a hand," Nic said, brandishing the wooden spoon. "I'd like to take you sailing."

"I'd love it," Catherine said, her face luminous. "If it's even half as good as you say it is, it'll be wonderful."

"That's settled, then" Nic grinned and turned back to stir the onions. "There's always enough depth to bring *Wayward* into your dock? We'll have to come in, if I'm going to drop you off."

"There's plenty of water for *Wayward*. Jimmy Ryan's fishing boat draws nine feet and he can get through the channel even at minus tides. It's deeper in the cove. But you don't have to drop me off. Stay a while, if you can."

Nic set the wooden spoon in a ceramic spoon rest and turned around to look Catherine full in the face. *We get on so well,* Nic thought, *but there's a barrier in her I can't breach. I come close and she backs away. Maybe all she needs is time. She's been alone so long, and this is moving so fast. For me, anyway.* Now Catherine had asked for more time, a request Nic herself hadn't planned to make until they'd actually brought *Wayward* around to the dock.

"I'd like that," Nic said at last, letting her face relax into a smile that reflected her happiness. "I'd like that very much. I've a couple of weeks, anyway, before I need to head north, if I'm going to make Alaska this season."

"Stay, then," Catherine said, sucking in a deep breath. She knew this was dangerous, but now that she'd found Nic — someone who laughed when she did, who liked what she liked, who seemed to know what she wanted almost before she did — she didn't want to let her go.

Catherine acknowledged that she was mostly content with her life. But despite it being a life she had chosen, sometimes the forces that led her to that choice made the island feel like a prison. *Hey, even prisoners are allowed visitors,* she thought. *Surely I can have Nic for two more weeks.*

⚓

That Friday afternoon, Janet went to the River Club for lunch. She wanted to review the Lowry file in undisturbed silence while she ate. She had decided to follow the chronology of the file if she could, and that meant interviewing Frank Vincent, the mate who had reported the *Valkyrie* missing, first. She had called to make sure he would be expecting her.

As she ate, Janet wondered if she was seeing ghosts. She hoped she was. All she had against Catherine was an apparent inconsistency. Catherine said she saw her stepfather on the 16th — Friday. Glen's neighbors had reported to the Coast Guard that they'd last seen the boat on Saturday, the 17th. Catherine's landlady said Catherine was gone all weekend, and turned up Sunday, the 18th, with a load of things from the house. It didn't necessarily mean Catherine had lied.

Janet fingered the pin fastening the collar of her ivory silk blouse. It was a platinum tennis racquet, the ball a brilliant-cut diamond connected to the racquet by a slender platinum chain. Catherine could have made a mistake on the date, Janet thought, thinking the 16th was Saturday. Alternatively, she could have stopped by the house on Friday, loaded up her car and gone somewhere else for the rest of the weekend.

At this point, Janet was not sure she could treat Catherine fairly. In trying to be fair, she could overreact, creating a bias against Catherine. Or she'd try to shield Catherine despite clear and convincing evidence. Or she'd bounce back and forth between extremes. She'd told Ed what she'd found out from Mrs. Svensen, and the detective had waved her suspicion away, using the arguments she'd just presented to herself.

Damn, she thought, hating the way her feelings about Catherine were clouding her judgment. Finally she wondered what Ben would say. *It's too early to draw conclusions,* she decided, *that's what he'd say. And he'd be right.*

She glanced at her watch. It was time to leave. She shoved the file into her briefcase, and left the River Club.

The River Club was located on a bluff on the northern, Charbonneau, side of the Salkum River. Janet followed the highway west, noting how the sun was burning off the morning clouds. The remains of an early drizzle had long since dried. Except for the occasional logging truck, she had the road to herself. She put the car through its paces as she sped through the woods. As she enjoyed the dappled brilliance of the sun through the trees and the unexpected greens and yellows and browns coloring the landscape, she could almost forget her mission, but not quite. Catherine Adams's status as a possible suspect in Glen Lowry's death preyed on her mind.

Janet turned left onto a two-lane county road, dodged a school bus before its stop lights went on, and entered farm country, with hayfields and pastures full of grazing cattle spreading out on both sides of the road. Minutes later, she breasted a hill, leaving the woods and farms behind as the ocean came into view. The coastal plain unrolled below her. Sprawling on either side of the road was her destination, Bridle Crest.

She turned into Larch Place, and saw a small orchard in the front of the ranch-style house. Here, playing catch with two children in the grassy half-moon of the drive, Janet saw a weathered man of fifty-something who must be Frank Vincent. He stopped the game and shooed the children around to the back of the house when Janet pulled into the drive.

"Come on in," Frank said expansively, after Janet introduced herself. He led the way around to the back of the house and opened a sliding glass door leading to the lower level. "This is my part of the house." He motioned Janet to a chair. "My daughter, Merilee, and her husband, they live upstairs. That way, I get to see my grandkids, they have a built-in baby-sitter, and they keep an eye on things for me when I'm out fishing. Works out for all of us. Want a beer?"

Janet accepted a beer, noting that it never occurred to Frank to offer a glass. He seemed a social, friendly person, inclined to talk. Some witnesses were like that. Having nothing to hide themselves, they enjoyed the importance of being on the inside of an investigation.

"You know, I can't hardly believe it. I've been out of town. After you called, I looked at the papers. They say somebody murdered Glen."

"That's right," Janet said, launching immediately into her questions, but carefully keeping her tone social. "You reported the *Valkyrie* missing on the 29th of March. Why?"

Frank Vincent looked at Janet as if he thought she must have lost her mind. That was good. She popped the top of the beer, keeping an expectant look on her face. She wanted him to feel a need to enlighten her.

"Because he didn't show up when he was supposed to, that's why. He was going to bring the *Valkyrie* in to the docks in Charbonneau to pick me up with all the stores — food and whatnot. Merrilee drove me down on her way to work, and I waited, but he never showed up, and nobody had seen him around the docks. So I called his house, and nobody answered. I tried to raise him on the VHF with no luck, either. So I waited some more, in case he was on his way in and wasn't monitoring the radio, and when he didn't show, I called Merrilee again, and she came and picked me up. We went by his house on our way home. There wasn't anybody there, and the boat was gone. So I called it in."

Janet nodded and sipped her beer before continuing. "From what I understand, Mr. Lowry had skippered an ocean-going boat for a number of years. Did it seem reasonable to you that he could have gotten into trouble right in the harbor, coming from his house to the port docks to pick you up?"

"You can find trouble in just about any boat, anywhere, any time," Frank said. "Out in the harbor, we got ships, we got tugs, we got boats, we got log booms. We got deadheads and sinkers all over the place. This was at night, and you can't always see those even in the daytime. They're logs, you know. Get away from the mills or the booms. They fill up with water till they're hard, like iron. Lots of times, they float just below the surface. Hit one, and you go down fast."

"Is that what you thought happened?"

"Most likely. What do you expect with all the mills and the timber trade we've got on the bay? Anything else, he would have showed up, or answered when I called, or the Coast Guard would have heard something right off."

"The Coast Guard concluded that the *Valkyrie* was lost going up to Hole in the Wall to take on fuel."

"That's after they knew he'd been gone for a while. I thought he'd come back from there long before. On the 28th, he was just coming in to pick me up so we could catch the slack on the bar and get a good weather window for the trip. Why would he go outside first? It always surprises me more people don't hit those deadheads, especially at night, and this was night, remember. It did surprise me when he didn't turn up. It was rainy, kind of squally, but that was supposed to be the end of the bad weather for a while. Didn't seem like the kind of night to be floating around in an Avon for fun, so I called it in. I figured they'd pick him up."

"What's an Avon?" she asked. She wanted to keep him talking.

"Life raft. *Valkyrie* carried a six-man. They come in canisters. Pull the string, the raft pops out. Flares, food, water, EPIRB to send out a satellite signal so the Coast Guard'll know where to come pick you up, it's all in there, but they're not real comfortable."

"Can you steer one of these Avons?"

"No," Frank explained. "That's not what they're for. They're round, see, when they're blown up. Like a couple of big inner tubes stacked on top of each other, with a floor and a tent on top. If you had a sculling oar, maybe, or could jury-rig a sail, and the weather wasn't bad, and you didn't have far to go, you might get somewhere, but that's not the point. That's what the EPIRB's for — so somebody'll know you're in trouble and come pick you up right where you are. That's the idea, anyway."

"The paper reported that the *Valkyrie's* skiff wasn't located. Does that seem reasonable to you?" Janet asked. She set the beer on a coaster on the lamp table next to her. She didn't really like beer.

"It doesn't and that's a fact," Frank told her. "We were heading out to sea. The skiff should have been up in chocks and lashed down on deck. I'd think it would have been with the boat. Might have broken loose and floated away. They have positive flotation, you see, so they won't sink if you take a big sea aboard them and they fill up."

"If you had to abandon ship, why wouldn't you take the skiff?" Janet asked, puzzled. "It's bigger than the life raft, isn't it? And it has its own engine."

"Doesn't work that way," Frank replied. "It'd take quite a bit of time to get the skiff into the water and away. If you had that much time, you'd have time to call a Mayday, maybe save the boat. You don't want to lose your boat if you can help it, lady."

"Could one person launch the skiff?"

"Sure. You ever been on a seiner?"

Janet shook her head. Frank seemed eager to show off his expertise.

"*Valkyrie* was set up like every seiner I've ever seen. Go on down to the docks and have a look. The skiff was cradled on the stern. The boat boom's right above it, with the block for hauling in the net. The net's stowed here, forward of the skiff, on the reel. Got it?"

Janet nodded. She'd seen seiners, of course, but Frank had worked on one for years, so from him she was getting the inside story with the kind of detail she hoped she'd eventually have to convey to a jury.

"To launch the skiff, you lower the halyard and hook the skiff up to it. Push the buttons on the electric control on the mast, over here, and you raise the skiff up, swing 'er over the side and let her down in the water. Get into the skiff, release the falls, start her up, and take her away. Even with a crew, it takes a lot longer than tossing the Avon over the side and pulling the ripcord. With one man alone, in trouble, well, he just wouldn't have that kind of time."

"What's the seiner doing when you launch the skiff?"

"Making way slowly with the wind on the opposite bow quarter from where you're putting the skiff in the water," Frank replied promptly. "Under normal circumstances, that is. If you're in trouble, it depends on what the trouble is."

Janet felt a stirring of excitement. Frank had given her a clearer picture of how a seiner worked. The missing skiff was a real problem. So far, she had heard nothing about a life raft. That would have to be followed up, too.

"You fished with Mr. Lowry for several years," she began, broaching a different topic.

"Three, all told." Frank set his beer can on an end table, leaned forward and folded his hands between his knees.

Janet picked up her beer again and took another sip before speaking. "Were you close?" she asked.

"You see an awful lot of a person when you're out fishing with him for a season. We got along OK. But there's other people I'd rather spend my time with when I'm in port."

Janet leaned back and considered. Frank Vincent was not being completely straightforward, which seemed out of character. He was concealing something. She'd have to try another approach.

"Who were Mr. Lowry's friends?"

"I couldn't tell you that. He didn't seem the type to make real close friends, though of course he knew everybody in the fishing business. He was president of that salmon fishermen's lobbying group, so he knew all the politicians, too. He spent a lot of time down at the Mermaid."

Janet raised an eyebrow questioningly.

"It's a saloon. There aren't too many of them left. Looks like a tavern, but serves hard liquor and a short-order menu. Down by the commercial docks in Charbonneau. You want to get ahead in fish politics, you hang around there. Most of the boys and girls off the boats go in there pretty often."

"You don't?"

Frank grinned. "Hell, no. Not much. Not when I own the Oyster Bar."

The expensive, upscale restaurant and lounge overlooking the Boat Basin in Salmon Bay was one of Janet's favorite haunts. Somehow, it didn't seem like Frank Vincent's kind of place.

"I haven't seen you there," she said neutrally.

Frank shrugged. "I get down there now and then. Jim and Merrilee split the managing. I got the idea and put up the money. They're buying me out a little at a time, until they own half. It works out."

"Are you still fishing?" she asked. She wouldn't have kept fishing if she owned the Oyster Bar.

"Sure. Good money, and I like the life, as long as I don't get too much of it. Gave up my own boat when I had enough put by, thought I'd do something else. But the way it turned out, when I started getting restless, Glen was looking for a mate, so I signed on. I crew on a herring boat in Alaska now. Shorter season, better money."

Frank Vincent smiled broadly, secure in himself and his success. Janet went to the next question on her mental list.

"The *Valkyrie* was reported to have left her dock the 17th of March, St. Patrick's day. So far, no one's been able to trace her after that. Do you remember the last time you heard from Mr. Lowry?"

Frank shook his head. "Can't say for sure. Couple weeks before we were due to leave is the best I can do. I stopped by the Mermaid. That's where we set up when he was to meet me and all."

"Do you know where you were the 17th?" Janet phrased the question as if it were solely an aid to Frank's memory of his last contact with Glen Lowry.

The fisherman's leathery face screwed up as he tried to remember.

"The 17th was a Saturday," Janet added.

"That's easy, then," he said with a smile. "Any Saturday, if I'm in town, I'm right here, watching my grandkids. From about four o'clock on, anyway."

"Would there be any way to verify that you were here that particular night? Pay records?"

"They don't have to pay me to watch my grandkids." Frank sounded shocked.

"They don't take a child-care deduction off their taxes?" It was Janet's turn to be shocked.

"I don't know about that, but I do know nobody has to pay me to watch my grandkids. And if I'm not home, the grandkids go visit Jim's folks for the whole weekend, not just Saturday, and nobody pays them either. Child-care deduction?"

"But you watch the children every Saturday night, if you're in town?"

"That's what I said."

"No exceptions?"

"None that I can think of. Friday and Saturday are the busiest nights the Oyster Bar's got. You say the boat was last seen on the 17th? That's St. Patrick's day, right? We did a special party for it. Do it every year. When I fixed it up with Glen, down at the Mermaid, it was just before then, Wednesday or Thursday, most likely. I remember now. I got the plan straight and got out of there. Bad business."

"What was?" Janet tried to sound casual, but sensed she was about to unearth something important.

"Oh, it had to do with this crewman, Vern. He'd been going out with us every year, but the year before, Glen caught him drinking on watch. Then, when we got in, Vern got pissed off over what he said was a short share. I thought Glen told Vern at the time it was his last trip, but either he didn't, or Vern didn't hear it, because Vern was down at the Mermaid the night I ran into Glen, and Vern seemed to think he was going, too, and got real bent out of shape when Glen told him he wasn't."

"What was the story on the short share?" Janet wanted to know.

"Vern was supposed to be supervising some of the kids we hired on as crew for the season, and a power winch got broken — I never did know exactly how it happened; none of my business, really. Glen didn't find out about it until later. The kid was long gone by then, and Vern should have told Glen about it when it happened. Glen held Vern responsible for it, and took it out of his share, even though the kid broke it.

If it'd been my boat, Vern wouldn't have been there at all. I would have fired him the second I caught him drinking on watch, got him off the boat the next time we put into port."

"What's Vern's last name?"

"Junker. You can find him at the Mermaid if you want to talk to him. Spends his time drinking and pissing and moaning about his hard luck. Damned fool way to behave if you're looking for a job, you ask me."

Janet held up the can of beer and said, "You drink. What was wrong with Junker drinking?"

Frank's square face became stern. "He was on watch, lady. He was responsible for the boat and everybody on her. Yes, I drink, and sometimes I booze it up pretty good. But only on shore. I never drink at sea."

Janet had an intuitive flash as data suddenly connected in her brain.

"Junker thought he could get away with it because Lowry drank, too, didn't he?"

Frank nodded, heavily.

"Too much. You could see it on his face," Frank said. "Glen had liquor on board — couldn't leave it behind is my guess — and he'd drink it when he wasn't on watch. First time we went out, I put it to him. I didn't like it. Captain's on call all the time. I was mate, and if he wasn't fit, that meant it was up to me, and I wasn't getting paid for that, even though I've got my master's ticket. So we worked it out. I didn't bitch about his drinking off watch and I'd be the one on call. The crew would know it, and I'd get a bigger share." Frank shrugged. "It worked out OK for me. But it gave Vern ideas. Glen couldn't do anything about the drinking off watch, if he was doing it himself, but drinking on watch is damned dangerous."

"What was Junker's reaction when Lowry told him he didn't have a job for the season?"

"He was mad. Plenty mad, and with some reason, if what I heard from Vern later was true."

"What was that?"

"That after that fight they'd had, about the shares, they'd talked it out and settled it, with Vern taking the short share, but getting his job back. But Glen said it wasn't like that, and Vern didn't have a job. What I say is, Glen should have made it clear. By then it was too late for Vern to get another Alaska boat, and it's been all downhill for him from there. But a lot of that's Vern's own fault."

"Did he make any threats?"

Frank shrugged. "Said he was going to call a lawyer. Never did, as far as I know."

Then the garrulous fisherman peered quizzically at the prosecutor. "You don't think Vern could have had anything to do with this, do you?"

"I don't think anything just yet, Mr. Vincent. But we will want to talk to Mr. Junker."

∼ 13 ∼

After Janet left Frank Vincent's house, she drove
out of Bridle Crest towards the coast. The road went through
North Jetty Park, then turned east to follow the bay shore back
to Charbonneau. As she crossed a bridge marked "Clark Creek,"
Janet slowed the car. She was nearing the house where Lowry
had lived. The road turned inland, curved away from the shore,
and then, on the left, a rural-route mailbox marked "Simpson"
appeared. Janet turned into the upland drive too fast, sending
up a cloud of sandy dust.

The house stood halfway up the hill. It was a classic
two-story Northwest craftsman design, painted white with green
trim. Janet mounted the steps to the wide porch and rang the
bell. The curtains were drawn against the afternoon sunlight.
No car was in sight, so she was not surprised when no one
answered. She turned to look at the expansive view across the
harbor and between the jetties.

From the porch she could see the back of another house
which stood below the road, by the shore. She saw a gravel
parking area in front of what appeared to be a single-car garage. Beyond the house, she could just make out the very end
of a long dock with a broad float. This would be the house
where Glen Lowry had lived. One reason she'd pulled into the
Simpsons' drive was to get an overview of the property. Since
she could see the end of the float, the Simpsons could have

seen the *Valkyrie* from their porch or noted her absence. They could also see anyone who came or went from the house. Janet wanted to talk to them. She also wondered what kind of car, if any, Vern Junker drove.

Janet drove across the road, down the slanting drive-way past the mailbox which was labeled "Hahn-Praeger," to park in the cleared area in front of the garage. She hoped the place would speak to her, tell her what had happened to Glen Lowry so long ago. Sometimes an examination of a presumptive crime scene enabled her to see exactly how a crime had occurred.

The lowland house was also built in the craftsman style, and was a little bigger than its upland neighbor. It was painted pale grey with slate-colored trim. Janet knocked at the back door. There was no answer, but a ginger cat came to curl around her ankles. She liked cats, and bent down to pet this one, but it flounced away. She brushed the ginger hair from her stockings, then circled the house in search of the front door, examining the place where Glen Lowry had lived and probably died.

The grounds were bordered by the woods to the west, the highway to the north, and the water to the south and east. The ginger cat followed her around the house, pretending that it just happened to be going in the same direction.

The wide front porch overlooked the harbor. No one answered this door either. Through the large, uncurtained front windows, Janet saw a cluttered living room, shabby and comfortable. Broad stairs rose to a barely visible landing. Janet could just see the top of the rail protecting the back stairs angling down to the kitchen. The big dining room table was covered with some child's project. There were dishes in the kitchen sink, visible through the open swinging door. It seemed like a happy place.

The inside of the house had changed so much since Lowry lived there, it evoked no response in Janet except to convince her the crime hadn't happened inside. Catherine or her tenants would have noticed something. *You can't cut someone's throat and not leave a mess. You can't get it all no matter how much cleaning you do,* Janet thought. That was a forensic fact. Well, at least now she had an idea of the floor plan, though craftsman houses were all pretty much alike. She abandoned the porch for the small and scruffy front yard.

She stopped and looked around, trying to get beyond the kids' toys and haphazard plantings to see into the past. The same problem applied to the yard as to the house. The killer couldn't have gotten rid of the mess entirely. Not only would the killer have had to move the body, he would've had to stand for hours with a garden hose trying to rid the ground of evidence visible to the naked eye. *No,* Janet thought. *Not here, either.*

A rough path led towards the water. Janet took it. The path branched. She took the wider fork leading to the dock. Steeply sloping mud flats fell away beneath the dock. A crab scuttled into waving eelgrass; suddenly the water was so deep Janet couldn't see the bottom. Tires had been nailed to the outside edge of the float to serve as bumpers. This was where the *Valkyrie* had moored. The water looked cold and forbidding.

A boathouse, sized and styled like a single-car garage, was tucked into the woods just west of the head of the dock. Janet peered through the grimy windows, but could see little beyond a collection of assorted orange, black and green containers, some the size of oil drums, and a huge pile of net edged with orange and white floats. What belonged to the tenants and what predated their occupancy was impossible to tell, but unless they also had a large boat, much of this collection must have belonged to the *Valkyrie.* Janet didn't see the boathouse as the crime scene, either. She fixed the empty water at the end of the dock with a gimlet gaze. *It happened on the boat,* she said to herself. *It's the only possible place.* She shivered suddenly and looked around. It felt like someone was watching her, but she saw no signs of another person.

The trees brushed up against the house on the west side. Some smaller specimens were even gaining a foothold in the

narrow space on the seaward side of the boathouse. A slender
path ran through the crumpled grasses and fallen needles, but
Janet suspected it had been made by the currently resident children and didn't take it. She'd found the crime scene, she was
sure. Now she wanted to get out of there. Crime scenes often
felt spooky to Janet, as if what had happened there imprinted
itself on the very atmosphere of a place.

     Retracing her steps, she returned to her car the way
she'd come. She opened the door, but didn't get in. She felt that
there was something more the house could tell her, if only she
would listen for it.

     Standing beside the car, she observed the scene around
her. The garage was open and empty except for gardening supplies. The paved drive ended in the graveled parking area, which
itself ended at the garage, but on the north side of the garage,
there was a wide flat area, almost exactly the width of the drive.
She closed the car door and walked over to it. It extended into
the woods, and was almost as wide as a road.

     Janet glanced up. The highway embankment rose steeply
on the right, hiding this area from the view of anyone in a
passing car, or even from the Simpsons in the upper house. A
casual observer would not be able to see a car parked back here
without actually coming most of the way down the curving
drive, and maybe not even then if it had been pulled forward
into the trees.

     Janet wondered if this might be part of the older, two-
lane road that would have preceded the highway. How far did
it lead before it petered out among the trees, or in the current
embankment? She stepped forward to find out.

     Immediately, she was in the woods. Huge, fragrant ce-
dars towered over her head, their fallen needles cushioning her
steps. Shafts of sunlight pierced the green darkness. A chip-
munk scolded as she passed too close to its territory. Janet
relaxed. There was nothing eerie about the path.

     Children used the path, Janet discovered, when she
found a multicolored ball in a deep rut. She picked it up. It

was the twin of one she'd sent her younger brother, Troy, for his last birthday. Brain-damaged in the accident that killed their mother, now an adult with the mind of an eight-year-old child, he lived in a congregate care facility near Lake Arrowhead. She visited often and wrote him every week, in fact had planned to do so tonight. She set the ball down gently and went on.

The trail which rounded the front of the boathouse ran behind the garage to meet this broader path. Other turnings led off into tiny glades. Through the trees, Janet could glimpse the bay. Then the wide path made an abrupt, but banked, right turn. A footpath branched off, going straight ahead. Janet followed that, to discover a huckleberry-covered slope leading to a broad stream.

She'd come farther than she'd thought. *This must be Clark Creek.* The channel was at least twenty feet wide. The lowered tide had left the creek much diminished, with the runnels bare between hummocks of stiff salt marsh grasses, but the channel was still navigable by a small craft.

One could slide down the slope to the flats to follow the creek's course on foot, but Janet, with due consideration for her Gucci pumps, decided against it.

She returned to the wider fork and followed it up a short slope, where it burst without warning onto the graveled shoulder of the highway. Maybe fifty feet to her left was the Clark Creek bridge. No houses were in sight. To her right, the highway curved inland, so this small abandoned road was invisible from both the Simpsons' house and the Lowry place. Janet felt a tingle of excitement. She crossed the highway and walked to the bridge over Clark Creek.

Standing in the center of the bridge, Janet looked upstream. The creek widened above the bridge; a good-sized island covered with grasses and dotted with a couple of stunted trees divided it into two channels, both of which looked navigable, at least by a very small boat, like a kayak, canoe or dinghy, or perhaps an inboard skiff. Beyond the island, the creek twisted out of sight.

From the bridge, Janet couldn't see a single sign of human habitation. Clark Creek's existence was common knowledge, she knew. It appeared on the navigation charts. It would take only a cursory inspection to learn the creek was navigable. Janet was now sure Glen Lowry had been killed on the *Valkyrie,* either by someone who came aboard while it was moored at the dock, or by someone Lowry had taken out with him from the house. The seiner had been scuttled to hide the evidence of the crime, and the killer had used the skiff to get back to shore.

Clark Creek was a perfect place to hide the *Valkyrie's* missing skiff, Janet thought, as she crossed the road and reentered the woods. After abandoning it, the killer could follow the creekbed to the footpath, climb up the slope, and retrace the path to retrieve a car hidden behind the garage. There would be total privacy. A killer who didn't know about the abandoned road might have had the luck to find it, or might have simply climbed up to the highway at the bridge and walked back to the house that way.

The abandoned road was wide enough and smooth enough to accommodate a car, she thought as she walked down it. The killer might have driven along it, rejoining the highway at the bridge, and then driven west in total safety, to circle around on any of the many secondary roads to whatever highway led home. This would have been the safest, most effective plan.

Janet sighed her satisfaction as she came out of the woods next to the garage. The house had spoken to her. She now felt sure she knew where the crime was committed, and how the killer had got away. She recalled Frank Vincent telling her about someone who knew the *Valkyrie* very well and could be presumed to know Clark Creek and Lowry's house. She got into her car and picked up the phone eagerly. She needed to talk to Ed.

～ 14 ～

Saturday morning, Nic was doing laundry in Catherine's small utility room. Catherine herself was in the living room editing the videos they'd taken of the sea lions. She looked up at a sudden roar overhead.

"Nic?" she called. "Did you hear that?"

"What?" Nic popped out of the utility room. Then she heard it too, and went to the window to look. "It's that helicopter again," she said. "They're going to land."

"What does she want now?" Catherine said, coming to join Nic at the window.

"It might not be Janet," Nic said, surprised that Catherine would assume it was the prosecutor coming back. "Remember, she said there might be detectives."

"They'll come up here, then," Catherine said. She turned to Nic and touched her arm. "Would you stay? I'll have to talk to them alone, I guess, but I'd like to have you close by."

"Of course," Nic said, reaching up to pat Catherine's hand. "I can just go on doing what I'm doing."

"Yes. Please. I just don't want to be alone."

A few minutes later, the two women watched as two men, one very large and sloppily dressed, the other shorter, slender and quite good-looking, made their way up the hill. The shorter one had to slow his natural pace to allow his hefty companion to keep up. They were unmistakably police officers,

Nic thought, though she didn't know how she knew that. They weren't wearing uniforms. Maybe it was the way they moved, with a kind of steady purpose. The smaller man finally knocked at the door. Catherine opened it.

"Yes?" she said.

"I'm Ed Nuñez," the handsome one said, proffering a credentials case. "This is Mick Taylor." He indicated his companion. "We're Sacajawea County Homicide Detectives. Are you Ms. Adams?"

"Yes. What can I do for you?" Catherine felt her heart pounding. She had never talked to a police officer before. She was the same size as the smaller man, and they were being polite, but she found their very presence intimidating.

"May we come in for a minute?" Taylor said. "We're just following up on a couple of things in connection with Mr. Lowry's death."

"I guess." Catherine stepped aside and led them into the living area, where they sat down. Nic had retreated to the laundry room. Catherine had been surprised at the amount of wash she had. It was going to take her most of the day to get it done.

"First off," Nuñez said, "we'd like to ask you about Mr. Lowry's estate. Did you expect to inherit from him?"

"It was a complete surprise to me," Catherine answered. "All there was, really, was the insurance. I thought that would go to *his* relatives, because we weren't really related at all, but Henry — Mr. Charm, my lawyer — said when there isn't a will, the law has a list of people the money goes to. They just work their way down it until they find somebody, and stepchildren are on it. That's how it happened. I had no idea."

"I suppose Mr. Charm would confirm that?" Taylor said in his deep bass voice.

"I don't know why he wouldn't. It's true," Catherine replied. Questions about the money part were easy. She hadn't asked for it, and didn't want or need it.

"What did you do with the money?" Nuñez, the handsome one, had a baritone voice. Catherine noticed a soft rounding to his enunciation that was not quite an accent.

"Nothing." Catherine sounded surprised. It didn't seem like that was any of their business, but she saw no reason not to tell them. "I didn't need it for anything, so I put it in the bank. The trust department invests it for me. That was all set up when I was a kid, with my father's estate. I already knew I was coming out here to do research when Glen died, so I just told Henry to have the other money added in."

"You work for the University, I understand?" Nuñez asked.

"And several other research groups. I own this island, you see. They come to me to do studies, or for permission to allow their people to come and collect data."

"Now, I believe you said you last saw Mr. Lowry on Friday, March 16?" This came from Taylor.

"I really can't remember. I think I figured out it was the day before they said he was last seen, but I can't be sure. It was a long time ago."

"Did you go out to his house after work?" Taylor asked.

Catherine paused, not sure if she understood what he was driving at. "Oh, I see," she said after a minute. "If I went out after work, it must have been Friday." She paused again. "No, I'm sorry, I can't help you. I remember I picked up a little cherry magazine table, and I remember it was dark when I left, and that's just about all I remember about the last time I saw him. There wasn't anything particularly significant about it at the time. It was only later that it seemed important to remember the last time I saw him, and that was only important to me. Then."

"Do you know what you did the rest of the weekend?" Nuñez asked.

"No. Come on, it was years ago."

"Please think about it, Ms. Adams," Nuñez said. "It might be important. Did you take the table right home?"

"I suppose — no, you know, I have a feeling that I might not have. I might have gone out to the park, the bird sanctuary in the wetlands, you know? That's nesting season. When I lived in town, I spent a lot of weekends camping out at North Jetty Park so I could be out early to watch the birds. The house is on the way."

"Do you remember if Mr. Lowry seemed upset about anything while you were there?" Nuñez asked. He seemed to be the leader, Catherine thought, with the other one, Taylor, chiming in occasionally to try and get her off balance.

"I don't remember noticing anything in particular. It was really not a big deal. I stopped by, said hello, got the table, and left, and that's it, as far as I can remember." Catherine reached up to finger the long braid hanging over her right shoulder.

"He didn't say anything to you about expecting anyone?"

"Not that I remember, but why would he?"

"Nothing that would indicate he was frightened of anyone, or had gotten threats of any kind?"

"Threats?" She shook her head. "I think I'd remember something like that."

"And you didn't see anyone else out there?" Nuñez persisted.

"I already told you I didn't." Catherine was getting exasperated, though she tried not to let it show. Nic could hear it in her voice. She didn't blame her. The questions were repetitious and Nic couldn't see what they were trying to prove. She wondered if she should interrupt. Suddenly the questions changed.

"Isn't this a lonely life for you?" Nuñez's voice was sociable, pleasant, even a bit flirtatious.

"I have quite a lot of company." Catherine's tone was dry. She'd had just about enough of this. It was time to change the situation. She raised her voice. "Nic? Come in here for a second, will you please?"

Nic came through the kitchen and into the living room. She faced Catherine.

"You called me?" she asked.

Catherine nodded. "Ms. Cavanaugh, this is Detective Mick Taylor, and this is Detective Ed Nuñez." She turned to the detectives. "Ms. Cavanaugh's boat was grounded here by the rogue wave we had last Monday night. She's my guest until she can make repairs. These gentlemen," she told Nic, "flew out from town to ask me some more questions about my stepfather's death." She turned back to the detectives and gave them an ironic smile. "For a person who lives by herself in a wildlife refuge, I think I have quite a lot of company. There's three of you here right now."

"Pleased to meet you," Taylor said, looking uncomfortable. Nuñez nodded and smiled at Nic, though he was a little worried. Janet had a blind spot when it came to Catherine Adams. How would she react when she found out Cavanaugh was a transient, not a permanent part of Catherine's life?

"How do you do." Nic glanced at Catherine. She could tell from the look in Catherine's eyes that she wanted Nic's support badly. So Nic sat down. Nuñez looked amused.

Taylor looked even more uncomfortable, but he said, "Can you tell us anything about the *Valkyrie?*"

"Probably nothing you don't already know," Catherine replied. "You can ask."

"When did Mr. Lowry buy her?"

"Right after he and Mom got married, when he sold his house. That's where he got the money for her. He came to live with us, in our house. He fixed up the dock so he could moor her right out in front."

"Didn't you worry about him, when you found out he was gone?" Nuñez asked.

"I didn't know he *was* gone, until the Coast Guard told me he was missing."

"But wouldn't you have? Isn't the middle of March early to leave for Alaska?"

"I don't know. I don't follow the commercial seasons. They're always changing." That was true enough. Catherine followed the fish runs generally as part of her work, but the commercial, sport and Indian fishing seasons weren't relevant to her. As a tribal member, she could fish for her personal use whenever she wanted to.

"How many crew did it take to run the boat?" Taylor wanted to know.

"Glen could run it himself. I don't know how many people he needed to fish. I remember he always seemed to have a few people around."

"Mr. Frank Vincent gave us the names of a couple of people who crewed for Mr. Lowry," Mick Taylor said. "I wonder if you could give us some more, maybe people in Alaska, or people who worked for him when you were growing up?"

"I'm afraid I couldn't. Frank would know a lot more about that than I do."

"Why is that?" Ed said in a smoothly insinuating tone that brought Nic up short. This man, she thought, was good. But Catherine was handling herself well.

"I hadn't lived there in a long time," Catherine said evenly.

"How long?" he asked, and Nic held her breath, though she didn't quite know why.

"Since I started high school. Salmon Bay had a special honors science program. To get into it, I had to move there. I boarded with John and Maggie Ryan."

"So you weren't close to your family?"

"I wouldn't say that. I grew up, that's all."

"Did you have any problems with your stepfather?"

"Why should I? He was my mother's husband." Catherine spoke easily, but Nic heard a reserve in her voice, and wondered what might be behind it. Apparently the detectives didn't notice it, because Mick Taylor then said, "I guess that's about it, Ms. Adams. Thanks for your help."

"Such as it is," she replied. "I'm sorry I don't know anything."

"If you think of something, will you let us know?" Ed Nuñez asked.

"Of course. But I can't think what."

"And we can reach you here, if we need to?"

"Where else?" Catherine smiled as she got up to let them out. Nic remained seated until Catherine closed the front door. Then, following an impulse she didn't quite understand, Nic went to make sure the back door to the lighthouse was locked. She returned to the living room.

"If you're OK, I'll just make sure they get off all right," she said to Catherine, who sat on the couch, staring at the dark glass of the fireplace insert.

"Sure," Catherine said quizzically, "I'm fine."

"It's *Wayward*," Nic continued, giving a nervous wriggle of her shoulders. "She's standing wide open and I'm uncomfortable with strangers wandering around like that."

"Go ahead," Catherine said with a smile. She wanted a little time alone, to review the conversation in her mind, to make sure she'd said nothing that could be misunderstood. The detectives seemed nice enough, but they were adversaries to anyone involved in a criminal investigation and she didn't dare forget it.

"You did great," Nic said as she went out the door. Catherine shook her head. The way Nic could read her mind was amazing.

Nic saw the two men walk quickly toward the clearing where the helicopter waited. She followed just far enough to see both detectives board. The helicopter took off immediately. Nic shrugged. Maybe she'd seen too many movies, but she still didn't like the idea of strangers having unimpeded access to her boat, especially if they were cops. She hurried down to the boat.

The police helicopter circled the island, coming in low over *Wayward*, before it left. Nic felt a curious sense of invasion. She locked the hatches before heading back to the lighthouse. She had barely reached the top of the headland when the helicopter returned.

No, by damn! she thought, *it's a different one!* There was a television logo on the door. "Oh, shit," she said aloud. "Reporters." She ran to the lighthouse door and stuck her head in.

"You want to talk to the press?" she asked.

"No." Catherine, alarmed, looked up from the couch.

"Come lock the door, then. I'll get rid of them."

Nic turned and hurried down the hill, taking up a position between a boulder and a rockfall on the path leading to the lighthouse from the landing site. To reach the lighthouse, they'd have to come up that path. Through her.

The helicopter landed. Half a dozen people poured out. They swarmed up the path and began talking to Nic all at once. She could only sort out bits and pieces of the babble — "...with Channel 6...." "What is your connection with...." "...your name is...." "...talk to Catherine Adams."

"You're trespassing. Get out," she roared

The babble rose again, insistently. They wanted to know who *she* was, since she obviously wasn't the woman they were looking for, according to the old photos they had dug up somewhere. Nic used a miraculously remembered phrase.

"I'm the owner's agent. This is a private island, and you're trespassing. Get out."

Someone thrust a microphone into her face. Furious, she grabbed it and threw it in the dirt at its owner's feet. A camera clicked.

"Go away," she commanded. "You're trespassing. Leave now or I'll have you thrown off."

A boom mike attached to a video camera brushed her hair. She swatted at it, connected violently and knocked the camera to the ground. The reporters withdrew a few feet into an agitated huddle, whispering among themselves. The camera operator scrabbled to regain his instrument, dropping papers in his hurry.

Nic held her ground and repeated in a voice deep with anger, "Leave now, or you'll be sued. Come back, and you'll be sued. This is a private island, and you're trespassing. Get out! Now!"

Glaring, she took a step toward the group. Almost in unison, they stepped backwards, then turned and fled. Nic followed them for several yards until she saw they actually were piling into the helicopter. Then she stood, arms akimbo, with a thunderous look on her face, until the helicopter rose from the ground and lifted away. She gave a sigh of relief, then giggled at her own fierceness, while she picked up the dropped papers. It felt good to do something concrete for Catherine. It would make a damned funny story, too.

Nic scanned the papers as she walked to the lighthouse. She had sections of three different papers, each containing a story about Glen Lowry's death. Presumably they'd intended to use these as a basis for an interview with Catherine. Janet Schilling figured prominently in each story. Nic began to scowl.

"Are they gone?" Catherine said from the door of the lighthouse. "I saw a chopper leave."

"They took off."

"Thank you so much." Catherine began to step outside, but Nic motioned her back in.

"They're circling, hear them? They might have long-range lenses."

Catherine nodded as she stepped back. She let Nic in, then shut and locked the door. "So tell me. How did you get rid of them?"

Nic dropped into a chair and set the papers on the round oak table. She uttered a short bark of laughter. "I told them they were trespassing, that they'd be sued if they didn't leave immediately, or if they came back. They seemed to believe it."

"I'm so glad you were here to do it," Catherine said gratefully. *If Nic hadn't been here, what would I have done?* she thought. *Hid in a corner listening to the reporters batter on the door until they got bored and left, most likely.* "I wonder what they wanted with me?" she asked.

"You'd better read these." Nic pushed the newspaper sections towards her.

As Catherine read, she pursed her lips, her face growing drawn and pale.

"I think," she said, "I better call my lawyer."

∾ 15 ∾

The Mermaid, across the street from the commercial fishing docks in Charbonneau, was a one-story concrete block building decorated in modern mock-tudor to resemble an English pub. There was a plank double door with an elaborately carved swinging sign hanging over it. This featured a buxom mermaid winking salaciously behind a wing of her blonde hair. Janet eyed it with distaste, but she had to go in if she hoped to find Vern Junker. She pushed open the left-hand door.

The room was big and dark, air-conditioned cool. Janet closed her eyes for a second to accustom them to the dim light. When she opened them, she saw a collection of round tables and captain's chairs clustered around a wooden dance floor, which sat in front of a bandstand located in the corner farthest from the bar. Huge speakers hung from the ceiling above it. Tonight, Saturday, the joint would be jumping, crowded with people out for a good time. This afternoon, though, it was quiet.

To Janet's right, the long bar ran around a corner of the room. A television set, tuned to a baseball game, hung from a wall bracket. This part of the saloon was separated from the larger area by a half-wall, with a series of pool tables strung along the bar side of it. At the end of the bar, a small kitchen area was walled off. Janet could see a blonde woman through the pass-through, manipulating a microwave oven. Frank had told her the owner's name was Vicky Davis. This must be her. There were no other women in sight.

Half a dozen men clustered on bar stools near the television. These were older men, with the air of habitués about them. A couple of kids in their early twenties drank draft beer and played desultory pool.

One of the men at the bar might be Vern Junker.

The woman left the kitchen, carrying a burger and fries and a cup of soup to one of the men. She collected for it at once, taking the money to the cash register to ring up the sale. Janet approached her there, out of earshot of the customers.

The woman slammed the cash drawer shut with the heel of her hand, said, "One second," and went to slap the change in front of the customer. She came back to the cash register and looked inquiringly at Janet, a half-smile on her face.

"Help you?" she asked.

"Is Vicky Davis in?"

"I'm Vicky," she answered. "What can I do for you?"

Janet slid a card across the bar.

"I understand you knew Glen Lowry. My office is looking into the circumstances of his death. I wondered if you could tell me something about him."

"Took you long enough," she said as she looked Janet over. The prosecutor's slim black jeans and pink crew-necked sweater might not look lawyerly, but despite Janet's clothes-horse tendencies, she knew she didn't need the costume to make a professional impression.

"Boats lost out at sea are in the Coast Guard's jurisdiction, not mine. You know his boat was found in the bay and his body was on it?"

"Hard to miss. It's caused a lot of talk. Sit down," she continued, indicating a stool right by the cash register. "Want a drink? We're a saloon, not a tavern, so we have the hard stuff. Or there's beer and soft drinks, if you want."

Janet accepted a club soda with lime. Vicky set it before her on a napkin and leaned up against the bar.

"Why should I be able to tell you anything about Glen Lowry?" she asked.

"I understand this is kind of a club for the commercial fishermen. Someone he worked with said he came in here a lot. You're the owner. You're here a lot. I thought you might know him."

"Club," Vicky said thoughtfully. "Yeah, I guess that's about right. We do a lunch and after-work trade for the marina people and local businesses. There's live music and dancing weekends. Afternoons, like now, and late at night on week-days, it's kind of slow. That's when it's more like a tavern, or a club, you might say. That's when the regulars are around."

Janet watched her as she spoke. She was Janet's own age, around forty, maybe a few years over, and attractive in a rough way. Her hair was yellow more than blonde, and her face showed the effects of too little sunlight and too much hard work. A line dragged down the corner of her mouth, and her blue eyes, behind a superficial friendliness, were cold and hard as cut crystal.

"I never got to know him really," Vicky said, "until after Alice, that's his wife, died. Before that, he'd come in for lunch or a quick one when he was passing by, so I knew who he was, that was all. And of course he was president of *Salmon Forever*. But after Alice died, he started coming in pretty often, almost every night. Showed up about four, and stayed pretty late. Like I said, it's afternoons and late evenings that are slow, so we talked. He liked things the way he liked them, just so. He paid cash, which made up for a lot as far as I was concerned. Never asked for a tab." She cast a jaded glance at the group around the television.

"He needed somebody to talk to, I think," she went on. "Most nights, I tend bar and cashier. Glen would sit right where you are, by the register here, and talk to me."

"What about?"

"This and that. Anything and everything, and nothing in particular. He missed his wife. Talked about fishing. Well, they all do that."

"Ever mention a Vern Junker?" Janet ventured cautiously.

Vicky laughed and gestured toward the group watching television. "Vern's usually sitting right over there."

"Today?"

"He's not here yet. He'll be in pretty soon, I guess. He usually is."

"He worked for Lowry, didn't he?"

Vicky tilted her head a little. Her mouth hardened. "Sounds like you know all about it."

"I heard he worked for Lowry," Janet said. "I heard there was some kind of disagreement. I'm interested in how they got along, if they both came in here often."

Vicky shrugged. "They got along. People don't get along in here, I kick 'em out. What happened, Vern and Glen got into some kind of hassle over shares, but they solved it, is what I heard. Then just before the season, Glen told Vern he wouldn't need him anymore. Vern was real put out by that, and it's hard to blame him. Person thinks they have a job, they don't go looking for another one. So Glen stopped coming around for a while, and then he went out and didn't come back." She shrugged again.

"Lowry talk about anyone else?"

"Alice, a lot. He missed her. And her daughter. Thought she was a bitch, kicking him out of the house. Well, it was her house. Her mother left it to her. And she wasn't exactly kicking him out. She was letting him live there for nothing till the season opened. I didn't see he had cause for complaint. He'd talk gossip, you know, and shop talk, about the other people who crewed for him, and what they were up to. Frank Vincent — I suppose that's who you talked to — he owns the Oyster Bar, and around here he's always good for talk. Fishermen like to hear about one of their own making good and getting out of the business. But Frank still fishes."

"Who else crewed for Glen?"

"Lots of kids. Good summer job for a kid in high school, or, more likely, college. Some of them want to do it regular, but you know kids. They change their minds, they move away. I can't think of anybody he used more than one season. Frank might know, or Vern."

"Did Glen ever mention to you being afraid of anybody? Getting threats? Any arguments, or fights, that you heard of? Anybody with a grudge against him?"

"I never heard of anything like that. Just this thing with Vern. I don't think that was all that serious, even though Vern sits in here and cries in his bourbon about it almost every night. He never has got another Alaska boat."

"Where would I find Vern?"

"He lives at the St. Charles Hotel. It's an SRO a couple of blocks from here." She jerked her thumb north just as the telephone rang. "Or he'll be in here later. 'Scuse me." She hurried to the wall phone by the kitchen entrance.

"Thanks," Janet called after her. Vicky nodded as she picked up the phone. Janet counted out the price of the soda from the change in her Vuitton wallet, listening with only half an ear to Vicky's end of the phone call. It concerned a car, and her tone, though sharp, sounded distinctly loving. While she waited for the conversation to end, she reviewed what she'd learned to see if there was anything else to ask Vicky.

"Hey, lady." Janet turned. The speaker was an old man, not too clean, with the wide muscles and tough, broad hands of a fisherman, though he was clearly many years past the work. "You a cop?" the man asked in a hoarse whisper.

"No," Janet told him, sliding another of her business cards towards the man. He read it.

"Prosecutor. Huh. That'll do." The man pulled himself up onto the stool next to Janet's. "Don't know what you're here for," he said, "but I can guess. There's something you should know that she" — he jerked his head toward Vicky, who was still on the phone but had moved into the kitchen area — "won't tell you. She knew Glen Lowry pretty well. They was almost dating, like. Then they broke up and he stopped coming around. She tells it like Glen stopped coming around 'cause of the trouble him and Vern had but that happened afterwards. Maybe she don't want to let on that she and Glen was close, not after what he did to Vern. Glen shouldn't have done that. Vern's a good guy."

Janet got the man's name and address, scribbling as unobtrusively as possible in her Vuitton purse notebook. This would have to be verified, maybe by Junker, maybe through another, more formal interview with Vicky. Thanking the man, Janet rose.

"Hey, lady."

Janet turned to face the old man.

"There some kind of reward?"

Janet's nose wrinkled involuntarily. Shaking her head, she left quickly.

～ 16 ～

Janet left the Mermaid and went directly to the St. Charles Hotel, where Vicky had said Vern Junker lived. She wanted to get to the man as soon as possible. Janet didn't like crime or criminals; they offended her sense of order. By prosecuting criminals, she pleased herself and did her little bit to make the world a better place. She enjoyed it, too. Litigation law was more challenging than Chess or even Go, and more interesting, too, since it happened in the unpredictable world of real life. Janet supposed it felt like big-game hunting might, only in her business, the game deserved what it got.

The St. Charles Hotel was in a poor part of town, near the docks, in among the warehouses. A single-room-occupancy building was not likely to be luxurious, but the St. Charles was hardly better than a flophouse.

The small lobby, with its cracked linoleum floor and sagging plastic-covered chairs, was crowded with old men, shirtless in the afternoon heat. The place smelled of disinfectant and old age. There was a checkerboard set out, but no one played. No one talked. There wasn't even a television. A couple of men pretended to read newspapers. All of them turned to stare at Janet. She ignored them. If Vern Junker was in, he would be in his room. He had the Mermaid to go to when he wanted company; he didn't have to endure the endless staring silence of the lobby.

No one stood behind the front desk. Through an open door on the other side of the desk, Janet could see an old-fashioned PBX switchboard, unattended. Although all the men continued to watch her, nobody spoke and nobody came to help.

A wooden rack for mail and keys hung on the wall behind the desk. Most of the slots had names next to the numbers. Vern Junker's name appeared next to number 314. Janet took to the stairs.

The halls were narrow, the carpet worn thin and bereft of all traces of its original color. The air was stifling. As Janet ascended the stairs, the sickening odor of disinfectant became underlaid with the musty smell of habitual uncleanliness.

The wooden door had been painted brown at some time long past. The paint was badly chipped and scraped; the "4" of the room number dangled upside down. Janet knocked. A scuffling, shuffling sound, like that of a burrowing animal, came through the door, and then it opened.

Vern Junker was probably in his late fifties, about the same age as Frank Vincent, but looked much older. His skin was pasty except for the high color splotches on nose and cheeks characteristic of the long-term alcoholic. His nose was outsized, as if swollen or mashed, covered with a network of broken veins. That and the jaundiced, bloodshot eyes testified to a long history of hard drinking.

Seeing the man, it was no mystery to Janet that Vern had been caught drinking on watch. The mystery was how he had managed to control his habit well enough to keep a job as long as he had. It was possible that this deterioration and the shuffling gait of a much older, weaker man were recent developments, but Janet didn't believe it. Given what Frank and Vicky had said about him, Janet thought she'd get the most out of the man if she played to his vanity. It would be tricky. Vern Junker had little left to be vain about.

She identified herself, passing Vern Junker yet another card. He moved aside to let her in. In the room, the musty smell completely overpowered the disinfectant. A window fan made a futile attempt at cooling, but only seemed to stir up dust. The single bed was unmade, the linens thin and grey. Janet began to feel sick.

A large color television set held pride of place atop a battered bureau. An overstuffed armchair squatted by the window. Its upholstery was faded and greasy, but it was infinitely preferable to the bed, and there was no other place in the room to sit. Janet took it.

She explained that she was trying to find out about Glen Lowry and trace the dead man's movements. She finished by saying, "I understand you crewed for him."

Vern was surly, but seemed to have no reluctance to talk. "Sure, I crewed for him," he said. "Three—four years. Then all of a sudden, he says he don't need me no more. Right before we was going out, too."

"Did he give you a reason?"

"Said I shoulda watched some kid better. Kid busted a power winch. Hell, he took it off my share."

"I heard there was something about drinking," Janet said carefully.

"That didn't mean nothing. Glen did it himself. That's just talk. Frank Vincent's talk, I'd bet," Vern said, with a shrewd gleam in his eyes.

"Hadn't the winch business been settled the previous season?"

Vern Junker nodded vigorously. "'Course it was. That's when the shares were paid up. It was all settled up. Hell, that other thing, it was just an excuse. Glen and me, we used to drink together, up in Alaska and down at the Mermaid, too."

"But Glen told you he didn't need you."

"I figured it was Frank Vincent's fault. Found some kid Glen could get cheaper, maybe even that no-good boy of his come back. Get a kid a lot cheaper than an experienced hand like me. If Frank made it a condition of his going, he'd have Glen over a barrel. Frank's got his master's papers, see."

"So you thought the drinking was just an excuse?" Janet shifted in the chair. She itched at the thought of what might live in its depths.

"Damned right." Vern nodded vigorously, and smiled. It was a parody of the smile a teacher might give a bright pupil. Janet found it dreadful, but it showed her tactic was working. She smiled back as she asked, "Did you try to get him to change his mind?"

"We talked about it some, but it didn't work out. I didn't mind," Vern said belligerently. "I figured I could get a better boat. One that didn't jerk you around about paying an experienced man what he's worth."

Vern obviously hadn't found one, but Janet forbore pointing that out.

"How many times did you discuss it?"

Vern shifted on the edge of the bed. "Off and on, from when he told me right up until he left."

"Where?"

"Mermaid, mostly."

"Where else?"

"Down at the docks. He was bringing the *Valkyrie* in to get her ready for the season. He did take care of that boat."

Janet thought of an area she'd failed to explore enough with Frank Vincent. She'd verify any information she got from Vern Junker, but the man should be able to provide an acceptable preliminary overview. It would also give him a chance to show off. People always talked more when they showed off, and trusted those who gave them a chance to do so.

"Was there a life raft on the *Valkyrie*?" she asked.

"Sure. Six-man Avon."

"Was it always kept on the boat?" Janet wanted to know.

"Except when it was being serviced. You gotta do that once a year. Glen brought it in to the shop every spring before we left."

Janet got the name of the repair service. The Avon life raft had not been attached to the *Valkyrie*. Despite what Frank had said, it was possible the killer had used it. This would have to be checked.

"Was there any other reason Glen would take the Avon off the *Valkyrie?*"

"It don't do you no good sitting on shore," Vern said emphatically. "I never saw the *Valkyrie* without the Avon lashed up in the brackets just aft of the wheelhouse unless she was in dry-dock. I wouldn't have sailed on her without one, and you can bet your last dollar Frank wouldn't have, neither."

"There was just one of these Avons?"

"How many do you need?" Vern asked. "There was only one I ever saw."

"Did Glen ever take gear off the *Valkyrie* and store it at his house? Might he have done that with the Avon?"

"I wouldn't know about that," Vern said sourly. "I was never out to his house."

"Even though you worked together for several years?" Janet was surprised, and let it show.

"We saw a lot of each other, on the boat, and at the Mermaid. Anyway, he had a wife, until she died."

"What exactly happened on the *Valkyrie* about the drinking?" Janet hoped the abrupt change of subject would force Vern to answer truthfully simply by giving him no time to concoct a story.

The old fisherman shrugged. "I had a couple of belts before my trick at the wheel. It wasn't no big thing. Glen did the same. But Frank, he goes to Glen and tells him I was drunk and raising hell. So Glen raised hell with me. But there wasn't nothing to it, not really. Glen did his share of drinking. He knew it was OK."

Janet doubted Glen Lowry had been the kind of drinker Vern Junker was. Vern bore all the signs of the confirmed and long-term alcoholic. Had Glen been the same, she doubted if Frank would have shipped with him. Frank's version was far more credible. Letting Vern save face for the moment, she moved on.

"I understand the Mermaid is kind of a club for the fishermen around here."

"Vicky runs a real nice place," Vern replied. "Makes us feel real welcome. I go down there most days, when I'm not working. After work, when I am."

"She seems like a nice woman," Janet said. "How long has she owned it?"

"Long time now," Vern replied. "Ten years. More. She's a real nice gal. Started out as a barmaid when it was Davy's Locker. She worked her way up — had some troubles here and there — but she got her own back, and now she owns the place. Doing real well."

"How old's her child?" It was almost pure intuition, but Janet was sure that Vicky's phone call had been from a child. It might not be relevant, but it seemed like a good way to lead the conversation into her relationship with Glen, if there ever had been any.

"Sally? Got to be eighteen, maybe nineteen by now. She's at the community college. Vicky says she's doing real well. Studying diesel mechanics. Wants to get her engineer's ticket."

"You like Vicky," Janet said smoothly.

"Everybody does."

"Did Glen?"

"Sure. She kind of went off of him, though, once she found out what he'd done to me."

"She agreed he'd treated you badly?"

"'Course she did. So did everybody. Letting a man hang on till the beginning of the season, thinking he's got a berth, then making up some story to tell him he hasn't? That's a pretty rotten thing to do, girly, but I wouldn't guess you'd know about things like that."

Janet ignored the commentary. "But Vicky liked Glen well enough before then?"

"Yeah," Vern said. "She liked him well enough." The man's face turned wary. "Vicky," he continued, "likes everybody. Long as they don't give her no trouble, that is."

Janet could see from the shift in Vern's expression that she wasn't going to get any more out of him today. He'd visibly closed down. The words confirming it came quickly.

"Listen, girly, I got somebody to meet. It's time for me to get going."

Janet ended the interview. There was no point in continuing, she thought as she fled to the relatively clean-smelling air of the hot street. Vern Junker's sudden caution was not necessarily significant. A lot of times witnesses talk readily, then suddenly realize the possible implications of what they're saying. So they stop until they can reflect on what they've said, what they could say, and if it could somehow help them — or hurt them.

Janet climbed into the BMW, pressed the buttons that opened the sunroof and the windows, then twisted the knob that turned on the air conditioner. She needed the fresh air to get the smell of that place out of her nostrils and her clothes.

But she wasn't done with Vern Junker. Not yet.

~ 17 ~

Janet inhaled deep lungfuls of fresh air as she pulled away from the curb in front of the St. Charles Hotel following her interview with Vern Junker. The miasma of the place seemed to cling. It was too early for dinner; she had no plans, since she was supposed to be in Seattle. Ed had a date, she knew. She tried him on the car phone, hoping to tell him about Vern Junker, but she got his machine, so he must have already left. Wallace and her other married friends would want some time with their families. At loose ends, Janet found she felt like driving, so she headed west on the highway, out of town.

The highway led her past Glen Lowry's house. She saw a car sitting in the Simpsons' drive. Braking abruptly, she turned up the hill. Finding someone home at the upland neighbors' house seemed almost like an omen.

The denim-clad back end of a large woman rose from the vegetable garden. Apparently, she hadn't heard the car drive up, because she didn't move until Janet slammed the driver's side door of the BMW shut.

Startled, the woman jumped and turned in the same motion. She brushed her mop of grey curls out of her face, and said, "Hello?"

"Mrs. Simpson?"

Janet handed her a card and explained the purpose of her visit. With small backhanded waves, Mrs. Simpson herded

Janet out of the garden to settle her on the porch in an old-fashioned rocking porch swing with a scalloped green awning on top. She excused herself to go in to wash her hands.

Janet pulled a pad out of her briefcase to make a quick outline of what she wanted to ask. Mrs. Simpson returned with a tray of iced tea. Setting the tray on a wooden table, she prevailed on Janet to accept a glass. As Janet took a polite taste, Mrs. Simpson started talking.

"Well," she said, settling herself comfortably next to Janet on the swing, "the last time either of us saw Glen's boat was on St. Patrick's Day, just like we told the Coast Guard officer when she came out and talked to us. It wasn't there on the 18th, and it never did come back. We didn't think anything about it. We just thought he'd left early for the season."

She paused to sip her own tea.

"I know it was a long time ago," Janet began, speaking slowly in an attempt to get Mrs. Simpson to do likewise, "but now that it appears Mr. Lowry's death was a homicide, anything you can tell me about that day, the 17th, or the day before, Friday, the 16th, might be useful. Anyone you saw visit or pass by might have seen or heard something that could turn out to be important."

Mrs. Simpson nodded, beginning her answer even before Janet had quite finished. "Wouldn't they come tell you themselves?"

"Not if they didn't know it was important, or didn't connect the day. They might not even remember unless they're reminded. It wasn't investigated at the time."

"The Coast Guard came out," Mrs. Simpson reminded her.

Janet agreed. "But they were only checking on the last sightings of the *Valkyrie* and Mr. Lowry. They weren't investigating a homicide. Do you remember that March 17th?"

Mrs. Simpson nodded decisively, giving Janet the impression that this explanation had scored points with her. The

woman set down her glass and wiggled backwards in the swing.
It began to rock.

"It's not a day I'm likely to forget. The Longline
Fishermen's Union puts on a big party every year, and that year
I had a new dress. It was made of blue silk brocade, and it had
a surplice bodice." She swept a hand across her ample bosom
as she continued. "Like this. And long sleeves. I'd had it made
from some fabric Cathy gave me that had been Alice's. Then I
went and fell off the steps here when we were coming home
and I broke my arm. Jack drove me back into town to the hospital, since that was faster than calling for an aid unit, and they
had to cut my dress apart to get at my arm. I fixed the sleeve,
but it's never hung right since then. I told them to cut through
the seams, but they didn't do a very good job."

"Alice Lowry? Her fabric? Were you friends?"

"Allie Miller, I always think of her. She was just about
my oldest friend. We grew up together down in Hoquium. Then
she married Jerry Adams and moved up here, and I married
Jack and we moved to Oakland, then just about every place
else, but we always stayed in touch. Then when Jack retired
from the Navy, we thought we'd come home. Allie had this
house for rent, and we thought we'd take it for a year, look
around, and then buy something, but we just haven't got around
to finding something we like better."

"Had you met Alice's second husband before you moved
here?"

"No. We hadn't, and I have to say he never really warmed
up to us. I suppose it was natural, really, because the rest of us
went back a long way, but Jack says he drank. After Allie died,
poor thing, I took over casseroles and things and tried to get
him to come over, but he never would, and Cathy had to return the dishes." Suddenly Mrs. Simpson sat up straight. "Oh,
of course, I almost forgot..." She nodded to Janet, "Cathy was
out here that Saturday."

"The 17th?" Janet tried hard to contain her emotions.
It could have been a mistake. "Saturday?"

"That's right. I don't think I saw anybody out here on Friday, but of course, I'm in and out. But Saturday, I remember, I saw her car, one of those little beetle cars, yellow with a black convertible top, pulling into the space beside the garage."

"What time of day was that?"

"It must have been about five, because I was just going in from the garden to change. We left for the dinner dance just before seven, and it was dark by then."

"So you don't know if she was still there at that time, or if she'd already left?"

"I don't know, but I know who can tell you. Vern something. Jack'll know his last name. He's a fisherman, used to crew for Glen. His car turned in just as we pulled out."

"You recognized him?" Janet arranged her face in its most neutral expression to conceal the excitement she felt. She had connected her best suspect with the time and location of the crime.

"His car, really," Mrs. Simpson said. "It's a leap-year car, the license plate, I mean, and it's always kind of tickled me. He's got an old Ford station wagon, with the old kind of plates, with the letters first, and the license is FBY-229. I'd noticed the car before I'd ever heard of Vern. You talk to Jack, and he'll tell you more about Vern. I've only met him once or twice."

"When will your husband be home?"

"Not till late, I'm afraid. He got bored a couple of years ago and thought he'd try his hand at some fishing, so he bought a share in a boat, the *Hepsiba*. He's down at the dock with his partners, doing some work on the engines. *They* say." She gave Janet an arch look which she interpreted as meaning that the fishing boat was more of a hobby than anything, and the "repair work" might be just recreational tinkering.

"So you saw Ms. Adams drive up about five p.m. Saturday the 17th, is that correct?"

"Absolutely." Mrs. Simpson nodded as she refreshed both glasses, then went on, anticipating Janet's next question.

"And then this Vern fellow pulled in just about seven, but I can't tell you if Cathy was still out here or not."

Janet made a quick note. Mrs. Simpson would have to give a formal statement. "You and your husband were together when you saw this Vern's car?"

"Absolutely." Mrs. Simpson nodded vigorously. "We were on our way to the dance."

"Both of you will need to give a formal statement. Someone from my office can call to set up a time. Or — could you make it Monday morning, early? Would that be OK? It'll take about an hour." Janet had a sentencing, but any of the Deputy Prosecutors could cover that.

"Of course. We're coming into town at ten, anyway, for the dentist. We'll just come in earlier. You can call us any time, if we can be of any help to you. Jack can put you in touch with this Vern fellow. I'd guess she left when he came if not before. Unless she was doing something in some other part of the house. When those fishermen get together, I tell you, all they talk about is fish." She wrinkled her nose. "Boring."

Janet nodded while draining her glass, thanked the woman, then rose to leave.

She no longer felt the need to drive out to the park. Instead, she turned back to town, driving at a surprisingly moderate pace. No longer depressed, she found herself humming a complicated riff. She left a second message on Ed's machine and another on Maud's voice mail at the office. Then she stopped to get some takeout Chinese food and a movie. By the time Janet reached the Salmon Bay side of the bridge, she doubted she'd ever watch the film. Her mind was working so furiously she nearly overshot her turn. Exactly how was she going to nail Vern Junker?

~ 18 ~

Sunday, Janet slept in until the phone woke her up. It was Ed Nuñez, back from his date and returning her calls. She updated him on her interviews with Vern Junker and Mrs. Simpson while she got a cup of coffee. She pulled back the curtains in her living room to check the weather. It was a gorgeous day.

"So that's it," she finished. "You busy this afternoon?"

"Not so you'd notice," Ed replied. "I could be talked into trying for rock cod." The sport salmon season was so regulated that bottom fishing trips had taken over the charter fishing business as well as becoming the choice of most private boat owners.

"We could run upriver and see if we can find a sturgeon," Janet suggested.

"There's new regs," Ed objected. "Did you see yesterday's paper?"

"Missed it. Rock cod's fine with me. You know we're not going to catch anything anyway. It's just an excuse to go out in the boat."

"Hey," Ed said. "Try me. Bet you five on it. How about I meet you in an hour?"

"Sounds good," Janet said, smiling. "Bring beer."

Janet never did see the movie she'd rented. She and Ed took the Grady-White outside, catching the bar at slack water. They went north, cruising close in to the rocks dotting the coast, looking for a place to fish. Since it was Sunday, lots of charter boats were out, clogging the best fishing holes. Finally, the two friends ran the boat out to sea until the shore was just a faint line in the distance. They sat in a companionable silence, watching the diamond-specked water until the sun began to go down and they had to rush to get across the bar during the slack. They were just a touch late, so the bar was building again by the time they started to cross, but the sunset was glorious. Janet whooped with pleasure as she made the boat jump the breaking waves. The Grady-White was the best toy she'd ever owned. She slapped it affectionately as she and Ed climbed off after the boat was back in its slip.

"Damn, that was fun," Janet said. "This is a hell of a nice boat."

"I'm glad you bought it instead of me," Ed laughed. "It's a hell of an expensive boat."

"Only the best," she grinned back. "Grab that cooler, will you?" She stopped at the head of the dock to watch the afterglow. "Gorgeous sunset, isn't it?"

"Yeah." Ed set the cooler down. "They last so long up here." He glanced at his watch. "And come so late. I gotta get home. It's after ten."

"See you tomorrow," Janet waved. She lingered a bit, enjoying the stars and the sweet night air before walking back to her condo.

*

"We read him his rights," Ed told Janet early Monday afternoon, "but I don't think he's taking this seriously. Anyway, he signed a waiver form, and agreed to talk."

"I think old Vern has the impression that all we want to do is confirm what he told you Saturday." Mick leaned up against the door frame leading to Janet's office. The two detectives had picked up Vern Junker to bring him in for questioning. She hadn't talked to either of them since she'd parted from Ed at the boat the night before.

"Jack Simpson verifies his wife's story," Janet told them. She had spent the morning confirming the license plates on Vern Junker's 1964 Ford station wagon with the Department of Licensing, and getting statements from the Simpsons. "He can't confirm whether Catherine Adams was still present when Vern showed up."

Mick was pursuing thoughts about Nic. "I'll bet that Kiwi gal's trying to get her boat off the rocks." He looked out at the silver haze overlaying the harbor. "She'll never get a higher tide. Adams is probably helping."

"She have a boat?" Ed asked.

"Boston Whaler Outrage," Janet told him, turning a yellow legal pad around on her desk so Ed could copy her notes. Distracted by the talk of Catherine, she forgot to pass on something else Mr. Simpson had said. "I asked the Department of Licensing about that as long as I had them on the phone."

"She couldn't use that to pull that Kiwi sailboat off the beach," Mick objected.

"No, but the engines they carry are pretty sizable," Janet replied. "I suppose it would have to be powerful if she uses it for transportation. Still, a Whaler seems small to me."

"Nah," Mick replied. "An Outrage is damned near as big as your Grady-White. Pretty near as seaworthy, too."

"Meanwhile," Janet went on, "we've got Junker in Interrogation A waiting for us."

Mick levered himself away from the doorframe. "Vern wasn't fully up when we got him. He's hung over. Dirty. He smells. We gave him coffee."

"He's expecting us to talk to him, Janet," Ed said. "So we want you to do it." He glanced at his watch. "He's had just about enough time to be getting nervous. When you show up in that classy black lawyer suit, it'll rock him. He'll know it's more serious than he thought, but he won't have time to figure out what's going on."

"Then you go after him with both barrels," Mick said.

Janet nodded. When a witness's integrity became suspect, psychological factors became increasingly important in eliciting the truth. What the detectives wanted was a courtroom-style confrontation, brisk and businesslike, conducted with a coldness and distance of manner that Janet, both as a person and as a prosecutor, could convey better than either of the detectives. She drained her coffee cup while reaching for her leather pad holder and Tiffany pen. Ed smiled. Janet knew that they were operating on the same assumptions. Without any kind of overt threat, the three of them would intimidate Vern Junker into the truth.

The atmosphere of the small, ill-lit interrogation room was itself intimidating. The room was windowless, hot. Mick stood by the door, facing the fisherman, expressionless. Ed stood behind the man, out of his line of sight. Janet sat at the scarred wooden table directly across from Vern Junker.

After establishing a formal record so the taped statement could be used in court, Janet led Vern through the salient points of his previous statement to her.

Finally, Janet judged it was time to attack. Rolling the pen in her long fingers as she leaned back in the hard chair, she made eye contact with Junker for the first time.

"Most of that story," she said coldly, "is a crock of shit." The deliberate vulgarity had its intended effect. The small smile on Junker's face faded as the color drained from his face.

"You were at Lowry's the night he disappeared."

"How..." Junker began, "how..."

"You arrived at approximately seven p.m., driving your own car. You were alone." Janet made a note on her pad, then looked up. "Do you want to change your story?"

Junker glanced over Janet's head in Mick's direction, but apparently got no comfort there. He glanced over his shoulder at Ed. Janet saw Ed's wolflike grin, and the predatory tilt of his head. Junker's gaze returned to Janet.

"I didn't see nothing," he said sullenly.

"You admit you went there." Janet made it a statement.

"Yeah, yeah, I went out there," Junker said. "But I didn't see nothing. Nothing happened while I was out there. Not a goddamned thing."

Janet leaned forward, stabbing the paper with her pen as she spoke. "You had a grudge against Lowry. You thought he'd treated you unfairly. You knew how to operate the *Valkyrie*. You knew how to scuttle it. You're the last person who saw him. You lied about it." Janet sat back and tapped the pen gently. When she spoke again, her voice was soft, her tone insinuating. "Was he telling people you were a drunk? Was he making it impossible for you to get another job?"

"No," Vern shouted, leaning forward and pounding his fist on the table. "It wasn't like that. You've got it all wrong. Nothing happened."

Janet met Junker's gaze, looking at him expectantly. He might still evade, would quite possibly produce a new set of lies. But most likely, much of what he'd tell would be the truth.

"I wanted to talk to him, see?" Vern said quietly. "I wanted to ask him if he'd take me on for the season, on probation, like. I thought if I told him I wouldn't drink no more on the boat, he'd give me another chance. So I went on out there. But there was somebody else there, so I left."

"Who?"

"He said it was his stepdaughter. He called her Cathy."

"Did you talk to her?"

"No. I didn't know her. But I saw her."

Janet waited.

"I went up to the door and knocked. Glen yelled to come in, so I did. I went in, and she was there, so I said I'd talk to him later and left."

"What were they doing?"

"Glen had the Sonics game on."

"Glen and Cathy were watching the Sonics game together, is that correct? And you said hello, and that you'd talk to him later, and left?" Janet's tone was incredulous, sarcastic.

"Yeah," Vern said, "Yeah, that's right. That's just what happened."

"Bullshit. Try again." Janet leaned back in her chair and folded her arms. She glanced at her watch, a calculated move to show impatience with Vern Junker's lies, since there was a clock on the wall beyond Ed.

"That's it!" Vern's voice rose. "That's all that happened."

Janet allowed her eyelids to droop. She felt the muscles under her eyes tense as her mouth drew into a narrow line. She regarded Vern for a second, then glanced once more at her watch, and over Vern's head to Ed.

"Book him," she said, and rose. "Investigation of homicide. Get him a public defender whether he wants one or not."

"Wait," Vern cried out. Janet ignored him.

"If he wants to tell the truth, have the PD call me." Janet turned away.

"Wait," Junker shouted. "Please. Wait. I did talk to him."

Janet had reached the door by this time. She turned back to Vern, very slowly. She stood near Mick, a couple of feet closer to the table. The two of them must have looked enormous to the seated man, confined in the small, windowless room. Janet leaned forward to accentuate the effect and waited.

"I did talk to him," Vern began. "I wanted him to take me on again. I thought he'd want to, see. And he said he might. He said he'd think about it. He didn't want to talk about it right then, he said, because his stepdaughter was there. He wouldn't want her to hear, I knew that. So he said he'd meet me across from the Mermaid Sunday, and that's when I saw her. She was up at the top of the stairs, on the landing. So I said I'd meet him Sunday, and I left."

Janet didn't move.

"That's what happened. It's the truth." Vern Junker leaned forward, and implored. "I swear it."

Janet took a single step toward the man.

"What didn't he want her to hear?"

Vern's head dropped, and his mouth screwed up as though he could hardly force out the words. Janet waited. Finally Vern spoke, his voice barely above a whisper.

"About Sally," he said.

Janet returned to the table and sat, focusing her attention on Vern, who had, she judged, finally gotten to the truth.

"What about Sally? Sally who?"

"Davis. Sally Davis. Vicky's daughter. From the Mermaid." The witness sat up and his voice got bolder. "She was just a kid then, fourteen, fifteen, and he'd been messing with her. She told Vicky, and that's why Vicky got all bent out of shape at him, it didn't have nothing to do with me. Vicky never said nothing, and she let it get out that she went off him 'cause of the way he treated me, but I knew that wasn't true. I'd heard things here and there, and I put 'em together. I figured, if I said I'd keep my mouth shut, he'd be glad to take me back."

"A favor for a favor?" Janet said dryly.

"Yeah, that's it. A favor. He wouldn't want that kind of thing getting around. Vicky wasn't going to say anything about it, and if she didn't, neither would Sally, and neither would I."

"He agreed?"

"No. That's what I told you. He said he couldn't talk about it, 'cause Cathy was there, his stepdaughter, but he'd meet me, and we'd talk about it. He said he'd give it some real serious thought, and could I leave on the 28th?"

"You say you saw the stepdaughter?"

"Saw a woman. She was in the shadows at the top of the stairs. Glen didn't see her, but he'd pointed upstairs when he said she was there, so I looked that way, and there she was."

"Then?" Janet was concentrated on getting the information; she realized she wasn't capable of analyzing it. Not yet. But she knew it disturbed her. Catherine had definitely lied about this.

"He said he'd meet me, like I said, and we agreed, and I left. She saw me leave. You can ask her. By the time I got outside, she was out sitting in her car."

"What kind of car?"

"VW. A bug, a convertible one."

That was consistent with what Mrs. Simpson had said.

"She saw you leave," Janet went on. "That means you left first?"

"Yeah. My car was in back of hers, between hers and the driveway. So I pulled out onto the highway and turned toward town. But she was right behind me. I saw her lights coming at me right after I went around the first bend. Going fast, too."

"Where did you go?"

"Mermaid."

"Did you tell anyone what had happened?"

"I mighta mentioned it looked like I got my job back, but that was all."

"What happened Sunday?"

"I showed up. He didn't. I went out to the house again, but he was gone, and then I heard he was gone for good."

This version sounded more like the truth to Janet. If it was, it potentially cleared both Vern and Catherine, given what Jack Simpson had said. They'd have to talk to Catherine again. *Why did she lie?* Janet wondered. *She couldn't have forgotten this.*

Vern regarded Janet expectantly, as if seeking praise, or absolution. But it was not Janet's job to provide either kind of comfort, and Vern Junker's story turned her stomach.

"Mr. Junker, this statement will be transcribed, and you'll be asked to review it," Janet said. "If it's correct, you'll be asked to sign it. Then you can go."

"I'm not under arrest?"

Janet looked down on him.

"No," she said tersely, barely able to disguise her dislike for the man.

～ 19 ～

"Just a minute, Mr. Junker," Ed said as Janet pushed open the door and walked out. Mick hustled to catch up with her minutes after she strode out of the interrogation room and into the narrow hall that connected the law enforcement facilities with the courthouse.

"Janet," Mick boomed, just as she stepped through the heavy door into the back hall of the courthouse. Janet turned in the doorway, holding the heavy metal door open with her shoulder as she faced the massive detective.

"What do you mean telling Junker he's not under arrest?" Mick began. "He's the perp, dammit. You know it and I know it. He's got the motive, the opportunity, and he knows enough about the boat to run it and to scuttle it." Mick ticked these points off on fingers the size of Havana cigars. "We've got enough to charge him now. Give me two days with him on ice and I know we'll get all the verification we need for a conviction."

"No." Janet was firm. "I won't agree to that." She punctuated her counterarguments by stabbing the air with her polished nails as if indicating them on a chart. "This case has been lying fallow for four years. Junker's not going anywhere. There's no evidence left to destroy. We don't know if Adams will confirm his story. She's denied knowing anything about this. Even if she alibis him, he could have gone back. We need to trace his movements for the rest of the night, and verify his story about the Davis girl."

Janet continued emphatically, "Even if that all checks out, we haven't traced the skiff or the life raft. Turning up physical evidence is going to be damned near impossible. And there's one more thing. I didn't get a chance to tell you earlier. Jack Simpson, the upland neighbor, saw a blonde woman in a dark-green Pinto turning around in Lowry's driveway at four a.m. the night of the murder. It's in his statement." Janet piled on the sarcasm. "That changes things a little, doesn't it? The Unknown Suspect. A defense lawyer's dream. I want her found before we even consider an arrest."

"I'm glad my client's not a blonde."

Janet whirled at the sound of a familiar voice. The speaker was a short, trim man in a rumpled brown suit, with a yellow shirt and a paisley tie. In one small hand, he carried an old-fashioned leather briefcase. His medium-brown hair receded from a round forehead, and his voice was mild, touched with a relaxed humor.

"Henry." Janet greeted the man calmly. Henry Charm was one of southwest Washington's best civil litigation attorneys, and the lawyer who had represented Catherine Adams in the probates of her mother's and Glen Lowry's estates. Even though Henry did no criminal defense work at all, Janet had met him often enough in the civil matters she'd tried for the county to regard him as a formidable opponent in any legal arena.

"Did I hear you say you want to talk to a client of mine?"

"Who would that be?" Janet temporized.

"Now, Janet. I heard you quite well. In fact, I suspect a lot of people did. You want to question Catherine Adams again regarding her stepfather's death. I will not allow her to answer any more questions unless she has counsel present."

"You, Henry?" Henry had never ventured this close to a criminal case before, as far as Janet knew. She would have expected him to insist on Arthur Beach, the criminal defense specialist headquartered in Aberdeen, for any client of his. Henry would, of course, be thinking of a possible defense.

"She's not a suspect, is she, Janet?" Henry shrugged. "I think I can adequately advise a witness. If it gets beyond that, I'll expect you to let me know. When do you want to talk to her?"

"If we arrest her, I think you'll notice," Janet began, rejecting Henry's demand for continuing updates on his client's status in the investigation process.

"It's just a matter of routine," Mick interposed, loudly enough to make Janet pull away to protect her ears. "We have a situation we're checking out, where somebody says Ms. Adams can alibi him. We need to verify that."

"That's on the night the boat disappeared?" Henry wanted to know.

"Yes, sir."

"I don't believe my client has a specific recollection of that night, Detective, as I think she's already told you. I'm not sure I see the point in troubling her further."

Henry, Janet thought grimly, wouldn't turn loose any information without good cause; that would be a legacy of his civil practice, where information meant money.

"There were special circumstances, Mr. Charm," Mick went on. "I don't want to go into them here. It's a question of an innocent person's privacy on a matter that, so far as we know, is unrelated. I think Ms. Adams might remember if she were reminded about the circumstances."

Henry dropped his gaze, treating Janet to a view of the spot on the top of his head where his hair was noticeably thin. Mick was handling it nicely, Janet thought, with the implication that Catherine's memory problems were deliberate and would resolve once she knew the investigators merely needed confirmation of whatever she was trying to conceal.

"I've met Ms. Adams, Mr. Charm," Mick went on. "I think she'd want to do her duty as a citizen and clear this individual if she can."

Janet could almost see the wheels turning under Henry's balding pate. Mick had made another hit. Fifth Amendment rights conferred a privilege against self-incrimination. There was no corresponding right to withhold evidence against another person. If Catherine's memory loss had been a convenient ruse, it would be better for her to change her story now rather than be discredited on the witness stand, under oath, with the concomitant threat of potential perjury charges hanging over her head.

"All right," Henry conceded. "When?"

"This afternoon, if we can."

"Do you want her to come into town?"

"That's not necessary," Mick said, shuffling his feet. "We can go to her. I don't think we can get the chopper. I heard it was going out fire-spotting up in the mountains. But we should be able to get one of the patrol boats. If you want to let her know we're coming, we can use the radio in the office when we call for the boat."

"Fine," Henry said. "Or we can take my boat." He waggled a finger at the detective. "If you'll just wait here a minute while I let my associate know where I'm going, we can leave now."

"I'll wait for you here," Mick said.

"Five minutes," Henry replied. "Janet," he said, nodding a farewell, as he scurried off down the hall.

"Don't arrest Junker yet," Janet warned Mick. "We have a lot of checking to do."

"Simpson's blonde complicates things," Mick admitted. "How in the hell are we going to find her if she was just a party-goer who made a wrong turn?"

"Exactly," Janet said. "If we arrest Junker and then have to let him go because we can't charge him, he'll know he's a serious suspect. His behavior will be less predictable. With a homicide suspect, you know how dangerous that can be." Janet smiled at the big detective and extended an olive branch since she'd won her point on the arrest issue. "That was damned nice work with Henry, Mick."

Mick grinned. "Wasn't it? I'd still feel better if we had Junker under lock and key, and I know Ed would, too. I'd like to keep the time frame as short as possible, whether he's in or out. You want to go talk to the Davises?"

Janet glanced at her watch. She could give her afternoon calendar to Wallace again. "Yes," she said. "Today."

~ 20 ~

Janet found Vicky Davis's house easily. The Mermaid's owner lived in Charbonneau, on the slightly sloping flatlands near the largest lumber mill. The houses were small, postwar frame cottages, well-kept and highly respectable. Janet thought it was interesting that the bar owner should choose to live in such a traditional part of town.

Jack Simpson had reported a blonde in a dark green Pinto backing out of Glen Lowry's driveway at four in the morning on what was almost certainly the last night of the murder victim's life. Given Vern Junker's story about Vicky Davis's daughter, and the fact that the woman was almost excessively blonde, Janet had run a rapid check with the Department of Licensing. That showed that she had owned a Mercury Bobcat at the time of Glen's death, a car that looked exactly like a Pinto. Though she had acquired a new Mercury Sable last year, she still owned the Bobcat.

The small white house stood on an oversized corner lot, surrounded by a four-foot chain-link fence. Janet glimpsed a closely-mowed lawn, a deck with a large barbecue, and the clean glint of new aluminum awnings. The area's constant rain kept the grass looking clean and fresh. The sight restored Janet as much as a dip in a swimming pool. Though the orange groves surrounding Janet's childhood home had been green, the leaves often looked dusty and tired even after one of the infrequent rains. As an adult, she appreciated fresh greenery wherever she found it. After pulling around the corner, she parked.

The Bobcat was parked on the side street, a "for sale" sign in its window. It was forest green. Janet felt her pulse quicken as she walked to the front of it to verify the plate. Examining the car, she looked for evidence that the color might not be original, or that the paint job was recent, but found neither.

"You interested in the car?"

Janet turned. A young woman in grease-stained jeans and a faded Evergreen State College sweatshirt approached the fence from behind the single-car garage that poked into the yard from the alley. She had a mop of light-brown curly hair, a round face, and freckles. There was a grease stain on her nose. From the condition of her clothes, and the crescent wrench she held in her grimy hand, Janet assumed she'd been working on yet another vehicle.

"Your car?" Janet asked.

"Yeah." She came up to the fence. "It's in my mom's name because of the insurance, but it's mine. I can tell you about it."

"You must be Sally Davis."

"That's right." She tilted her head warily. "How'd you know that?"

"My name's Janet Schilling." She walked up to the fence, pulling her card case from her bag. "I'm a prosecuting attorney." She passed a card across the fence. Sally Davis swiped at her jeans and took it, but still left black fingerprints on the card's white surface. "I need to talk to you," Janet said.

"What about?" Sally stuffed the card in her back pocket, looking up at Janet curiously.

"Glen Lowry."

"You want to come in?" Sally pointed Janet to a back gate next to the garage. She led Janet to a small, tidy kitchen, cheerfully wallpapered, and directed Janet to sit at a Formica table while she cleaned her hands with a cream.

"Coffee?" Sally asked when she was finished.

Janet accepted a cup when she saw the pot of the automatic coffee-maker was already full. After pouring, Sally joined Janet at the table, and looked at her expectantly.

"You're what? Nineteen?" Janet asked.

"That's right."

She looked at the younger woman for a long second before speaking. "You don't need to talk to me. Even though you're an adult, if you want your mother present, that's fine. If you'd rather talk with another woman prosecutor or police officer present, or a friend of your choosing, that's fine, too."

"Oh, hell," Sally said. Her hand jerked and a little coffee slopped out of her cup onto the shiny surface of the table. She jumped up to get a cloth to wipe it up. Once she'd folded the damp cloth over the faucet, she came back to the table and slowly sat down.

"I don't mind," she told Janet. "It's OK. Go ahead."

"You know that Mr. Lowry's body was found in the harbor?"

"Who doesn't? The paper says somebody murdered him. Is that right?"

"That's what it looks like. That's how we're investigating it."

Sally nodded sharply, her face solemn.

"We need to talk to everyone who knew him at the end of his life. I understand he was a close friend of your mother's for a time."

"Mom felt sorry for him. His wife died, and he was kind of at loose ends, I guess. She had him over a few times. They weren't dating or anything, but I think it was heading that way. He was a regular at the Mermaid. But then..." She shrugged.

"We've been told your mother ended her friendship with Mr. Lowry because of something he did to you. Is that right?"

"Mom," Sally said distinctly, "is going to have a cow. She made such a big deal about it, and never wanted anybody to know, like it was some kind of secret or something. But it wasn't my fault, or hers, either. We don't have anything to be ashamed of. What happened was, first he got fresh, and then he got grabby, so I slugged him, and then I told Mom, and she had a fit. But nothing serious happened. Not to me, anyway."

"You actually hit him?" Janet grinned. She liked Sally's attitude. She wished more girls had that kind of guts.

Sally grinned back. "You bet I did. Gave him a shiner. I wasn't taking that kind of crap." She shivered. "It was creepy."

"You said, 'not to me,'" Janet said, homing in on a serious point. "Was there something about what happened that made you think it wasn't the first time he'd tried it?"

"Oh, sure," Sally said. "It was like he had all his lines set out and ready to go, like guys do when they're coming on to you. It was weird. He talked about how much he liked me, and then about teaching me things, and how he had a responsibility or something. He was like hugging me and stuff and it seemed like he was taking it too far and in the wrong direction. He was twisting things around when he talked like he was trying to convince me that I had some kind of duty to go along with him. Then he actually started ripping at my shirt and grabbing me. Made me real mad. That's when I popped him one, told him off and split." She swallowed coffee. "But it sure sounded like a line to me. I could see him conning some girl who didn't know any better. Somebody younger, maybe. Who hadn't been around."

"When did this happen?"

"Oh, like February. I don't remember exactly. Mom made me go see a shrink in case I got a complex or something, so somebody's probably got it written down somewhere."

"How'd you feel about him afterwards?" Janet found Sally's perspective on the incident refreshing. It was certainly a change for the better.

"I was real glad Mom got so pissed, because she wouldn't have him around any more. It would have been creepy to have to see him, and I sure wouldn't have wanted to be alone with him."

"And when he disappeared?" Janet wondered how Sally would feel about that.

"Good riddance. That's what Mom said." Sally's tone was severe.

"Do you remember when he disappeared?"

"The papers say it was St. Patrick's Day."

Janet nodded. "Do you remember anything about that particular day?"

"I was thinking about that when I was working on my motorcycle yesterday. You know, where was I, that kind of crap. I remember that day pretty good. I was a sophomore at Holy Family, and there was a big all-county dance over at Lincoln High in Salmon Bay. That was the first big dance Mom ever let me go to. She'd only let me go to the Holy Family ones before. None of us could drive, so Judy Mitchell's dad took a bunch of us, and picked us up. He took us for burgers afterwards."

"Do you know what time you got home?" Janet remembered those kinds of dances. She'd been so tall most of the boys didn't want to dance with her. Then she discovered — and was discovered by — the basketball team, who were themselves uncomfortably taller than most of their potential partners.

"Ten after one." Sally laughed. "My curfew was one, and I was scared Mom'd call to make sure I was home, and she did, too, but not till a quarter after."

"So you were probably in bed by one-thirty."

"Oh, no. Creature Feature."

"What?" That one went right over Janet's head.

"Creature Feature. Horror movies every Saturday night on television. Mom gets home about two-fifteen Saturday nights, and she used to let me watch it and wait up for her. It goes off at two. We'd make cocoa and talk and stuff. She doesn't open the Mermaid till late on Sundays, so they do the cleanup before they open, instead of at night on Saturdays."

"You remember very well." Janet smiled at the girl. If she had a daughter, she'd want her to be a lot like Sally.

"It's kind of weird thinking about it now," Sally said, wiggling a little in her chair. "I mean, him getting killed that night and all. If that's when it happened. But that dance was a pretty big deal."

"Would you be willing to sign a statement about what we've talked about today?"

"I guess." She sounded dubious.

"What's a good time to call you?" Janet asked, rising.

"I'm home by two most days," Sally said. "I'm in the Marine Diesel program at the Community College, and we go seven to one-thirty. Sometimes there's something special, like we get to go on a ship or something. But we've got an answer machine if you want to leave a message. Why do you want a statement?"

"If we're going to call you," Janet said, "it'll probably be this week. A statement is your words, signed by you to show you've looked at it, so it's more accurate than just having my memory of what you said. In law, we like to have our files as accurate as we can get them."

"Oh, OK," Sally said, nodding. Janet smiled again, and said good-bye. Sally was a thoroughly sensible and very nice young woman. Janet wished she'd had that kind of confidence at that age. She remembered herself as a shy four-eyed grind when she was in college, even though she'd never worn glasses.

Sally's story indicated Vicky Davis could not be the blonde in the Pinto. From the way Sally had handled Glen Lowry, as well as the way she'd responded to Janet's questions, there was virtually no chance she'd lie under oath. More important, Janet thought a jury would be as convinced of Sally's honesty as she was. A big dance was just the kind of thing a teenager would remember in detail, and Sally's memory of the dance could be corroborated. Vicky's alibi for Glen Lowry's murder also seemed secure. But there was one question she hadn't asked Sally. For the answer to that one, she'd better talk to Vicky.

~ 21 ~

Monday morning, Nic rose early to catch the low tide. If she set her kedging gear then, when the tide reached its peak, she should be able to get *Wayward* off the beach with a minimum of difficulty. The patch had dried well. She regarded it critically. It didn't even look too obvious, though it would always show, since the new material would age differently than the original. *At least the hull's sound,* she thought. The successive high tides over the past week had revealed no leaks. The batteries were up, the broken shroud replaced, the electronics back on line, and the engine had turned over smoothly. *Wayward* was ready to go. Nic couldn't wait to get back out in open water.

⋆

By late morning, when the tide was almost full, Nic was ready to begin. Catherine sat in the cockpit, watching as Nic started winching. She couldn't help. There was only one windlass, and Nic was the one who knew how it worked. She held her breath as the line strained and the boat creaked. Sweat popped out on Nic's bare arms. The boat didn't move. Nic bent over to adjust something, then leaned into the crank to apply leverage. Sweat stained the back of her scarlet tank top and ran down her bare legs. Catherine wondered if the boat would ever come free, and what Nic would do if it didn't. Then, suddenly, she felt a ponderous shudder and the boat began to slide. Nic cranked harder. Catherine jumped up to shove a fender that had rolled onto the deck with the movement back between the boat and the cliff. Nic looked up.

"Thanks," she called. "I think we've got it."

"Great," Catherine shouted back. She kept a critical eye on the fenders until the boat was clear of the cliff. She returned to the cockpit to watch as Nic adjusted the kedging gear to turn the bow out to sea. Nic continued cranking to work the boat through the needles and cushions of rock to open water, where the kedging anchor lay buried in the sand.

"Whew," Nic said when the boat rode over the anchor. "For a minute there, I wondered if it was going to work."

"Me, too," Catherine said. "What now?"

Nic looked around. The sea was calm and there was no wind. That was good for kedging, but bad for sailing. Nic expected a north wind would build later. She had noticed that usually happened here when the weather was good. She wished it would happen soon. She was eager to show her new friend what sailing was all about.

Out to the west, she saw a hint of glitter on the long ocean swells. Wind!

"How about I take in the kedging gear and get the engine started while you put together some lunch?" Nic asked.

"Sure," Catherine said. "But I thought we were going sailing."

"We are." Nic grinned. "The wind's out there," she pointed. "We'll use the engine to take us to it, and have lunch on the way."

Nic set her course so that the trip back to the island would be downwind. It was the easiest point of sail, and the most comfortable. She set the autopilot, then went forward to get the cruising spinnaker ready to raise. She returned to the cockpit as Catherine came on deck with sandwiches, chips and cans of soda.

"I like this boat," Catherine said. "I've been snooping down below. It's so comfortable. There's even a guest room! You've got everything you need, don't you?"

Nic took the plates and put them on the cockpit table. "That's the idea. I'm a turtle. I take my house with me wherever I go." She was pleased Catherine admired the boat, since *Wayward* was her own design. "Don't fishing boats have living quarters?" she asked.

"Not like this. Most of a fishing boat's taken up with gear and cargo space. There are cramped little bunks and crowded little galleys, and a table that's usually covered with charts and dried-out coffee cups. This is great!" She sat down and helped herself to a sandwich. Then she noticed the wheel move by itself. She jerked upright in alarm.

"What's that?" she asked.

"Autopilot. It steers so I don't have to."

"I didn't think you'd have one on a boat this size." Catherine relaxed and sat back. "Fishing boats have them, of course, but they look different."

"Different makes for larger boats. Have a look at these." Nic ran below and flipped a switch, turning on the navigational instruments mounted around the wheel.

"I like this one," Catherine said, pointing to one which looked like an outline of a sailboat with an arrow overlaid on top of it.

"Wind indicator. It's pointing straight ahead because we're moving forward faster than the wind. If the wind's faster than our speed, the arrow shows the direction it's coming from. Down here," Nic indicated a digital display, "it shows the wind speed. An easy way to set your sails when you're going upwind is to trim them until they are at about the same angle as the arrow."

"When do I get to sail?" Catherine asked impishly.

Nic laughed. "Soon. See the wind? We're almost there."

Half an hour later, Nic and Catherine had finished lunch, cleaned up after it and reached the patch of wind. They'd been traveling over an hour at six knots, Nic saw. They'd probably get three or four knots out of the spinnaker, giving them a pleasant sail back to the island. Nic turned the boat downwind, pulled the throttle back to slow the engine speed and set a new course. Catherine watched with interest. Nic slipped on her safety harness, attaching the tether to the jackstay running fore and aft on the side deck.

"Why the getup?" Catherine wanted to know.

"I'm leaving the cockpit and we're out at sea. It's a standard safety precaution. If someone went overboard out here in the swells, there'd be hell to pay trying to find them to get them back on board. This way, you can go off the side, but you can't get lost, and even if you're by yourself, you can haul yourself back onto the boat." Nic grinned. "It's a sailboat thing. I'm going to bring up the chute. Watch!"

The cruising spinnaker was huge, made in panels which were all the colors of the sunset. When Nic freed it, the lightweight sail filled like a hot-air balloon. Nic came back to the cockpit, adjusted the sheet until the sail was drawing properly, then cleated it off. She reached across Catherine to take the engine out of gear. Catherine felt the sail take hold even as the boat slowed down. Nic shut off the engine and grinned down at Catherine. "You're sailing."

Catherine looked around. "It's so quiet."

"That's one of the best parts. Listen to the silence."

Catherine listened. Gradually, she heard the creak of the rigging, the rush of the ocean as it whooshed past the hull. She leaned over the side, only to be mesmerized by the boat's wake as the hull glided through the water.

"Can I go forward?" she asked.

"Sure," Nic said. "Slip on this harness and hook up." She helped Catherine untangle the unfamiliar webbing contraption and buckle it across her midsection. "Go out on the bow," Nic told her with a smile. "Duck outside the sail — grab it if you need to, you can't hurt it — and get way out on the pulpit."

Catherine nodded. She was so overwhelmed with the beauty of it, she couldn't speak. She caught the sea rhythm easily as she moved forward, Nic was pleased to see. *She's right at home out here,* Nic thought happily.

Catherine glanced back at Nic before dodging around the sail. Nic smiled and nodded. Catherine gripped the pulpit and stepped out into nothingness. She felt like the figurehead on an old-time clipper ship, her hair blowing wildly around her. She had the security of the anchor platform beneath her feet and the rails protecting it, to which she clung, but it felt like flying. She looked down. *Wayward's* bow parted the sea, sending rolling waves tumbling to either side. The swells came from behind the boat, lifting the keel and rushing beneath. The sail collapsed a little every time the bow went down. Catherine gasped the first time it did that. Then it snapped as it caught the wind when the bow rose up. There was a pattern to the movement, Catherine discovered quickly, and though the swells were huge, it didn't feel dangerous.

She stood on the bow for a long time, relishing the experience, wishing she never had to leave it. Then she saw Seal Rock, and realized they were getting close. It was time to go back to the cockpit.

"It's fabulous," she said, as she shed the harness and settled in next to Nic.

"I thought you were going to stay up there forever," Nic replied with a grin.

"I'd like to." Catherine opened her arms to the sky. "I love this. The boat feels alive. She's happy to be sailing, isn't she?" Catherine reached out to stroke the teak coaming at the edge of the cockpit.

Nic felt her heart yearn with longing. That was exactly how she felt about *Wayward.* Suddenly she knew she wanted this woman forever. But she restrained herself. Something about Catherine's reticence made her cautious. In some ways, Catherine

reminded her of a wild animal. Intuitively, Nic sensed she must
be quiet and careful, respectful, until Catherine freely came to her.

"Is it always like this?" Catherine asked, her eyes shining.

"Sometimes," Nic replied. "Always. Never. It's always
changing, and it's almost always better than anywhere else. I'm
glad you're here. You make it better still." She reached out and
touched Catherine's hand with her own. Catherine stiffened,
but didn't move. Then Nic became aware of an insistent buzz-
ing just as Catherine withdrew her hand.

"Powerboat," Nic said with disgust.

"Where?" Catherine asked, answering her own question by kneeling on the seat and looking in the direction of the
sound until she spotted it. "They're heading this way. I think I
know that boat. Nic, do you have binoculars?"

"Here." She handed them to Catherine.

"I knew I recognized her," Catherine said, her tone be-
traying her dismay. "It's Henry, Henry Charm. My lawyer. And
he's got those two detectives with him."

Nic doused the spinnaker and prepared to follow the
lawyer's boat into Seal Rock's tiny eastern harbor.

Henry Charm had tied his powerboat up to the dock,
leaving just enough room for *Wayward*. It was a Scarab, its low,
planing hull built for speed. The name *Hot Pink* and the accent stripes were painted on the metallic grey hull in the name-
sake color. Henry waved as they neared. He wore charcoal-grey
slacks, Topsiders and a black rugby shirt with *Hot Pink*
monogrammed on the left chest to match the graphics on the
boat. His baseball-style jacket, in a grey that matched the boat,
sported the colorful logo of an offshore race across the back,
and a winner's patch on the sleeve.

Nic remembered Catherine saying that Henry was a
different person professionally than personally, his quiet, ab-
sentminded and slightly rumpled professional persona meta-
morphosing during his off time into this sophisticated owner
of a racing powerboat. It was clear to Nic that Henry Charm's
companions had never seen him like this. Mick, the big detective

with the bass voice, appeared disconcerted whenever he looked at the lawyer. Ed, the handsome one, was visibly amused.

As Catherine got off *Wayward,* Mick said, "We just have a few more questions to ask you, Ms. Adams. Sorry to interrupt your sail."

"We were heading in anyway," Catherine replied. She had to stay calm. It was probably nothing. But Henry had come. That scared Catherine. It meant this was important. Whatever it was, she wanted to get it over with. "Fire away," she said.

"Would you like to go up to the house?" Ed asked. Nic turned to go below on *Wayward.*

"There's plenty of room on the boat, isn't there, Henry?" Catherine said to the lawyer and indicated *Hot Pink* with a wave. She wanted Nic to hear whatever they had to say, without having to make a point of including her.

"Certainly," Henry said, holding out his hand to help her aboard. She took it, giving her lawyer an ironic smile at his old-fashioned courtesy. Henry and the detectives followed her aboard. He and Catherine took the two chairs in the front of the cockpit, leaving the bench seats astern for the detectives.

It was a neat finesse on Catherine's part, Nic thought, as she settled herself comfortably under. *Wayward's* forward hatch. There was no room for Nic on *Hot Pink.* But Nic could hear perfectly well from *Wayward.* She felt protective. If it involved Catherine, it was her business, too. Whether Catherine knew it or not, or wanted it or not, Nic was feeling the beginnings of love.

Mick began. "We understand that the *Valkyrie* carried an Avon life raft, but we haven't been able to locate it. Would you know anything about that?"

"I don't know what the *Valkyrie* carried," Catherine said, sighing slightly with relief. "There's a lot of spare gear stored in the boathouse over there by the dock at the house. If you mean one of those barrel-shaped rescue rafts, I think I remember one of those."

"Mind if we go take a look?"

"In the boathouse? I don't, but I don't want my tenants bothered. Henry?"

"Do your tenants use the boathouse, Catherine?" Henry asked.

"Of course. There was so much stuff out there, and I was trying to get this place ready, so I just pushed everything aside until I could get to clearing it out, and I simply haven't done it."

"Would you be able to tell what's theirs and what's yours?" the lawyer wanted to know.

"Probably not. Except for the fishing gear. That would be left over. The tenants run a tug," Catherine told him in businesslike tones.

"But you couldn't be sure of any of it?" Henry wanted to make sure.

"Not really. It's been years since I was in there."

"Is it kept locked?" he asked.

"I have no idea." Catherine was beginning to sound annoyed. "Glen always kept it locked as far as I know, but I don't keep tabs on Lisa and Luke."

Nic hadn't been able to see where Henry was going with this, but it became clear when the lawyer addressed the detectives.

"I don't think we'll permit a consent search. My client thinks she remembers seeing a barrel-shaped life raft in the boathouse. Is that correct, Catherine?"

"Yes. When I was getting the house ready for tenants." She spoke crisply.

"At this point, the property's been out of her direct control for some years, the tenants are mariners, and there would be no probative value to any fruits of a search of the boathouse now. Whether or not a life raft is there now has no bearing on whether one was there several years ago, and that has no bearing on whether there was a similar raft on board the *Valkyrie* when she went down. Such a search would only disturb the tenants without adding anything to your investigation. Catherine?"

"Whatever you say, Henry. I've got good tenants. I don't want them bothered."

Nic nodded her satisfaction. Henry's voice had been brisk and decisive, his position clear and logical. Catherine had a good advisor. She settled back on her elbows, relieved, and curious about what would come next.

"But the raft was there in the boathouse after Mr. Lowry disappeared, Ms. Adams?" Ed asked.

"I believe *a* raft was there, Detective," Catherine said.

"I understand that," Ed continued. "There's just one other thing. Several witnesses have told us that you were out at the house on Saturday, March 17th."

"So?" Catherine's voice was cool.

"You told us before you were out there the 16th."

"I believe I told you I thought it was the day before he disappeared. I also told you I wasn't certain. It was a long time ago and there wasn't anything special about it at the time." Nic sat up. Catherine's voice was still crisp and businesslike, but Nic thought she could detect an undercurrent of fear.

"Wasn't there?" This was Mick.

"One of the witnesses is a man named Vern Junker. He crewed for Mr. Lowry," Ed said. "He's sure you were out there that evening. He tells us he saw you."

"That was *that* night?" Catherine sounded, Nic thought, both surprised and alarmed. She held her breath, waiting apprehensively.

"Do you remember that night now?"

"Some. I hadn't connected it."

"Mr. Junker's story needs confirmation, Catherine," Henry interjected. "It would make it easier if you could tell the detectives what you remember about the incident. If they have to ask questions, it'll take a long time."

"OK." Nic could almost see her nod, but she sounded dubious. The chair creaked as Catherine turned.

"I was out at the house to pick up a cherrywood magazine table I wanted, and to do some more sorting," she began.

"I knew Glen would be leaving pretty soon, and I wanted to get an idea of how much work there would be to get the place rentable, since I was going to be coming out here. I was up-stairs, and Vern — that's the only name I heard — came to talk to Glen about a job for the season. I guess there had been some trouble the year before. When I was loading the table into the car, this Vern left, and I did, too."

"You followed him?" Ed asked.

"Pretty much. I wasn't right behind him, but close."

"Did you go back in the house to say good-bye to Mr. Lowry?" Mick wanted to know.

"Henry?" Catherine asked uncertainly. Nic sat up. There was something wrong.

"Ms. Adams?" Ed said.

"Just a minute, Detective." Henry's quiet voice rose. "Catherine, I think you should know that they know about Sally Davis. Vern Junker told them."

"Oh, no." Catherine's voice was faint. Nic fancied that she could feel her slump in the chair "This isn't going to make any trouble for Sally, is it? I mean, it's over now, she's grown up. She doesn't need to have this dragged up after all this time, have to live through the whole thing again."

"How did you find out about the Davis girl, Ms. Adams?" Mick asked.

"Henry?"

"Just tell them, Catherine. I think it's best. Do you want to tell me privately, first?"

"No. It's OK. If they already know, I guess it doesn't matter if I say. It happened just like I said, except that this Vern told Glen he knew Glen had tried to molest Sally Davis. He actually laid hands on her, tried to force her, but she got away. Sally told her mother, and Vicky had thrown Glen out, but nobody else knew. Vern said he would make it public if Glen didn't give him his job back. Glen shut him up, told him I was there — I'd come to the top of the stairs when I heard someone come — and they agreed to meet later, the next day, I think it was. That's all."

"What did you do, Ms. Adams?" Mick's deep voice was surprisingly gentle.

"I was upset, of course. I didn't think I could stand to look at Glen. I grabbed my purse and ran down the back stairs to my car. The table was already in it. I felt sick. I was sitting in my car when Vern came out and got in his car and drove away. I followed as soon as I could. I didn't want to talk to Glen."

"Why didn't you tell anybody?" Ed asked. "It was a couple of weeks before you knew Lowry was gone. Weren't you worried about the girl?"

"You don't understand," Catherine told him. "It was clear from what they said that Sally had told her mother. I know Vicky, not well, but well enough to know she could handle it. Making it public would have been hard on Sally. People talk in small towns. Being a victim sticks to you almost as if you did something wrong yourself. Vicky sure knows that from personal experience. As long as Vicky was taking care of it, the best thing I could do for Sally was keep quiet. Vern's lever was against Glen's reputation. The important thing was that the abuse had stopped."

"What did you do after you left?" Mick wanted to know.

"Drove around. I didn't want to go home. My landlady then was an old dear, but I knew she'd want to talk, see what I brought home. So I got something to eat and went out to the park and went home in the morning."

"Which park?"

"South Jetty. The county park, the one with the camp-sites in the dunes."

Catherine's story made Nic queasy. The idea of some-one molesting — abusing — whatever you want to call it — a child made her furious. She thought of her stepchildren, and what she might do if anyone like that threatened them. If Nic were looking for suspects in Glen Lowry's death, she sure as hell would begin with the Davis girl's parents.

∾ 22 ∾

After leaving Sally Davis, Janet stopped by her condo for a quick snack and to pick up her mail. She pulled one letter from the stack of bills and junk. The postmark was Puerto Escondido, Mexico. *Rosalinda,* Janet thought, with a fond smile that softened her face. The housekeeper who had raised her after her mother's death wrote her every week. She remembered how Rosalinda had made her feel loved, how the small, white frame foreman's house tucked into the groves behind the chilly mission-style main house had quickly become Janet's real home as her father slowly drowned in depression and alcohol.

Years later, after Janet's father died, Rosalinda Diaz had returned to her hometown in Mexico, where her pension, investments and the annuity he'd left her in his will allowed her to live in a comfortable villa overlooking the beach, with a housekeeper of her own.

Rosalinda had given Janet more than a kind housekeeper's attention and fluent Mexican Spanish. Rosalinda had given her a family. She put the letter in the center of the blotter on top of the desk in the room she used as a home office. She would write Rosalinda tonight. She glanced at her watch. It was time to go back to work.

After finishing the afternoon Omnibus calendar, Janet returned to her office to find Ed and Mick waiting to tell her the results of their second interview with Catherine Adams.

"What's up?" she said, circling her desk to sit down.

"It's just like we thought," the big detective said. "Adams confirms Junker's story. She left after he did. Hearing about the Davis girl made her sick, she said. So she didn't want to see anybody, especially Lowry. She picked up some takeout and went to camp at South Jetty."

Janet nodded. It was the most plausible explanation. "What about the raft?" she wanted to know.

"We got a bonus there," Ed Nuñez said. "Adams thought she remembered one in the boathouse, so we called the company that serviced it when we got back. We found somebody who remembered it and looked it up. The company's records show it was picked up by Lisa Hahn on July 15th. She's one of the tenants in the Lowry house. I talked to her, too. She and her husband run a river tug. The company called right after they moved in. They didn't change the phone number, just the name on the account, because it's cheaper. The company wanted to know what to do with the raft. So Hahn told Adams, and Adams said stick it in the boathouse, if they didn't want to use it."

"So that takes care of that," Janet said thoughtfully. "This means finding the skiff is all the more important. That's the only way the killer could have got back to shore after sinking the *Valkyrie*. It's too cold and the current's too strong to swim."

"We'll assign some people to go house-to-house asking questions about the skiff next," Ed said.

"Excellent," Janet replied. She quickly recounted her conversation with Sally. "Now," she finished, "I'm on my way to the Mermaid to talk to Vicky Davis."

※

By six p.m. that Monday evening, Janet, having changed into slate-blue silk slacks and a matching V-necked sweater, sat at a small table near the Mermaid's bar and ordered a Scotch from a waitress. A few minutes later, Vicky Davis brought it over and slammed the glass onto the table in front of her. "I want to talk to you," she said ominously.

"I have a few questions for you, too, Ms. Davis," Janet replied. "Is there someplace..."

"Come into the office," she interrupted, and marched off, pausing only to call out to a lanky woman with high, country-singer-styled brown hair, "Betsy. You're in charge till I get back."

Vicky faced Janet across a small desk in a tiny office behind the kitchen area of the Mermaid, her face ugly with anger. Janet perched on the single visitor's chair, wedged in between the stacks and piles and cabinets of all the record-keeping associated with a business.

"You've been talking to my daughter."

That Sally had called her mother had been obvious to Janet from the moment she'd seen Vicky's face. She shifted on the narrow chair. If she wanted information, she had to defuse Vicky. If that was possible.

"If you've talked to Sally, and you have," Janet began calmly, "you know the first thing I did was make sure she was a legal adult. The second thing was to tell her she didn't have to talk to me at all, and the third thing was to tell her she could call you and have you or anyone else she wanted present. She didn't think it necessary. She talked to me quite willingly. I like your daughter. She's a very mature, very nice young woman."

"Oh, shit." Suddenly, Vicky's face crumpled. "It's so damned hard to let them go. She's been the center of my life ever since she was born. She's grown up, mature, responsible, everything you say, I know. I worry about her anyway."

Janet decided this was as close as Vicky Davis would get to an apology for her anger. She decided to accept it as obliquely as it was offered.

"I think you have a daughter you can be proud of."

Vicky regarded Janet solemnly. "I didn't want any of this getting out. Sally doesn't understand the real world yet.

Blame the victim, that's what the real world does. I don't want her carrying this around for the rest of her life like it's her fault."

Janet's voice was deliberately soothing. "Sally doesn't see it that way. She knows it's not her fault, or your fault either. That might make a difference for her." Janet hoped she was right.

Vicky shook her head. "It doesn't matter how she sees it. What matters is how everyone else in this county would see it. Even if nothing happened beyond some advances, and there was more to it than that. He ripped the buttons off her blouse before she socked him. If a man takes advantage of a woman, even if she's just a child, it's always the woman who pays." Her voice was bitter.

Janet had no response to make. What Vicky said was all too often true. Even when dealing with the best-intentioned people, being known as a victim caused a double-take that made everyone concerned uncomfortable. Janet was very familiar with that kind of double-take. She could see why Vicky would want to spare Sally from it.

"Right now, what happened to Sally is wholly peripheral to our investigation," Janet said, then added with real concern, "As long as she's not personally involved, I'll do whatever I can to protect her from publicity. If she'll accept that protection."

Vicky stared at Janet for a long moment, taking the prosecutor's measure. Finally, she rewarded Janet with a faint smile.

"You got that right. Sal has a mind of her own. But she's so young. She hasn't been around the block yet, and I hope she never takes the trip." Vicky fished in the desk for a tissue, spat on it, and dabbed at her mascara. "How do I look?"

"Fine," Janet told her. "You look fine."

"Sure." Her smile was wry. "Sorry I blew up at you when you came in. I guess I'm overprotective. Shit, I know I am. But Sally's just about all I've got." She paused to take a breath. "You said you had some questions?"

Janet nodded. "I want to ask you about Vern Junker," she said. "The night Lowry disappeared."

"Hoo-boy," Vicky sighed. "As if I could remember. But I'll try."

"He said he came here and got drunk."

"Nothing new about that. It's what he does most nights. The surprise would be if he didn't."

"He said that he told several people that night that Lowry was going to take him back. Did you hear anything about that?"

"Did he say he told me?" Vicky's face screwed up in puzzlement.

"No, he didn't. I'd think he knew you wouldn't be pleased with his knowing about what happened to Sally, or how he used the information. Do you know how he found out?" Janet wanted to see how much Vicky knew.

"I always suspected he knew something he shouldn't." Vicky sat back in her armchair. "I sent Sal to a psychologist, to make sure she was OK over it. She might not have told me everything that happened. Or it might not have been the first time. Sexual-abuse victims don't always tell their mothers everything. At least that's what our doctor said when I asked her if she thought I should do anything more than what I already had. I had to call around to find somebody good, and I talked to a bunch of them until I found somebody I liked. Well, a couple of times I had to use the phone out there," she pointed toward the kitchen. Janet remembered the wall phone just outside it. She'd seen Vicky use it before.

"Sometimes, I was the only one here," Vicky continued, "and I couldn't leave the register to use the phone here in the office. One time, I was telling one of them what I wanted, and I'd turned to the wall. When I turned back, Vern was right there. He claimed he'd just come in, hadn't heard a thing. I wasn't sure I believed him, so I kind of sat on him. Told him if he had heard anything about my private affairs and I found out that anything I might have said on the phone had gotten out, I'd know it was him, and I'd make sure he never came in this place again. Well, that would pretty well end his social life, so I thought he'd keep his mouth shut."

"It sounds like he wanted Lowry to pay him for the same service — keeping his mouth shut — by giving him his job back."

"Never trust a drunk," Vicky said sourly. "I ought to know."

"Did you ever confront Lowry about his behavior?"

"Of course I did." Vicky slapped the table. "As soon as Sally told me, I went out there and read him the riot act. I told him if I ever saw him around my daughter, my house or my business again, I'd have him thrown in jail."

"What did he say?"

"Denied it. Said Sally misunderstood."

"And you said?"

"That was a load of crap. From what Sally told me he said and did, and the way he acted when I talked to him, it sounded to me exactly like it sounded to her. First he tried to seduce her and when that didn't work, he attacked her. If she hadn't known how to fight and hadn't had the sense to do it, he would've raped her. Then he started whining at me, and I told him to shut up before I killed him. Oh, shit, I didn't mean to say that. Figure of speech."

Janet nodded. "When did this happen?"

"February. About a month before he left. It happened fast. He attacked Sally, and she told me, and I went out there, all in a couple of days."

"Did he ever try to get in touch with you after that, despite what you'd said?"

"Once. I hung up on him."

"Can you tell me who all knew about this incident?"

"Sally. Me. Glen, obviously. The shrink. The doctor. Vern, maybe, if he overheard something I said on the phone and put two and two together, and anyone he told."

"Sally's father? Did you tell Sally's father?"

Vicky grimaced in surprise. "I thought the whole world knew about that. It's twenty damned years and people still talk and point. Sally doesn't have a father. Not a legal one, and not a practical one, either. He took off before she was born, as soon as he found out I was pregnant. We weren't married. As far as I know, he's never been back, and he's certainly never been in touch with me, or with Sal. Somebody might have told him he had a daughter, but he's never shown any sign of interest in her."

"Do you have any idea where he is?"

"Don't know and don't care. I don't think anyone around here does. He might be dead for all I know."

～ 23 ～

Janet dropped her letter to Rosalinda off at the post office on her way to work Tuesday morning. Sometimes she walked, but she drove if it was raining or if she might need her car during the day. Most days, it was one or the other or both. Ed Nuñez climbed out of his red Bronco just as she pulled into her reserved space.

"*Buenos dias,* Ed," Janet called cheerfully. "*¿Que pasa?*"

"Two things." Ed's tone was serious as he hurried across the lot. He stopped beside her, pausing for a second to catch his breath. "First, somebody cold-cocked Frank Vincent in the parking lot at the Oyster Bar last night. He's in County Memorial, unconscious."

"Has he come to, at all?"

"Not since he was found. He's badly concussed, possibly comatose. It might have been robbery. His wallet was on the ground beside him. There wasn't any cash in it, but his credit cards were intact. His daughter didn't know if he had any cash on him. Her husband came down with the flu, so Frank had gone over to close up the place for them."

"What about the restaurant receipts?" Janet began walking to the courthouse, Ed accompanying her.

"Vincent counted them, made out the deposit slip, entered the numbers in the books, and the bartender and bouncer made the deposit on their way home. That's SOP. They're both longtime employees and pretty hefty guys. Bodybuilder types."

"They ride together?"

Ed nodded. "Live together, too. That's how the system started, the daughter told me. The bank's on their way, and with the two of them, it seemed safer than sending one person alone, and easier than having somebody follow somebody else. They're both bonded and they've worked at the Oyster Bar since it opened."

"Was that deposit made?" Janet pushed open the door to the courthouse.

Ed nodded. "First thing I checked. It was made, and it's complete. The employees I've talked to all verify that the two regulars took the deposit at the usual time. They weren't the last to leave, either; the kitchen staff was. All of them left together at about twenty past twelve, and they all saw each other drive out of the lot. That left Frank alone to lock up. A patrol car doing a routine pass found him just before two."

"Where was he?" The two colleagues continued talking as they climbed the stairs to the second floor. They had to dodge County employees, lawyers and their clients waiting for the morning court calendars as they walked to the Prosecutor's Office.

"His car was parked around back of the building. There's a slot in front of the dumpsters that the owners use. The rest of the staff park along the far side of the lot, in the last row. He was next to his car, but on the passenger side, away from the building."

Janet opened the door to the Prosecutor's Office. "What about Vincent's keys?"

"Intact. As far as Merrilee — that's his daughter — can tell, there's nothing missing from the restaurant or his car. The patrol officers say both were locked."

"Good morning, Janet, Ed," Maud Fleming said as they passed her desk. "Coffee?"

They accepted and went into Janet's office, where they sat down.

"So he might have been robbed, but only for the cash he had on him, if any?" Janet summed up.

Ed nodded. "That's what it looks like. But Merrilee reported something odd. Frank got two calls last night after he'd gone to the restaurant. The first one, she just said he wasn't home and was there a message. They said they'd call back. The second one, she told them Frank was at the Oyster Bar."

Janet braced herself for a punchline. Ed was grinning so hard the ends of his mustache were sticking out almost horizontally.

"Why'd she tell the second one where he was?"

"The caller used your name."

"What?" Janet rose in her chair.

"Relax, Janet." Ed, still grinning, flapped a hand. "I know you didn't call him, and I know you didn't cold-cock him."

"How?" Janet wanted to know. Her initial anger and alarm had retreated before Ed's obvious amusement. "Besides your general knowledge of my sterling character," she added as she settled back into her chair.

"I had a tape of a press conference in my car. I played it for the daughter, and she positively unidentified you. Said your voice is higher-pitched, more feminine. The caller just said 'Prosecuting Attorney Schilling.' She wasn't even sure the caller was a woman."

Just then, Maud Fleming came into the office, carrying with her a tray of coffee and Janet's phone messages. She deposited both on the desk, reminded Janet of her morning appointments, and left.

Ed picked up his cup. "So we can guess that this wasn't a straight robbery. This was somebody who was looking specifically for Frank Vincent, and somebody who either knew you'd talked to Vincent recently, and why, or someone who just picked up your name from all the publicity you've had lately and used it to get an edge. It's likely whoever it was knew Vincent's connection to Lowry."

Janet grimaced. "You know how the nut cases come out of the woodwork in homicides. It's possible the attack has nothing to do with the Lowry case. The call could be a setup to make us think it does. If Frank wasn't home on a weeknight, and his daughter was, where's the most likely place for him to be? They could have called the restaurant and found him there, and placed the second call to muddy the waters. Or the second call could have been a prank, and the assault unrelated."

Ed nodded, then said, "This doesn't look like a random mugging. They didn't take the credit cards, they didn't take the car. The manager answers the phone at the Oyster Bar, takes the reservations, all that kind of stuff. So if somebody called Frank there, he'd be the only person who'd know about it."

Janet leaned back in her chair, sipping at her coffee. "What are the odds of Vincent identifying his assailant?"

"The longer he stays under, the worse the odds get. They're hoping he'll come out of it soon. They say he's pretty strong for a fellow in his sixties. But even if he comes out of it today, he'll probably have short-term memory loss. For a while, anyway. At least there's no intracranial bleeding. If whoever hit him was trying to kill him, they didn't do a very good job of it. It could even have been an accident. Looks like the injury resulted when Vincent hit the ground. It's all gravel and rocks back there."

Janet nodded. "I've seen the place you're talking about. I thought Vincent was younger than sixty. He must be in good shape."

"We can hope."

Janet knew she didn't have to ask whether routine procedures had been followed. If a weapon had been found, Ed would have told her. Forensic specialists would be examining the place where Frank was found for evidence of what happened and for clues to the assailant's identity. Patrol officers would be searching for witnesses and correlating data to see who might have known that Janet had seen Frank, or who might have known Frank was at the Oyster Bar, or who might have a grudge against him. Someone would be monitoring the injured man's condition so he could be interviewed as soon as possible.

"You said there were two things, Ed?" Janet set her cup on a coaster and regarded her friend quizzically.

"Yeah. What did you find out from Vicky?"

"She backs Sally up. Says she told Lowry off, told him to stay away from them both. Vicky thinks Vern might have heard her trying to line up a shrink for Sally and that was how he found out what happened. Then he got his bright idea of using it to blackmail Lowry."

Ed frowned. "I wonder if more happened than they're letting on. Getting the kid a shrink seems like an overreaction."

"Not to me." Janet reined in her temper. Some people still thought if it wasn't a violent rape, abuse somehow didn't count. But Janet knew sexual abuse was most often committed by friends and family members, and they tend to rape and molest through seduction rather than by force. The long-term damage to the victim was usually caused more by the violation of trust in the relationship than by any physical invasion, which might seem relatively minor. Ed, as a cop, should know that as well as she did. "It didn't seem like an overreaction to Vicky or their family doctor, either," she went on. "Vicky asked their doctor what to do. The doctor recommended a consultation to make sure Sally was OK. Too much trouble's caused by not talking about things like this. Giving Sally the opportunity to talk it out with a professional wasn't out of line at all."

"Nobody else wants to talk about it, though," Ed said thoughtfully. "Adams lied to us with the idea of protecting the Davis girl. That was pretty obvious. Sounds to me like she thought if she told us, the Davis girl would be worse off than if she didn't, even after all this time."

"Vicky Davis would agree with that," Janet replied. "Vicky's awfully big on nobody knowing about the assault. I don't completely agree, but I can see her point. I think she's

afraid of the distancing factor. Knowing somebody's been a
victim of rape or sexual abuse makes people pause. It's something
outside of most people's experience. They don't know how to
react." Janet smiled as she remembered Sally's reaction. "Sally
herself couldn't care less. It's no big thing to her. She knows
who was wrong, and she knows it wasn't her. I suspect the five-
minute double-take would pass right by her. I wondered about
Sally's father, but according to Vicky, he's not in the picture,
never has been."

Ed made a sour face. "I suppose we're going to have to
find out who Sally's father is. Where he is. What he does."

"You're not going to get much cooperation from Vicky,"
Janet replied. "I think that's another reason why she's so insistent
on keeping Lowry's assault on Sally a private matter. From what
she says, she feels victimized by Sally's father. She says he ran
out on her when she found out she was pregnant. They weren't
married. I gather she's taken some flack about it over the years.
It's that distancing factor again. The five-minute double-take.
You get that even if people don't make judgments."

Ed frowned, then nodded. "There's still a lot of people
who look down on a woman who has a baby without getting
married, like it's all her fault or something. Hard on her and
hard on the kid. And there are still plenty of assholes who think
the victim of any crime, especially a sexual assault, was asking
for it." He shook his head and went on. "Listen, I also want to
tell you what we have on the *Valkyrie's* skiff. That Loretta Rogers
in Patrol came up with a witness. Mick's gone out with her to
bring him in."

"Who?"

"His name's Curtis Spencer. He lives inland from
Lowry's place, on Clark Creek. According to Loretta, he saw
the skiff."

~ 24 ~

Janet and Ed went immediately to join Officer Rogers and Mick in the same interrogation room where Janet had questioned Vern Junker. Officer Rogers' discovery, Curtis Spencer, was a small, wizened man who had to be over seventy. He had a stubble beard and sported a buffalo plaid hunting jacket. His grin revealed missing teeth.

"Mr. Spencer," Officer Rogers said, "this is Detective Nuñez and Ms. Schilling, the Prosecuting Attorney."

"Good morning," Janet said, extending a hand. The old man's callused hand gripped like iron.

"Morning," Curtis Spencer replied. He settled in his chair, making much of the attention he was getting.

Janet took the field incident report from Loretta Rogers and scanned it quickly. Curtis Spencer's address was on an inland county road, but his property bordered the western side of Clark Creek, just north of the property rented by Catherine Adams to the Simpsons. She handed the report back to the officer, then sat down opposite the witness. After obtaining Curtis Spencer's consent, on the record, to a recording, she had the man recite his name and address.

"Now," Janet began. "Will you just tell me what you told Officer Rogers and Detective Taylor?"

"Well, this gal," Spencer said, pointing at Officer Rogers, "come up to the house yesterday, asking about boats in the creek, so I told her. Then she come back this morning with this big fellow here" — he pointed at Mick — "and I told him the same thing. What I seen."

"Did you see a skiff, the kind used by a purse seiner, up Clark Creek?"

"That's what I seen." Curtis Spencer nodded vigorously.

"When was that?" Janet asked. Curtis Spencer obviously didn't understand the importance of repeating his information on the record for a written statement. Janet was going to have to pry it out of him line by line.

"Four years ago and a little more. Right after Lowry went down."

"How did you happen to see it?"

"I'm a logger by trade, but I like to fish. Get up far enough, and you get some good fishing in Clark Creek. Freshwater fish, not all them bullheads and dog sharks you get in the bay. I was up the creek fishing when I saw the boat."

"Can you come a little closer on the date?"

"Well, we figured out it was after Lowry left, but before anybody knew he was missing. I thought the skiff was abandoned, see?"

Over Curtis's head, Mick executed a solemn wink. Janet had to control her face. Obviously, Mick believed that Curtis hadn't really thought for one minute the skiff had been abandoned.

"Go on," Janet said.

"Well, it was a pretty nice boat, one of them big double-hull aluminum inboards they use as skiffs on the seiners, and there didn't seem to be nothing wrong with it at all. So I pulled it up on the bank and thought I'd wait and see if anybody claimed it."

Janet turned to look over her shoulder at Officer Rogers. "You've seen where it was?" The officer nodded. Janet turned back to Curtis. "Then what happened?"

"Nothing. Not for a couple – three weeks or so. I didn't have any call to go back down there, and I kind of forgot about it. I didn't hear 'bout anybody losing any skiff, though. Then there was one of those spring storms, and it brought down a tree right by the creek. I went down to cut it up, get a start on my firewood for the winter, and there was somebody taking that aluminum boat away."

"Did you know the person?"

"Nope. Didn't recognize them."

"One person?"

"Yep." Curtis Spencer nodded vigorously. "Just one of 'em. That's all I saw."

"Could you tell if it was a man or a woman?" Janet wanted to know.

"Wearing rain gear and a watchcap. Could have been either. I don't see distances real well any more."

"How tall?"

"Medium, I'd say from seeing them on the boat."

"Fat or thin?"

Curtis laughed, showing his missing teeth. "Miz Prosecutor, everybody looks chunky in rain gear. Not a real blocky person, as I recall. If I had to say, I'd say medium. Not fat."

"Could you tell anything about this person's age?"

"Medium. Not creaky or shaky the way somebody my age is, but not jerky or clumsy like a kid either."

Janet scribbled a note on her pad.

"What did you see the person do?"

"They was running the skiff out of the creek, like I said. Towing some kind of other boat behind it."

"What time of day was this?"

"Morning. Real early in the morning, just about sunrise. I don't sleep real well at my age. I'm seventy-six, you know. Seventy-two, then. I get up early."

"Did the person running the boat see you?"

"I doubt it. I didn't wave or nothing." Curtis Spencer thought about it for a minute. "No, I don't think they did. I didn't have my saw on yet, and I was kind of behind them."

"Did you think the boat belonged to the person driving it?"

"Now, how would I know something like that?" Curtis's tone was scornful. "But they must have known where to find it. People don't go up Clark Creek by accident. Except kids, and this wasn't no kid."

"What did you do?"

"Kissed off the idea of getting me a free salvage boat and cut up that tree."

Janet leaned back in her chair, crossing her long legs and tapping her silver pen on her pad.

"You said you pulled the boat up out of the creek?"

"I pulled it up on the bank. No sense it drifting away. In case somebody was looking for it," Curtis added, with what Janet was certain was entirely spurious virtue.

"Was it drifting when you found it?"

"Awash, like, not drifting. Like somebody hauled it up at low tide and didn't get it up quite high enough."

"Heavy boat?"

"Heavy enough. I couldn't have got it much higher. But the tide was up, so I didn't have to."

"Did you see anything on the boat that might identify the owner, or the seiner it was off of?"

"Nope," Spencer said. "If I had, I would've had to call it in. I didn't see any numbers on it, and there wasn't a name, either. Might have been something in the steering console, maybe an engine number or something, but I didn't think to look there. There weren't any papers or anything like that."

Janet thought it possible that Curtis Spencer had destroyed any papers that might have identified the skiff. He'd obviously regarded the boat as his, free and clear as salvage, as soon as he'd seen it. He seemed to take an easy come, easy go attitude toward its loss, but that didn't mean he hadn't been willing to exert himself in an underhanded manner to keep it.

"Did you see the boat again?"

"Saw it through the trees running out in the bay."

"Where was it headed?"

"West, towards the jetty."

"Anything special or different about it? How did you know it was the same boat?"

"Stands to reason, don't it? I suppose it might have been one just like it, but I saw it up the creek with somebody driving it out, then I saw one out in the bay right after that. Stands to reason. Anyway, it was towing one of those little whatchacallems. Flat, kind of scoopy bow, real low down to the water, and with one of those consoles you stand behind with the wheel on it."

Janet's hand clenched around her pen. "Boston Whaler?"

"Yeah. That's what it was." Curtis Spencer leaned forward triumphantly. "Now how likely is it there'd be two skiffs towing them Whalers out in the bay at six in the morning? It was the same boat, no question."

"You're sure it was a Boston Whaler?"

"I didn't remember the name until you said it, but now I'm sure. The shape's what you might call distinctive. Them Whalers don't look like nothing else."

"Do you know a man named Vern Junker?"

"Fisherman? Crewed for Lowry?"

"That's right."

"I've seen him around."

"Do you know Catherine Adams?"

"Alice's girl?"

"Yes."

"Haven't seen her since she was a kid, except in passing. I'd know her if I saw her on the street, I guess. She moved out pretty young — still in school. Sent her to live with some of the Ryans over in Salmon Bay."

"And you didn't recognize the person who took away the skiff?"

"Nope."

"Is there anything else you'd like to add to what you've said this morning that might give us a clearer picture of the situation?"

That was the catchall question with which Janet liked to end interviews and depositions. The information people didn't volunteer unless given this specific opportunity was often vital. But Curtis Spencer was indignant.

"I don't know nothing about any 'situation,'" the old man said, his face growing red. "This here girl comes around asking about a skiff up the creek four years and a bit ago, and I told her. Then I told that big fellow, and now I told you. But I don't know about any 'situation.'"

Janet nodded. "Thank you for your cooperation, Mr. Spencer. Officer Rogers has to get back on patrol, I think, but if you'll just go with the detectives, what you've just told me will be typed up in the form of a statement. We'll ask you to look it over, and when it's correct, to sign it. Then the detectives will take you home."

"How about some breakfast while we're waiting? I get awfully hungry without my breakfast."

Janet looked up at Mick and raised an eyebrow.

"Good idea," Mick said. "You come along with us, Mr. Spencer. We'll take you to the Main Cafe up the street here. They do a real good breakfast."

"Want to come along, Janet?" Ed asked.

"No, thanks, Ed. I've got to get back to my office." But as she watched the three men leave the small interrogation room, she knew it wasn't just the pressure of time that stilled her appetite. It was something quite different, the growing suspicion that this investigation was moving in a completely wrong direction — one she definitely didn't like.

~ 25 ~

The beeper went off as Mick and Ed were driving back to town after taking Curtis Spencer home. They'd spent most of the morning with the old man, between breakfast and watching him carefully review his statement, and that was plenty long enough. Ed pulled the beeper off his belt, read the number it displayed, and dialed it on the car's cellular phone. He spoke briefly.

"Head for County Memorial," he said as soon as he disconnected. "Frank Vincent's awake."

The intensive care unit was quiet, with dim lights, and a circle of wedge-shaped private rooms surrounding a central nursing station. They'd had to buzz for admission into the unit; here, at least, Ed thought, the patients were kept secure from the parade of people passing through most hospital wards.

The detectives found Frank Vincent's room easily: a uniformed officer stood outside the door.

"He's kind of drifting in and out," the uniformed officer, a middle-aged man named MacKenzie, informed them. "Ms. Murchison, the nurse in charge of the ward, said we couldn't talk to him until the doctor has a chance to look at him, but I thought you'd want to be here."

"Yeah," Mick said. "We do. When's the doctor coming?"

"Should be here any time. None of them like having me on duty here," Officer MacKenzie said. "They don't understand the security risk, but, hell, anybody could show up and say they're a family member or something."

"Has anybody shown?" Mick shifted, looking around the unit. Ed tried to catch the nurse's eye. He liked the look of her. She was a thin, sharp-featured woman, with plain brown hair cut in an uncompromisingly efficient style and a brisk, economical way of moving. Ed would bet she was a real firecracker. He barely heard MacKenzie's reply.

"The daughter stayed until the doctor said he was stable," MacKenzie said. "I hear she's called, but she hasn't been back. Nobody else has come looking for him, except the medical people, and I verified all of them."

"I'll go talk to the head nurse," Ed said, winking, and crossed the room to the central desk.

"Ms. Murchison?" he said, showing her his best smile.

"Can I help you?" her tone was frosty.

"I'm Ed Nuñez." He proffered his ID. "I understand Mr. Vincent's conscious?"

"Yes. But I cannot allow you to talk to him until his doctor has examined him."

"That's not a problem." Ed raised his hands in a conciliatory gesture. "We can wait. We don't want to jeopardize his recovery or disrupt your unit. What we want is to see if he remembers anything about his attacker. If he does, maybe we can eliminate the guard once we make an arrest. We want to make sure he's protected."

"So do we." The nurse's tone was tart, but not as chilly.

"With that in mind," Ed continued, "I want to get some idea of how clear his memory is likely to be, how pointed we should make our questions, and how long, more or less, we can have with him without tiring him out too much."

A buzzer sounded. Ms. Murchison leaned into a funnel-shaped noise damper and spoke briefly.

"Doctor Reinhardt's here," she said. "He'll let you know if Mr. Vincent can be questioned and for how long." She turned away. Ed wondered what it would take to make an impression on her. He'd have to ask Janet if she had any ideas on the subject.

Dr. Reinhardt breezed by the detectives and the guard, waving them away until he had consulted with a tall man who had been in Frank's room. They vanished behind the drawn curtains.

They emerged fifteen minutes later. The tall man was introduced as Frank Vincent's special nurse.

"It's looking good," Reinhardt said. "I won't bore you with the jargon, but I think he'll be all right. It was a pretty near thing. The injury was a bad blow to a part of the head prone to subdural hematoma. He's lucky. It looks like there's been no internal bleeding. Right now, he's tired and he needs quiet so he can rest. You can have five minutes."

"How clear is his mind, Doctor?" Mick had anticipated Ed's question.

"He's oriented to time and place, competent and co-herent. Don't tax him with complex questions. Keep it slow and simple."

"Can two of us go in?"

Reinhardt looked from one detective to the other. "Two," he said, "but not three. And only one of you talks. The special nurse will be present to monitor the patient's condition."

Ed nodded at the doctor as he followed Mick into the small room. Longtime partners, the detectives didn't have to consult to agree that Mick Taylor should be the one to talk. Mick's rapport with the man had been instantaneous. Ed would have to work for it, and they didn't have time for that.

Frank Vincent looked like he'd shrunk, Ed decided. His skin had an unhealthy pallor. Janet had said Frank Vincent looked younger than his reported age; now, Ed thought he looked older, with a grey stubble beard, and missing bridge-work. The skin hung slack on his big hand, the IV needle taped in place on the back. The hose from a catheter snaked out from under the sheet to the bag hanging on the bed rail.

"Mr. Vincent," Mick began, after placing himself squarely in Frank's line of sight. "Are you awake?"

Frank moaned, his bandaged head shifted and his eyes opened.

"It's Detective Taylor, Mr. Vincent. We met before. Can you tell me who hit you?"

Frank's head moved back and forth, a negative.

"Was it a stranger?"

The injured man moved his head in the negative pattern again.

"Was it an employee of the Oyster Bar?"

"No." The word came out haltingly once, then twice. "No."

"Was it a man?"

It took a minute, but Frank's head moved up and down, affirming he'd been hit by a man.

"You didn't know him?"

Frank shook his head again.

"Did he speak to you?"

Frank's head moved back and forth. Mick looked at Ed, his face crinkling with dissatisfaction. His answers were not consistent. Either he didn't remember, or...

"Ask him if it was Vern Junker." Ed had to stand on his toes to hiss the suggestion into his partner's ear. Mick shrugged.

"Did Vern Junker hit you, Mr. Vincent?"

The effect on Frank Vincent was galvanic. His eyes popped open and he stared at the detectives in shock.

"It was Junker, wasn't it?"

"Yes." The word came out softly.

"Why?"

"Money. He wanted money. To get out of town."

Ed saw Mick nod. He agreed. Vern Junker was the kind of man who might run.

"Did you give him any?"

"No."

"Did you have money in your wallet?"

"Yes. Hundred, hundred twenty."

"Your wallet was empty when you were found, sir," Mick said.

"Won't get far," Frank said with a ghost of a smile.

"No," Mick said. "That won't get him far."

Ed was itching to ask one more question. Once more, Mick anticipated it.

"Do you know why he hit you, Mr. Vincent?"

"Wouldn't give him money." Frank's hand began to shake.

"Why would he come to you for money?" Mick asked.

Frank appeared visibly distressed. The nurse moved closer, taking Frank's hand, even though his pulse was clearly visible on the monitor. The nurse looked up at Mick and said, "I think that's enough for now. It's been more than five minutes."

The detectives looked at each other and shrugged. They had their name. The details could be filled in later.

"Wait." Frank Vincent's voice was stronger. "I want to ask."

Ed stepped back toward the bed as Mick turned to face Frank.

"Vern said Glen molested a girl. That right?"

"Yes," Mick told him. "At least, he tried to, but she got away and told her mother. According to the girl, nothing happened beyond that, but her mother wasn't so sure."

"Who?"

"We know who it was, sir, but we can't say at this point. It's confidential."

Frank let out a heavy sigh, and it seemed to Ed that some kind of tension left his body. He spoke. "Vern wanted money not to tell about that. Not to tell you, not to tell the papers. Don't know how he knew."

"We think he overheard the girl's mother talking on the phone."

"Probably." Again, the smile crossed his face, then, with effort, he went on.

"He got mad at me when I said I didn't have enough money. Guess he thought I'd have the money from the restaurant.

Didn't want to wait. Said he'd be arrested if he didn't leave. Then he'd have to tell about the girl. I knew he'd already told the police. Wanted to put him off. Call, report him. Black-mail."

"Payment for silence? Yes, sir, that's blackmail. Seems to be one of Mr. Junker's habits."

Frank Vincent nodded.

"Mr. Vincent, one last question, and we'll leave you alone for now. Why did Mr. Junker think you'd pay for him to keep quiet about this incident?"

Frank Vincent smiled as he said, "Sally's my grand-daughter. My son's child. Doesn't matter they never got married. Doesn't matter he left town. Haven't heard from him in years. Alcoholic, drug addict. Don't know where he is. Could be dead. Sally's here. I love that girl. Want to help her. Doesn't need people's attention, people's pity, charity. Help out all Vicky lets me. Stubborn woman. Independent. You protect her, too." His last sentence was half question, half plea.

"Yes, sir," Mick told him. "We are. We don't see any need for publicity. Like I told you, it's confidential."

"Good," Frank said. Then, visibly spent, he collapsed into his pillows. The nurse turned to his patient as the detectives left.

"We can take off the guard now," Ed told the head nurse. "He was able to tell us who assaulted him. Just don't let any-body in you don't know already, until Detective Taylor or I call."

"I go off shift at three," Ms. Murchison objected.

"We'll have him in jail by then."

～ 26 ～

After questioning Curtis Spencer, Janet returned to her office just long enough to assign her scheduled work to subordinates, then went home to change into jeans and a sweater. She left her condo on foot, walking out the jetty path and down the stairs bolted into the rock to the beach. She often thought her mind was at its best watching the surf crash against the shore, and she wanted her mind clear now.

Janet walked below the tide line, on the hard-packed wet sand, heading south, into the wind, head bowed, hands shoved into the pockets of her leather flight jacket.

She wasn't satisfied with the case against Vern Junker. There were too many unanswered questions. "I don't think Junker did it," she said aloud vehemently. "There's somebody behind him, using him as camouflage." The concurrent events surrounding Sally Davis might have nothing to do with Glen Lowry's death. Or maybe these events, particularly the attack on Frank Vincent, were relevant, but not central, to the original crime. They could be occurring independently, snowballs set in motion by the avalanche of the murder investigation.

Climbing to the top of the first set of dunes, Janet found shelter behind a stand of Scotch broom and sat down. She stared at the sea. Its inexorable motion comforted her.

"If there *is* someone behind Junker, there's only one person it could be," she thought, her heart sinking at the prospect.

It could only be the person whose headlights Vern had thought he'd seen behind him as he left Glen Lowry's house. The person who knew the landscape better than anyone else. The person who had practically grown up on the *Valkyrie*. The person who owned a Boston Whaler. The person who had lied. Catherine.

Janet wrapped her arms around her knees and pulled them into her chest. What was she going to do about her suspicions? That was the crucial issue. The homicide detectives were sure Vern Junker was guilty. Janet knew there wasn't enough evidence to convict him. Jack Simpson's testimony about seeing the blonde in the Pinto on the night of Lowry's death was enough to guarantee Vern Junker would be acquitted at trial. Filing felony charges was within her discretion, no-one else's, no matter what Chief Daniels might think. Janet knew she could make sure Vern Junker was never tried.

If she refused to file charges against Vern Junker, then what? Could she allow the file on Lowry's death to join the many unsolved, unsolvable, but still open homicide files that plagued every law enforcement agency? Or would she have to insist the detectives pursue her suspect?

"Ed'll think I'm going after her because I'm still in love with her and I'm overcompensating," she said to herself. "Mick will think I'm out for revenge because she dumped me." Janet smiled grimly, got up and walked down to the waterline, where she let the wavelets lap at the toes of her waterproof Norfolk boots. "Daniels will be out for my blood. And none of that's important if she's the one who killed him."

Giving in to what other people thought or wanted of her wasn't her style. It never had been. She stood on her own feet, made her own choices, did what she thought was right and took the consequences.

And her father hadn't spoken to her from the day she told him about Gloria until his death. She stared at the ocean bleakly and felt the pain of that bit of necessary honesty stab her yet again.

Actually, she hadn't needed this walk to come to a decision; she'd made it long ago. Whatever events people set in motion by their crimes, they alone were responsible for the subsequent effects. Her responsibility was not to make choices about her job, but to perform it, honestly and thoroughly. She couldn't do it any other way.

"Integrity may be all I've got," Janet said aloud, "but by damn I've earned it. And I'm proud of it." She turned her back on the ocean, her long legs carrying her swiftly through the dunes directly to the courthouse. This wasn't going to be easy. She'd just as soon get it over with.

She strode down the hall, told Maud she wasn't to be disturbed, sat at her desk and flipped open the file on the Lowry case. She wanted to find the inconsistencies in Catherine's statements and locate any information which could be independently verified or disproved.

The termination of the lighthouse lease was the first thing she found. Catherine's statement said she had found out about it before Glen Lowry's disappearance. That could be verified. She telephoned the Coast Guard Station and asked for Lieutenant Fitch, who had been the officer the detectives had worked with in getting the overdue-vessel report for the Lowry homicide file.

"Fitch, here," a soprano voice said as she came on the line.

"This is Janet Schilling at the Sacajawea County Prosecutor's Office. I need some information regarding the termination of a lighthouse lease on an offshore island. Can you tell me who I'd call for that?"

"If it's in Washington, we'll have the records here. I can get them for you."

"It's the one just offshore. Seal Rock."

"Can you hold?" Janet held.

Lieutenant Fitch came back on the line quickly. "I have the file," she said. "What do you need to know?"

"Do you have any correspondence showing when the lessor was first contacted about terminating the lease?"

There was silence on the line, except for the sound of rustling paper.

"Let's see," Lieutenant Fitch said. "We have a letter that was sent to the lawyer for Alice Miller Lowry's estate, a Mr. Henry Charm. We show her estate as the owner. It's dated April 10th...oh. Is this connected to the Lowry murder case?"

"Possibly. Why?"

"The letter is from the same year Mr. Lowry died, the lessor's name was Alice Miller Lowry and the name of the executor is the same as the name we show in our overdue-vessel investigation file for Lowry's next of kin." Fitch sounded exasperated that Janet would ask such an obvious question.

"And there's nothing before April 10th?"

"I don't see anything in the correspondence section. Oh, here it says the Aids to Navigation Department didn't even decide to terminate the lease until the week before, but they'd been considering it for a while. At least that's what it says in the memo transferring the file to Legal."

"Was there a map of the island provided the new owner, or her attorney, at any time?"

"Let me look. Here. Yes, we sent a map with the April 10th letter. And photographs, showing the improvements. We built a small dock on the east side. Then there was the lighthouse itself, and a separate keeper's cottage, which was pretty dilapidated. The lighthouse had been automated for years."

"Anything about the geology of the island?" Janet tapped her silver pen on her pad.

"What do you mean?" Fitch sounded puzzled.

"Are there caves on those islands? And does anything you sent out show them?"

"Oh, yes. Those islands are riddled with caves, just like the coastline. The sea lions use them for rookeries. And it says here in the original letter that the lighthouse has stairs going down into an underground chamber that opens up right under the middle of the island. The letter says it's where the keepers used to moor their boats before we blasted out the cove and built the dock. There's a memo here." She paused, then continued. "It looks like the Legal Division was trying to get the owner to take the place back without demanding the improvements be demolished. That was her right. 'Returned to its natural state,' it says in the lease. It looks like they were trying to show the owner how it was already prepared for use as a summer house, or something. I guess there's a big demand for these islands as private residences, and they sell for huge prices with the improvements. Or at least that's what the letter says."

Janet slashed a triangle on her pad with the silver pen. She did not like what she was hearing. Caves under the island. Access directly from the lighthouse. A place where someone had once moored a boat. There would have to be access from the sea, too. Janet felt bleak. She couldn't think of a better place to hide an unsinkable skiff.

"Will I need a court order to get copies of that file?" She turned the triangle into a pyramid.

"Let me check with my Commander and call you back. I think I can send you regular copies, but if you want certified ones, I'll have to have the order."

"Regular ones will be fine for now," Janet told her.

Once she'd hung up, Janet flipped through her own file once more, checking her memory against the written record. Her next call was to the Department of Licensing.

"I need a trace on boats registered to a particular person." She gave them the year of Glen Lowry's death, and Vern Junker's name. The clerk was back on the line in seconds.

"No boats titled to anyone by that name anywhere in the state, ma'am, in that year."

"Try this name. Same year. All year." She gave the man Catherine Adams' name, with all the addresses she might have used. As she waited for the clerk to run a computer search, she drummed her nails on the desk, and found herself clenching her teeth. She didn't like doing this, but she had no choice.

The clerk came back on the line a few minutes later, sounding pleased. "In that year, I show a fourteen-foot Boston

Whaler registered in that name at the Church Street address.

"When was it purchased?" Janet asked.

"Two years before that," the clerk told her. "I also show a new Boston Whaler Outrage 23 registered in July of that year, but the address is different." The clerk gave it. It was Catherine's bank.

"Thank you," Janet said automatically, and hung up. She slammed her fist against the desktop. How the devil had they missed it? There were two Whalers, and the small one fit Curtis Spencer's description perfectly. Grim determination showed on Janet's face.

Why did she do it? Janet wondered as she leaned back in her chair. *It wasn't the money she got through Lowry's estate. Catherine didn't need the money; she hadn't touched it. But then, motive isn't an element of proof in homicide, because one person's motive is another's annoyance. Still, juries like to hear it.* More than that, Janet herself wanted to know. She sketched another pyramid while she thought, and began filling it in.

Curtis Spencer had said Catherine had moved away from home when she was very young. Catherine talked about it quite openly. She'd lived with some of the Ryan clan, she'd said, when she was in high school, so she could get into some special science program at Lincoln High in Salmon Bay. *That doesn't make sense,* Janet realized suddenly. All the Sacajawea County schools were in the same district. You didn't have to move to go to one or the other, and hadn't as long as Janet had lived there. Janet made a note to call the school district to check Catherine's story, but the offices closed for lunch, and it was noon. She read through Catherine's second statement.

Catherine could confirm that Vern Junker had left Glen Lowry's place, though she said she hadn't seen Glen after that. Vern could have killed Glen before he left, then returned later to hide his tracks. More likely, if Vern had killed him, Glen hadn't been killed until later.

In her last statement, Catherine had said that she followed Vern away from Glen's. Now, Janet realized, by that time Catherine knew Vern had said she followed him into town. She just confirmed his statement. By doing so, she gave Vern a partial alibi, but she also gave one to herself.

On reviewing Vern's statement, Janet saw that Vern could not have positively identified Catherine's car as the one he saw behind him as he drove back into Charbonneau. All he'd seen was headlights behind him after he'd rounded the first bend away from the house.

What if Catherine never left? Janet wondered. She reviewed what she'd discovered in her mind.

According to the Coast Guard's records, it wasn't true that Catherine had known about the termination of the lighthouse lease before Lowry's death, though she had said so more than once. She had also lied about the last contact she had with Glen Lowry, though the detectives were willing to conclude that she had done so to protect Sally Davis.

"Why would *Catherine* want to protect Sally Davis?" Janet said aloud as she swiveled in her chair, staring out the window. "Surely *that* was an overreaction, if ever there was one."

Janet could see Vicky's perspective. Vicky intimated that she, as an unwed mother, had been the victim of charity, pity, some notoriety and a certain amount of disapproval. All of that would have attached to her daughter. Illegitimacy wasn't the same kind of burden to bear today as it had been years ago, but it was still a burden.

Being a victim was a burden, too. Janet knew that sex crimes often went unreported simply because the victim didn't want to be identified as such. *Even if she's not blamed for being a victim, it's something people notice, something they talk about, even if they think they're being kind,* Janet thought. *Vicky wouldn't want to see her daughter have to bear that additional burden. But Catherine?*

Suddenly, an idea came to her, one so startling in its enormity she had trouble believing it. *It makes sense,* Janet thought, coming upright and sitting tall in her high-backed chair. *Total and complete sense. It explains why Catherine left home when she did and why she'd go out of her way to shield a girl she hardly knew.* It was a motive for murder that made far more sense than the insurance money Catherine hadn't touched.

"If I'm right," Janet said aloud, "I can prove it in an hour." She grabbed her briefcase and left the courthouse.

Janet drove too fast in her hurry to get to the Juvenile Court complex. It was a newer building, dating from the late sixties, situated on spacious grounds outside Charbonneau. She waved to the counter clerk, slipped under the lifting counter gate and headed for the indices.

The older indices were handwritten in huge books, each of which would be used until one letter's allotted space was filled completely, at which time a new book would be started. Janet found what she was looking for in minutes, copied the case number on a slip of paper, and took it into the microfilm room.

Original files were never actually destroyed. Courthouse space was saved by retaining just the films of older cases there, with the actual files stored in a warehouse. She found the right spool and inserted it into a reader. What she read confirmed only part of her suspicion. Though her mother was living, Catherine had been declared a dependent child, made a ward of the court, and placed in foster care. There were periodic reviews of status, but no changes. To get the details, Janet knew, she would have to get the Social File, which was the casework history, indexed separately, numbered differently, and subject to different rules of confidentiality.

She hurried upstairs to the casework department, where she got the number of the Social File. Back downstairs in the microfilm room, she pulled the spool and fed it into the reader while she slid into the uncomfortable chair. Scanning the file first, then reading it slowly, she slumped against the back of the hard wooden chair, feeling queasy and very sad.

～ 27 ～

Ed Nuñez and Mick Taylor hurried from Frank Vincent's hospital bedside directly to the St. Charles Hotel. Mick poked a finger into the clay pot of a sorry-looking split-leaf philodendron in the lobby as he passed it, then held the finger up for Ed to see.

"It's been watered," he said, "but it still looks half dead."

"Might be depressed," Ed replied as he mounted the stairs.

"Or maybe it's the smell."

When they reached the third-floor hall, they saw a middle-aged man running a vacuum cleaner over the faded carpet in the hall outside Vern Junker's door. Ed reached the door first and knocked, loudly. There was no answer. He tried again, as Mick rumbled, "Junker, it's Nuñez and Taylor. Open up." Again there was no answer.

Mick turned to the man with the vacuum and asked, "Are you the manager?"

The man said, "That's me." *Mexican,* Ed thought, switching to his California Spanish. The man's face lit with a pleasant smile, and he replied in the same language. Ed turned to Mick and translated.

"This is the manager, Fidelio Martinez. He hasn't seen Vern since he came in last night. He's been cleaning the halls all morning, and hasn't seen Vern leave. Vern usually doesn't go out before twelve or one. He didn't get in until about two-fifteen this morning."

"You saw him?" Mick asked Fidelio.

"*Si,*" Fidelio replied, and continued in Spanish, addressing Ed.

"Fidelio lives here," Ed translated. "There's a night clerk, six to six, but he didn't show up last night, so Fidelio was on call all night. He says this happens a lot; the clerks are usually either students or drunks. When they don't show up, he locks the door at ten, and puts out a sign that says 'Ring for Entry.' If somebody rings, it wakes him up and he goes out and lets them in. That's how he knows when Vern came in."

Ed asked the man another question and translated the response.

"Fidelio says he unlocked the door at seven this morning. Vern hadn't gone out before that, because the door's on a dead bolt. Needs a key to open it from either side. So anybody who wanted to leave had to get Fidelio up, too. Nobody did."

Mick nodded thanks at Fidelio, then turned and pounded on Junker's door. Fidelio had stopped the vacuum cleaner, and stood watching, alert and cautious.

"Vern," Mick called. "You OK?"

There was no response.

"Ed, ask Fidelio if he's got a pass key."

"I got a pass key," Fidelio replied in English.

"Use it," Mick commanded.

Fidelio turned to Ed. They spoke in Spanish at some length.

"He doesn't want to," Ed reported. "But I told him that we're worried about Vern, and we want to make sure he's all right. I promised we wouldn't go in if he wasn't there."

"OK," Mick said.

Once Mick had agreed, Fidelio abandoned his vacuum cleaner and moved toward the door. He, too, knocked.

"Vern," he called. "It's Fidelio. These men just want to see if you're OK. If you're there, open up, otherwise I'm going to have to use my key."

But Vern Junker didn't answer.

Ed looked at Mick. He could feel a vein throb in his left temple. The right corner of Mick's mouth went down, and he shook his head slightly. Ed nodded imperceptibly. He could tell they shared the same hunch, and neither of them liked it.

"Open it, Fidelio," Ed said.

Fidelio turned the key in the lock, pushing open the door as he did so. He gasped, pressing his hands to his face. Mick shouldered him aside. Vern Junker lay sprawled on his bed. Mick crossed the room swiftly to pick up a flaccid hand.

"Don't do that here," Ed said to Fidelio. Mick turned to see him hustling the man out into the hall. "In the bucket," Ed said, and Mick heard the sounds of someone being sick.

Ed stuck his head back into the room. "He'll be OK," he said. "You want an ambulance?"

"No," Mick said, letting Vern's dead hand down gently. "Medical Examiner. And Crime Scene."

"He is dead, then?" Fidelio's face, pale and slightly green, appeared at the door.

"He's dead," Ed said. "Come on out into the hall."

The three of them waited there until the Medical Examiner and the Crime Scene technicians showed up in their respective vans. A group of curious residents collected. Ed assigned Fidelio to crowd control. Then he followed the technicians into Junker's room.

"It's going to take the autopsy to make it official," the Deputy Medical Examiner said, "but I can give you a preliminary cause of death right now. I've seen this one before."

Ed and Mick both approached the bed.

"It's pretty straightforward, actually. I don't think the autopsy will change things. From his eyes, you can see his liver was just about shot, and I'll bet he was overdue for a coronary, but barbiturates and booze is my preliminary determination. Probably suicide. Here's the booze." The doctor indicated a glass by the side of the bed. Ed bent over it. The fumes of bourbon wafted up.

"Where's the bottle?" Mick wanted to know.

The Deputy Medical Examiner shrugged. "That's your problem."

"Whiskey bottle's right here," a fingerprint technician said.

"I meant the pill bottle," Mick said.

"Haven't seen it."

"Look at this." Ed pointed out a crumpled piece of plastic wrap on the night table.

"So?" Mick asked.

"They sell pills in twists of this stuff because it sticks to itself. Smaller and easier than plastic bags. Cheaper, too."

"We'll need this handled carefully," Mick told one of the technicians. "Check it for traces of barbiturates and other drugs, and gelatin from capsules." He turned to Ed. "You're thinking he did it himself?"

"Maybe." Ed shrugged. "Who else? He was in bad trouble. From what Frank said, he knew we wanted him for the Lowry killing. Then he assaulted Frank, but didn't kill him. Maybe he couldn't after he saw Frank on the ground. Or maybe they scuffled and Frank getting hurt so bad was an accident, and it scared him. If Vern killed Glen Lowry in anger, or with a single thrust, that makes sense. Killing somebody's a shock. Then, when Vern didn't get enough money from Frank to leave town, and he knew Frank would identify him, he didn't have a lot of choices left."

"From talking to him," Mick said, "I would have thought Vern would leave a long, drunk note justifying everything he ever did. But I could be wrong. Half the suicides don't leave notes."

"Maybe he was too drunk," Ed said. "Hell, it could even have been an accident. We'll want to check on how much money there is in his wallet. Something else we need to check. Fidelio said Vern got in about two-fifteen. Where was he between the time Vincent was hit and when he got home?"

"Talk to Fidelio," Mick suggested.

Ed nodded and left the room. He found the manager out in the hall, trying, unsuccessfully, to get the residents to disperse. Ed was suddenly glad of his Spanish. He could talk to Fidelio right in front of the crowd, and would bet that none of them would understand what was being said.

"Fidelio," he began, "what kind of shape was Junker in when he got home last night?"

Fidelio shrugged. "About the same as usual. Maybe a little dirty, like he'd fallen, or something. He sometimes did that. When he had too much to drink."

"You mean when he was drunk? Was he drunk last night?"

Fidelio lifted his hands and shrugged in a gesture of gentle futility Ed recognized. "He was about as usual last night. He had been drinking, yes, but I would not say he was drunk. He liked to drink. There is a bar he went to with his friends almost every night."

"Was he unhappy? Grouchy? Angry? Sad? Cheerful? Happy?"

"I can only say that he seemed to me much as usual. We didn't really speak."

"Thank you," Ed said. He turned. Mick had managed to come up behind him without Ed being aware of it. Ed stepped away from the group.

"What'd he say?" Mick asked in low tones.

"Vern was just about as usual when he came in last night, which means, as near as I can tell, that he was pretty well lit. You know what that means."

∾ 28 ∾

Janet hurried back to her office from the Juvenile
Court complex. She was too intent to care about stopping for
lunch, though it was one-thirty and she knew she ought to be
hungry. She sat at her desk and opened the Lowry file. She'd
been working half an hour when the door burst open without
warning.

"Dammit, Janet," her boss, Ben Davidson, the County
Prosecuting Attorney, shouted as he stormed into the room.
"What the hell do you think you're doing?"

"What's the matter?" Janet knew she was going to have
to tell Ben what she was doing. She was going to need his support. But she had planned to do it in her own time and on her
own terms.

"You tell me." Ben planted himself in front of Janet's
desk, gripped the edge of it with his hands, and leaned
forward. "Vern Junker's dead."

"Oh, shit." Janet fell back in her chair, shocked. "What
happened?"

"Barbiturates and booze, according to the ME on the
scene. Possibly suicide."

"How did you hear?"

"Police radio. I *listen* to mine." Ben jerked a thumb in
the direction of the scanner sitting silent on Janet's window
sill. "You weren't around so I called homicide for an update. As

soon as the switchboard heard my voice, I got put through to Daniels. No damned thanks to you that I know anything about this case at all. You've not only been keeping me in the dark about this Lowry thing, but now Daniels is telling me you're screwing it up. Do I need to say Daniels thinks Vern Junker would be alive if you'd authorized his arrest on investigation? Why in the hell did you let him go?"

"We didn't have a case, Ben." Janet allowed her voice to become emphatic. She felt anger rise as Chief Daniels' accusation sank in. The damned old bigot thought by going to Ben, he could cause trouble for her. Well, he was wrong.

"We *never* had a case against Junker," Janet said. "That's my decision to make, not Daniels'. If Daniels had a problem with it, he should have come to me. When you look at the evidence, all we've got against Junker is motive, and motive isn't enough." Janet stabbed at the notes on her pad.

"We have to assume the crime scene was Lowry's house or on the *Valkyrie*," she told Ben. "I think it was the boat, where Lowry's body was found. It was seen moored at the house that afternoon and wasn't seen again after it left there. Junker was confirmed leaving the house in his car by someone who was behind him, and was seen at a bar later. Nobody saw him going back to Lowry's. The upland neighbor saw a blonde woman in a Pinto turn into Lowry's drive long after we know Junker left. We can't identify her, though I think I know who she was. So we can't place him at the scene.

"Furthermore," she continued, "we have a witness who saw what we believe was the *Valkyrie's* skiff up Clark Creek. We can't connect Junker to the Clark Creek location at the time the skiff would have been abandoned there or when it was moved later. Junker had no demonstrable connection to the only physical evidence we have. The only thing we had was motive. We simply didn't have enough to justify an arrest."

Ben pursed his lips, pulled a side chair up and sat. Janet was glad to see some of her superior's anger had evaporated. At least, he wasn't mad at *her* anymore.

"Did you know Frank Vincent identified Junker as the person who hit him?" Ben asked.

"No. When?" Janet leaned forward, her face grim.

"Couple of hours ago. Mick and Ed talked to him at the hospital right after he woke up. They found the body when they went to pick Junker up on the assault. Janet, if you saw a problem coming, you should have brought me in. That's what I'm for. Maybe I could have helped you before it got this bad. Christ, woman, at the very least I could have backed you up. Now Daniels is involved; he thinks you're wrong, and if you give him a chance, he'll turn this into a goddamned political circus."

"You *can* help. I hope you will." Janet sighed heavily. "I was going to come see you as soon as I finished this. What I want to do isn't going make it any better. I'll need all the support I can get." She leaned back in her chair. "Vern Junker assaulted Frank Vincent," she said thoughtfully. "Was Vincent able to suggest a reason?"

"According to Vincent, Junker was looking for getaway money."

"Why would he think he'd get it from Vincent?" Janet asked.

"Vincent's the Davis girl's grandfather. Vincent says his son is the man that ran out on her mother, and Vincent's been trying to make it up to both of them ever since. Junker was trying to sell silence on Lowry's assault on the Davis girl in exchange for hard cash."

"Junker had a one-track mind," Janet said. "He'd tried blackmail before." She grimaced. "We were pretty hard on him, I think." Janet expelled a huff of air and drew small circles on her pad. "Just because we didn't have a case doesn't mean Junker didn't think we were going to try to pin it on him."

"Daniels sees his death as consciousness of guilt," Ben said.

"He's wrong. I see it as fear," Janet replied. "Fear that we were going to take the easy way out and nail him for something he didn't do."

"Daniels said Lowry's stepdaughter was an old girlfriend of yours who dumped you. He claims you ignored the evidence against Junker because you want to nail her."

Janet grimaced as she thought about her options. Finally she decided to short-circuit that issue entirely. Ultimately, the truth was her best defense.

"Considering her as a suspect wasn't easy, Ben," Janet told the older lawyer. "Focusing on Junker was. But I have to consider her. We all have to consider her. The evidence is there." She leaned forward and laid her hands flat on the top of her desk. "Ben, I think she killed him."

"Oh, hell, Janet." Ben tilted his magnificent head and skewered Janet with the laser gaze he used on recalcitrant witnesses.

"I'm serious, Ben. Listen. Junker could place Adams at the house. She could testify that he left, but there's no real confirmation that she left after he did. She's stated she knew she was going out to Seal Rock to live before Lowry vanished, but the Coast Guard file shows she wasn't notified that they wanted to terminate the lighthouse lease until three weeks later." She took a deep breath and looked at Ben. His expression was thoughtful. At least he was paying attention.

"There's more," she went on. "The skiff was abandoned up Clark Creek. Adams grew up on that creek, so she'd know it better than anyone else. She'd need to bring the skiff in to shore near where she'd left her car at Lowry's. There's a way to get from the creek to the house on foot without going up on the road. It's a path that's wide enough for a car. It leads out onto the highway right by the bridge, where there are no houses in sight. She's the only person we have who connects all those facts together."

Ben leaned forward, propping his elbows on the desk, and listened intently. Janet continued, relieved. He was giving her theory serious consideration.

"Here are the clinchers," she said. "The skiff was taken away by a person who fits her description well enough, who

came in driving a Boston Whaler. Adams owned a small Whaler
for years, including the year of Lowry's death. She owns a bigger one now. Junker never has; he didn't own any boat at all at
the time of Lowry's death. Seal Rock is riddled with caves, including one accessible from the lighthouse where the keepers
used to moor their boats. The timing of the Coast Guard's letter describing that cave coincides with the time the skiff was
moved.

"This is the major point against her," Janet said at last.
"No one else had any reason to move that skiff. The Clark Creek
location connects with Adams; she's familiar with it, she even
owns it. It doesn't implicate anyone else. She's the only person
with a more secure place to put the skiff — on the island."
Janet repeated this point to emphasize it. "Catherine Adams is
the only person who had a reason to move the skiff and the
only person with a better place to put it. It's double-hulled
aluminum. Apparently you can't sink the thing, and it would
take a welding torch to cut it up. Then what would you do
with the pieces?" Janet sat back and fussed with the papers on
her desk. She didn't like to say this part, but she had to.

"As to motive," she continued, "Adams admits that when
she heard about Lowry's assault on Sally Davis, it made her
sick, physically sick. It wasn't just general sympathy. I've checked
into her background. She didn't move to Salmon Bay to get
into an honors science program like she said. She was a ward of
the court and was living in foster care." Janet paused before the
next words and took a deep breath. "Lowry had raped her. Re-
peatedly. The records are all over at Juvie." She shot him a sad
look as she finished.

Ben considered her words, the planes of his patrician
face hardening into granite as his lips thinned. "It rings true,"
he said, "but you can't prove it. If you can't bring charges,
Daniels will say that he's thought all along that Junker was guilty.
That Junker could and should have been arrested on investigation. If he had been, he probably would have cracked, and we
could have closed the file with a confession. I don't agree with

that kind of law enforcement and you know it," Ben said as Janet jerked angrily in her chair. "Even if he didn't confess, even if he wasn't guilty, if Junker was in jail, he couldn't have assaulted Vincent, and he'd still be alive. That's what Daniels will say."

Janet was so angry she couldn't speak. While she was trying to get her temper under enough control to make a reasoned reply, Ben went on, "He'll claim you prosecute from emotion, for personal reasons, rather than acting on evidence for the public good. Janet, if he goes public with this kind of bullshit, it could cost you the election."

"Daniels has the problem," Janet retorted with some vehemence, stabbing her pad with her silver pen. "I don't think I do. There wasn't a goddamned case against Junker, and I will not countenance arresting people we don't have grounds to charge. We can't arrest people just because they *might* do something stupid or foolish. We have to have a reason." She paused to marshal her arguments. She knew she might have to repeat them to the press.

"There is no way that having Vern Junker in jail would have made it any easier to get evidence against him on this crime," Janet continued. "All it could have accomplished is to have intimidated a confession out of a possibly innocent person. That's no substitute for doing the investigative work necessary to arrest the actual perpetrators. Our job, Daniels' job, too, is to investigate crimes, arrest the guilty and bring them to justice. We aren't in business just to close files, Ben. Or are we?" She slapped the pen on her desk.

"You know we're not," Ben replied. "I'll go on record that it was appropriate to let Junker walk, if the file backs you up."

Janet nodded. "It does."

"OK," Ben said thoughtfully. "Fine. It'll work. If we both attack Daniels' ethics and performance strongly enough right now, I think we can keep him from going public with his opinions. He'll never be your friend, but at least he'll be defused. I'm afraid we'll have to leave the Lowry case unsolved. I don't like it any more than you do, but you can't charge Adams if there's no case you can prove against her, either."

"Have a look at this." Janet held out the paper she'd been working on. "It's a warrant application for a search of Seal Rock. There's a sailboater who was washed up there by the rogue wave. Her name's Cavanaugh. She's our guarantee that Adams hasn't disposed of anything relevant, including that damned skiff. Cavanaugh's been there since before Lowry's body was found."

"Without that skiff you don't have shit, Janet." Ben's face registered shock.

"I know," Janet said. "I'm betting it's there."

"Do you know how much you're betting?" Ben, with a look of concern on his distinguished face, spread his hands on the desk and leaned forward, speaking earnestly. "If you go ahead with this warrant, it's a direct and public challenge to Daniels. If you come up empty, he'll see that you get crucified. He'll paint you as a vengeful woman scorned. If you come up empty, you'll lose the election and end up unemployed when Halliday fires you."

A tremor of fear ran though Janet. She looked her boss square in the eye. "I know the risk, Ben. But it's one I have to take."

~ 29 ~

After Vern Junker's body had been taken to the
morgue and the crime scene technicians had finished their work
and sealed the room where the fisherman had died, Ed Nuñez
and Mick Taylor went directly to the Mermaid. Ed had never
been in the Mermaid during the daytime before. It was disconcerting how walking through the double plank doors into the
cool, darkened room turned day into night.

"There's the owner," he said softly to Mick, "the blonde
by the register."

"Ms. Davis?" Mick asked as they approached the bar.

"Yes?"

"We're police officers." He flashed his identification.
"Can we have a few minutes of your time?"

"Come into the office." She looked at Mick dubiously.
"I suppose there's room. Betsy, take over the register." She led
the way through the small kitchen into her office, where she
sat behind her desk. She laid her hands on it, tapping her index
fingers, and said, "Well?"

"We're sorry to have to tell you, ma'am," Ed said, after
he had sat down in the room's only other chair, "that a patron
of yours, Vern Junker, has died."

The only reaction Vicky Davis displayed was that the
tapping of her fingers stopped. She looked from Ed to Mick,
and back again. "Well?" she said.

Ed glanced up at Mick, who shrugged so slightly that even Ed could hardly see it. He turned back to Vicky Davis.

"The preliminary Medical Examiner's report indicates that it wasn't a natural death," Ed said.

"Vern wasn't my family, or even a close friend," Vicky Davis said. "He was a customer, and I don't like to lose my customers, but you wouldn't have come here just to tell me he died. How can I help you?"

"Was he in here last night?" Ed asked.

"Yes, he was."

"Can you tell us what time?"

Vicky leaned back and rubbed her index finger across her upper lip. "I remember seeing him about eight-thirty. He was watching a Mariners game. Then he left for a while. I didn't see him go, but I saw him come back in. I think it was about one o'clock. He stayed till we closed."

"Was he drinking?" Ed already knew the answer, but he wanted to hear it from Vicky.

"Sure he was."

"What?"

"Bourbon and water," the bar owner replied. "His usual."

"Did you talk to him at all during the evening?" Ed asked.

"Of course. We passed the time of day. I didn't notice anything unusual that I can think of offhand. Can you tell me what happened to him?"

"He was found at home in bed a little while ago," Mick told her. "It looks like an overdose of drugs, Ms. Davis."

"He didn't buy drugs in here." Vicky Davis's voice rose, and her tone hardened.

"We're not saying he did. It wasn't the kind of drugs people usually think of with an overdose, anyway," Ed assured her. "It was sleeping pills."

"I wouldn't think Vern would use sleeping pills," Vicky said. "He usually puts away enough liquor to fell an ox."

"We didn't find a prescription bottle," Mick said. "Have you ever gotten word of anybody selling pills around here?"

"He didn't buy drugs in here," Vicky repeated harshly. "I won't tolerate it, not in the building or in my parking lot. I can't control what goes on anywhere else, but I sure as hell can on my property, and I do. This is a clean place, Detective."

"We're not accusing you of anything, Ms. Davis," Ed replied. "What we are saying is that, in your position, you might have heard that someone was a source for some particular kind of drug. If you did, what would you do?"

She shrugged. "Keep a close eye on them. Make sure they didn't do their business or any part of it in my place. If I caught them at it, I'd throw them out and keep them out."

"Exactly," Ed said with approval.

"Everybody knows that, though," Vicky said, nodding, as she relaxed back into her chair. "Anybody who wanted to do that kind of business around here would make darned sure I didn't find out about it."

"So you can't help us pinpoint a source of the drugs?" Mick asked.

"No. Pills? No."

"Capsules, really," Ed clarified. "They're called reds, or yellow-jackets. Blue Bonnets, sometimes."

"Like *Valley of the Dolls*? Or what Marilyn Monroe took?"

"That's right."

"They still make that stuff?" Vicky sounded incredulous.

Ed nodded. "It's made primarily for sale abroad, but it gets diverted before it leaves the country, or people bring it back, like from Mexico. A lot of things that are prescription here you can buy over the counter in Mexico."

"I remember hearing that when I was in Cabo last winter. But doesn't everybody know it's dangerous to mix that stuff with liquor? I mean, I'd even expect Vern to know that."

"We still see cases of it," Ed told her. "Sometimes people do it on purpose."

"Are you saying you think Vern killed himself?"

"We don't know what happened yet, ma'am," Mick said. "We're trying to find out. Can you tell us what you noticed about Mr. Junker when he came back in? You said that was around one?"

Vicky nodded. "He seemed like he was dirtier than he was when I saw him before. I wondered if he'd fallen down. It happens. If he'd been driving, I wouldn't have served him, but he always walked down here from his place."

"Anything else?"

"Well, he had a headache, he said. Matter of fact, I think that was just about the last thing he said to me. Wanted to know if I had anything for it. I gave him some painkillers from the bottle under the register and told him to go home and sleep it off. He said that was what he was going to do."

"Did he do that often?" Ed wanted to know. "Ask you for something for a headache?"

"Pretty often." Vicky Davis shrugged. "Maybe a couple of times a month. I think he asked me so he wouldn't have to buy the stuff himself."

"Can we see the bottle?" Mick asked.

"Sure. Excuse me," Vicky said as she maneuvered herself out from behind the desk to lead them back through the kitchen to the public room, where she took them behind the bar.

"It's right here," Vicky said, showing them a shelf under the cash register, where an assortment of toiletries was kept in a small cardboard box. "This is the bottle."

Mick lifted the box to the counter.

"What's up, Vic?" Betsy came up to them.

"Don't say anything," Vicky Davis told her softly, indicating the customers grouped at the bar, "but Vern Junker died last night. They think it was an overdose of sleeping pills and liquor."

"Suicide?" Betsy breathed, her eyes widening.

"Accident, most likely," Vicky said. "They just want to look at the headache pills I gave him before he left."

Ed examined the bottle. It was a standard plastic bottle of generic acetaminophen capsules.

"That's the new bottle, Vicky," Betsy said. "I just opened it this morning. Didn't you give Vern the last out of the old one?"

"Oh, yes." Vicky appeared flustered. "I guess that's right."

"Where would the old bottle be?" Mick asked.

"Out in the dumpster," Vicky said. "I tossed the empty in the trash, here, so it would have gone out this morning. But it was just like this one. I always get the same kind."

"That's right," Betsy confirmed. "She gets them at one of those warehouse places, four bottles at a time. They're all over the place. Here, in the cabinet in the Ladies' restroom — you even keep a bottle in your purse, don't you, Vic?"

"I don't think they care about that, Betsy. And keep it down."

Ed bent over to replace the box on the shelf. It seemed to be a catchall shelf, holding purses, sweaters, an umbrella or two, even a thermos.

"Did Mr. Junker eat or drink anything else while he was here?" Mick asked.

"Besides bourbon?" Vicky Davis wanted to know.

"Well, it would help to know how many bourbons he had after he came back in."

"I fixed him one, no, two. How about you, Betsy?"

"I didn't fix him anything to drink after he came back in, but earlier, he had three or four drinks that I know of myself, and then he had dinner about nine."

"What did he eat?"

"Some of our chili. It's real good, with cornbread and a small salad, and he got one of those chocolate chip cookies to take home."

Ed looked in the direction Betsy indicated. There was a rack of assorted cookies, supplied by a local bakery. They were wrapped in heavy-duty plastic wrap. Ed looked at Mick. His mustache twitched. Mick inclined his head once, to the left. The cookie was the obvious source of the plastic wrap found on Vern Junker's nightstand. If that turned out to be true, and they were sure it would, then where did Vern get the sleeping capsules?

∼ 30 ∼

Nic Cavanaugh, dressed for the job in dark green shorts and a leaf-green halter top, a canvas sun hat from Australia on her head, spent Tuesday afternoon giving *Wayward* a good cleaning, inside and out. She had almost finished scrubbing the boat's decks when she heard a powerboat's roar. It was the Scarab, *Hot Pink*, owned by Catherine's lawyer, Henry Charm. Nic squirted the hose over the last unrinsed part of the deck, then jumped to the dock to catch the Scarab's lines.

"Where's Catherine?" Henry asked as soon as the boat was tied up, and the two were standing next to *Wayward* on the dock. He'd traded his office shoes for boat shoes, Nic saw, but she could see his business shirt and tie under the ragg sweater he wore against the cold wind generated by the ocean and the speed of his boat.

"Out," Nic said, alarmed by the haste Henry's failure to change his clothes implied. She pointed to the empty davits over the cradle where the Whaler Outrage normally rested. "She said she was going to the puffin nesting area."

Henry frowned. "I need to speak to her. Did she say when she'd be back?"

"I'm not sure," Nic told him. "I expect her back in a couple of hours for dinner, but if you don't want to wait, I can run you out in my dinghy. It's too shallow for that," she said, nodding towards *Hot Pink*.

Henry's frown deepened. "Is there a place to land? I need to talk to her privately."

"Not much of one, but there should be a little beach at this tide."

"All right." The lawyer nodded decisively. "Let's go."

Henry helped Nic launch her dinghy and attach the outboard. They tossed in life jackets from Catherine's boathouse. Nic started the engine while Henry cast off the lines. Nic hoped the lawyer was as competent at his work as he was with a boat. Anxiety rose in her as she shifted the outboard into gear. She wished she could simply ask Henry what was going on, but the lawyer had said he wanted to talk to Catherine alone. Nic would have to wait and she didn't like it. She goosed the little engine to its top speed.

Nic spotted the Outrage drifting off one of the islets, and ran her dinghy up beside it. Catherine caught the dinghy's side. Her eyes widened and the color drained from her face when she saw Henry. She'd thought the investigation was over; she'd hoped it was over, but Henry's appearance meant that it wasn't.

"We have to talk, Catherine," the lawyer said. "This is important. We can go back to *Hot Pink* or your house, or Nic says there's a beach we can land on."

Catherine couldn't think. Her mind seized on the last thing she heard. "The beach is right over there."

"We'll meet you there," Nic said. She pulled away as Catherine started her boat's engine. But Catherine had put it into gear too soon and it died. *Shaky,* Nic thought. *Scared. Can't blame her. I am, too.* Nic held the dinghy off the beach to let the Whaler, large but still beachable, nose into the packed sand first. Then she brought her dinghy alongside.

"Henry says he needs to talk to you alone. I'll go for a walk while you talk," she offered, "unless you want me to stay." She stared hard at Catherine, who nodded quickly in reply.

"I'm afraid you can't," Henry said gently. "This needs to be privileged. I can't be forced to tell anything that passes in a privileged conversation. That doesn't apply to you."

Catherine looked from one to the other with dismay. Whatever Henry had come to tell her, she wanted to know it *now*. Whatever the worst was, she wanted it over. But she wanted Nic there, too. She needed the support of a friend. She twisted her long braid in her fingers. Her mind *still* wouldn't work. Suddenly she thought of a way to please Henry but still let Nic hear. She latched on to what Nic had proposed. "You can't walk on this island," Catherine said. "You'll disturb the birds. Why don't you just stay in the dinghy? Come over here, Henry. We'll go below. It's not *Hot Pink*, but there's a cabin." She rose and turned to the lawyer, beckoning impatiently. "Come *on*."

Henry climbed onto the Outrage. He and Catherine went below. Henry closed the companionway hatch, but no-one went forward to close the hatch over the v-berth in the bow. Nic arranged the life jackets in the dinghy into a comfortable nest. Catherine obviously wanted her to hear what the lawyer had come to say. *Clever of her,* Nic thought as she settled in, *to fix it so I can hear, but he won't know.* Nic figured she had her own version of what was privileged. You might call it a convenient memory. If anyone asked her, she simply wouldn't have heard a thing.

Without any preliminaries, Henry said, "Janet's got a search warrant for the island, Catherine."

"What? A search warrant? For the island?" Catherine couldn't take it in. It felt like the sky was falling around her. Nic twisted in the dinghy and stared at the Outrage. What the hell did that mean?

"Yes," Henry went on, "a search warrant. It specifies several items — letters and papers of various kinds, mostly — but principally the skiff off the *Valkyrie*. Since it's an unsinkable double hull, and it hasn't turned up, she's decided you've got it out here."

"That's ridiculous. How could she get a warrant? Doesn't she have to have some reason?" Catherine knew she was dodging the real problem, but she couldn't help it. She had to have time — she couldn't *think* — what on earth was she going to do?

"She's got reason enough," Henry said patiently. "You admit to being at Lowry's house that night, there's no one who can say when you left, there are inconsistencies in your statements about when you knew you were getting the island back, you've owned Whalers for years, and they've got someone who saw a skiff being taken out of Clark Creek towing a Whaler."

"What about that man, that fisherman? He said he saw me leave." She felt like she was falling down a well.

"He's dead, Catherine. That may be a break. I'm not even sure if his statement is admissible now — I haven't looked it up — but if he were alive and cross-examined, he'd have to say he assumed it was you he saw behind him. I've read that statement carefully. He couldn't positively identify you."

"What happened to him?" Catherine felt the well getting deeper, herself falling faster. This was more than she could assimilate.

"Drug overdose, barbiturates and booze, according to the preliminary medical report. Accident or suicide, apparently. He tried to blackmail Frank Vincent for money to leave town, and when Vincent wouldn't give it to him, Junker hit Vincent and robbed him. He'll be OK."

"Oh. Good," Catherine mumbled. At least she didn't have to worry about Frank.

Catherine's voice sounded faint to Nic, flat, as if she were responding mechanically. Nic edged closer to the open hatch, careful to keep out of sight.

"I might have been able to keep them away from you," Henry went on, "if Janet hadn't come up with a humdinger of a motive, right in the public record. Catherine, why didn't you tell me?"

There was anger in Henry's voice. Nic found that surprising. She would have thought Henry would express his anger by roaring across the ocean in his powerful boat rather than show it in his voice or his work.

"Tell you what?" Catherine queried sharply. She hoped she didn't know exactly what Henry was talking about.

"That Lowry abused you, for Christ's sake. That you were placed in foster care because of it. I understand you might not want it to be common knowledge, but in a murder case, there's no such thing as privacy, and I'm your lawyer. I need to know. I can't protect you if you won't let me."

Nic barely heard the last part of this, because her stomach was turning somersaults and her muscles tensing with anger. She would have liked to beat the son of a bitch to a pulp. If someone hadn't already killed him.

"How did they find out?" Catherine asked Henry.

"Janet started wondering why you'd lie to shield Sally Davis. That got her thinking, so she went over to Juvenile Court to check out her hunch. The files are closed to the public, but any lawyer can get them."

Catherine felt disoriented, as off-balance as if the boat were pitching and rolling in a head-sea. She shook herself. She had to pull herself together. To listen. To defend herself.

"You're lucky," Henry continued. "Janet didn't have to tell me about this warrant in advance, but she did. I think she wants to give you every possible break."

"She could have just left me alone," Catherine cried out in despair.

"No, she couldn't." Henry's voice was firm. "Not with the facts she's got. She's a prosecutor," he said. "This is her job."

"But, Henry, why is what happened to Sally a motive for me?" Catherine cried. "What happened to me was long over. Sally was taken care of. She told her mother, and her mother protected her. Yes, hearing what he did to her made me sick. I knew exactly what she'd gone through. No, I couldn't go home after hearing that, so I went to the park to be alone. I didn't want to talk about it, and there was no reason to." Finally, finally, her brain was kicking in.

"I understand why you'd think that, Catherine. I'm sure keeping it quiet seemed like the most reasonable thing for you to do. Given your history, however, a prosecutor could argue Glen's assault on Sally provided you with an adequate motive for murder. Remember, the prosecution doesn't have to show the reason why you did something, just that you did it, and they only have to show that beyond a reasonable doubt. But juries like to know why, and motive's important in establishing the direction of an investigation. As I said, without this motive, I think I could have kept them away from you entirely. But this isn't the time to talk about that. The warrant has been issued."

"Oh, damn him. Damn him." Catherine's voice was strong with passion. "I hope he rots in hell!" Nic realized her own fists were clenched, the nails biting into her palms. She hated Catherine being subjected to this. It was a continuation of the horror the dead man had inflicted on her.

"Catherine, I know this is upsetting for you," Henry said softly. "That's why I came out to prepare you for it. Warrants are usually a surprise. You have to call your lawyer after it's served. But when the search is done, it'll all be over. They'll have to close their file, and you'll be cleared."

"What would happen, Henry?" Catherine sounded resigned.

"We'll be out in the morning, about eleven, in a police harbor patrol boat. They'll search the island. Then they'll leave, and that will be the end of it."

Nic nestled back into the life jackets, relieved. Catherine only had to endure one more day. Then it would really be over. She examined the red marks her nails had made on her palms. *Maybe after tomorrow, Catherine can put this whole mess behind her once and for all,* Nic thought.

"No," Catherine said, sounding shaken. "I mean, what would happen if Janet decided to have me arrested?"

Henry sighed and explained. "If you were arrested, you'd be taken into custody until I could get you released on bond, and I probably, but only *probably,* could. At the same time, I'd get a criminal defense specialist to handle the defense. It's not my area of concentration, as you know. Then it would be necessary to evaluate the strength of their case to see if it should be

tried, or if we should attempt a reduction in charge in exchange
for a guilty plea." His voice became brisk, his tone positive.
"But that's academic, Catherine. You can't be arrested unless
you're going to be charged. Janet won't charge you unless she
believes she can get a conviction. She can't get anywhere close
to a conviction unless she finds that skiff."

"Oh." Catherine sounded depressed. *Why?* Nic wondered.
What Henry had said sounded like good news to her.

Henry's tone became professional, crisp and guarded as
he asked the question he knew he must ask if he were to do his
duty by Catherine.

"Catherine, I assume there's nothing to find out here
that might possibly connect you with this crime. If by chance I
am wrong in that assumption, or if there's anything, anything
at all, that might help me represent you better, or anything you
want to tell me, whether it's related to this case or not, I want
you to tell me right now." His tone softened. His voice became
that of a friend again, impassioned and sincere. "I cannot help
you unless I know." This was not strictly true. If he were de-
fending her against a murder charge, it would be better not to
hear her admit it if she was in fact guilty. But since he wouldn't
actually defend her, knowing would help him get a criminal
defense lawyer hired and on the island before the warrant was
served. That would be the best service he could provide her.

There was a long interval of silence.

"No, Henry," Catherine said at last, in a flat tone. Nic
heard the Outrage creak as someone rose. She lay back and
pulled her sun hat over her face. "Thank you for coming out,"
Catherine added as she and Henry emerged into the Outrage's
cockpit. Nic sat up and settled the sun hat firmly on top of her
head.

"I'll run you back to the dock, Henry," Catherine said.
"You'll come with them tomorrow?"

"Yes. I'll accept service of the warrant for you, if you
want me to. Maybe you could stay on your friend's boat while
they search." He cast a questioning glance at Nic. She nodded.

"Yes," Catherine said, smiling at Nic. "I think I'd like that. I guess we're ready to go in."

"Right," Nic said. She pushed the dinghy away from the Outrage and started the little engine. She waited, engine idling, until Catherine got the Outrage going. Henry helped her shove the bigger boat off the beach.

Catherine's Outrage, with its big engine, was much faster than Nic's small dinghy. By the time Nic got back to the island, Henry had helped Catherine attach the davits and hoist the boat into its cradle. Nic attached the lifting sling to her dinghy and winched it onto *Wayward's* deck while the other two said good-bye.

"I'll see you in the morning, Catherine." Henry got aboard his boat, but before he started the engines, he turned and said, "Catherine, I'll be at home tonight, and in the office until about a quarter to ten in the morning. *Hot Pink* is a lot faster than anything the harbor patrol's got. If you think of any questions you want to ask me, or if there's anything that comes to mind that you think I should know, call me. I can beat them out here in the morning and we can talk about it. Will you do that?"

"Of course, Henry, thank you. But I really don't see what else you can do."

"Thanks for the ride," Henry called to Nic. *Hot Pink's* huge engines started with a roar and the racing boat slid away from the dock. Nic nodded and waved an acknowledgment. She jumped off *Wayward* and approached Catherine.

"You did want me to hear that, didn't you?" she asked.

"Yes." Catherine grinned. "I'm glad you picked up on that. I didn't want to have to repeat everything Henry said."

"I'm sorry," Nic said awkwardly. "If there's anything I can do?" Suddenly she understood Catherine's reluctance to have someone else initiate touch. "It must have been terrible for you. To have it come back like this..." Nic shook her head sympathetically.

Catherine glanced at Nic briefly, her eyes reflecting an old pain. "It'll be over tomorrow," she said at last. "Nic, if you wouldn't mind, I'd like to be alone tonight."

"If you like," Nic said. "But if you need somebody to talk to...well, I'm not going anywhere."

Catherine smiled. She reached out and touched Nic's cheek. "Thank you, Nic. For everything."

～ 31 ～

After Henry left the island, Catherine walked slowly back to the lighthouse, leaving Nic on board *Wayward*. She looked around the island as she walked up the path, wanting to imprint every detail of its pristine beauty on her memory. It had been a very precious prison.

Catherine was no lawyer, but she sometimes read the papers. She knew that even an accusation could take years of a person's life and all their resources. It didn't matter if the person was ultimately acquitted. If they were convicted, of course, it was worse.

Janet had obviously decided she killed Glen Lowry — it didn't matter why, really. "My garden will go wild," Catherine said to herself. She gave it one last loving look before opening the lighthouse door.

Janet is totally committed to whatever she thinks is right, Catherine thought. *That's why she's so dangerous. She won't give up. Henry expects her to play by the rules of their lawyer game. He's wrong. Janet doesn't believe in defeat. She just tries another tactic.* With a heavy heart, Catherine shut the door and shot the bolt.

"It's *his* fault," she cried aloud as she rested her forehead against the door. She remembered the relentless probing fingers, the smarmy inducements that confused her until she didn't know what was right or wrong, until she was convinced that she was as guilty as he was. It had taken her years to learn otherwise: That *she* was the victim. That *he* was the criminal. Now, ultimately, his crime would destroy her life.

It was all his fault.

She crossed the living room, touching surfaces here and there, picking up a book, stroking the back of the couch.

I don't think I could stand it if they arrested me, Catherine thought. *Not again. Not the doctors poking and the shrinks asking questions and being locked in those tiny cells with all the talking and singing and screaming and no way to get outside.* She shivered, remembering. *And the courtroom, with all of them looking at me like I'm some kind of bug. I think I would lose my mind."* She stared at the fireplace. "Actually, it would be worse if I didn't," she said aloud.

Catherine steeled herself. She straightened up and faced the plank door leading to the caverns beneath the lighthouse. She still had a chance. There was still something she could do.

⚡

On *Wayward,* Nic scowled at the GPS. All the data it contained had been erased when the power crashed. Even though half her mind was preoccupied with thoughts of Catherine, she was trying to recreate her planned route north. The device would compute its current position from the satellite signals it received and direct the autopilot to steer the boat to the next place on its programmed route, but only if Nic entered the latitudes and longitudes of the places where she wanted to go. But she kept making mistakes. *By now,* she thought, *I've probably got it steering me overland to New York.* She turned the instrument off in disgust. She couldn't concentrate because she was worried. Catherine's farewell had seemed so final. Too final. As she stared at the blank screen, a sudden notion flickered through her mind.

"Oh, no," she breathed, straightening abruptly. It was shocking. It was horrid. It was possible. "Hell," she said aloud. Then, grabbing her waterproof torch, she jumped off the boat, and ran for the lighthouse.

Though it was only just dark, there was light in all the windows. Nic reached the front door and pounded. "Catherine," she called. There was no response. Impatient, Nic tried the heavy front door. It was locked. Through a crack in the curtains, she could see the padlocked door at the base of the tower stairs. It was closed, but the hasp swung free. That was where Catherine must be, down in the depths of the caverns below. Nic had to find her.

Nic raced to the back. She remembered that the shed door locked from the outside with a padlock. With relief she saw that it was open. The inner door leading to the utility room was a simple interior door, its lock designed more to keep it shut than for security. Nic tried it first, then, when it didn't open, she raised her foot and kicked.

The door was so flimsy that Nic's foot went right through it and she lost her balance. When she regained it, she was able to reach in, turn the knob and go inside.

Nic had never seen what lay below the lighthouse. The stairs were dark. Her red-shaded light revealed a small landing hung with ropes, a couple of oil lanterns, and old yellow oil-skins. Stone steps descended into the darkness. Following the eerie glow of her red torch, she went down.

At the bottom of the stairs, she paused, shining the light around. The stairs opened into a natural cave, carved by the ancient sea, but now dry. Bolts of canvas, piles of stretchers, and racks of finished paintings lined the walls. Nic didn't stop to examine them, for down a tunnel to her left she saw a glimmer of brilliant white light.

Nic hurried over the striated rock floor. The crashing of the sea became louder, filling her ears. At the end of the tunnel, at the edge of a circle of light given off by a camper's gas lamp, Nic stopped, blinking, as her eyes adjusted to the bright light. Even though she'd more than half expected it, her stomach sank as she saw what lay in front of her.

The missing skiff floated in a tiny basin, tied to rings mounted in the slab of rock on which she stood. That slab slanted steeply downward into the water; another rose at a shallow angle to the edge of the cavern. Jumbled rocks at the edges of the cave showed that at some time in the past, it had been blasted to make it larger. Nic squinted at the lantern, which sat atop a boulder. Then she saw Catherine, sitting in the shadow of the boulder, facing the sea.

"Catherine?" she called softly.

Catherine leapt to her feet, turning, her hands pressing against the boulder, her face shocked. "Go away," she cried. "Go away. Please, Nic. Just leave."

"What are you doing?" Nic strode over to her and saw she had been working with a tangle of rope and an anchor. "I won't let you do it," Nic said.

"What do you know about it?" Catherine's temper flared.

"I won't let you kill yourself." Nic grabbed the anchor and pulled it from Catherine's arms.

"You can't stop me," she said. "I'll find a way."

"I don't want you to kill yourself," Nic repeated firmly. "I want you to tell me how it happened."

"No. Leave me alone." Catherine edged toward the basin.

"You killed him, didn't you? Tell me how it happened."

"Leave me alone." Catherine backed up further, a haunted look in her eyes, until she stood at the basin's edge. "Why do you care? This isn't important to you."

"It is. Anything about you is important to me. I care about you, dammit. I want a chance to love you. Don't you know that by now? Whether you care about me or not, I don't want you to die."

"You'd like it better if I spent my life in jail?" Catherine blazed.

Nic shook her head. "I don't think so. Tell me how it happened."

Catherine stepped back and nearly fell as her foot overshot the edge. Nic lunged for her, seized her arms and pulled her upright.

"Let go of me," Catherine said, a mix of fear and fury in her voice.

Nic released her immediately and dropped her hands to her sides. She realized that physical force would only panic Catherine, and she didn't want that.

Suddenly, Catherine slumped, visibly drained. She turned, stepped aboard the skiff and sat down by the engine controls. "I'll tell you, then. I guess I don't have any choices left." She looked hopelessly at Nic. "You heard what I told the detectives. That was true. Hearing what Glen tried to do to Sally made me sick, but what I was sick with was anger. I didn't leave the house when Vern, that fisherman, did.

"I marched back into the living room and confronted Glen. I told him I was going to Sally's family and tell them all about him. I said I'd see they pressed charges. I'd see him put away."

"What had he done to you, Catherine?" Nic didn't want to hear the details of the abuse, but if they were to have any future at all, Nic had to hear the truth and Catherine had to tell it. Catherine's response was bald and her voice was harsh and loud.

"He raped me. For three sickening years, until one of my teachers convinced me to tell her about it. She meant well. Oh, they all meant well, but sometimes I wonder if I wouldn't have been better off not saying a word and just leaving home as soon as I could."

Nic reached out to her, but Catherine ignored the outstretched hand and went on. "After all the hell that I went through with him, I got a whole new hell afterwards with all the doctors and the social workers and the courts and having to leave home. They believed him when he said he wouldn't do it anymore. I was the one who was punished. That night, I decided it was *his* turn." Her shoulders lifted, she shivered and her face twisted as though she were suppressing tears.

"What happened, Catherine?"

"I underestimated him." She regained her composure and shrugged. Her voice was flat as she went on. "He lunged for me; he grabbed me and shook me, and said I'd never get that far. He said he'd see me in hell first.

"He was drunk, of course, like he always used to be, and then he grabbed my breast and he said I'd always liked it. I kicked him and broke away. He was between me and the kitchen, so I ran out the front door. He caught up with me in the yard. I got away from him again, but I couldn't get around him. There was only one other way to run."

"To the boat?" Nic asked. Catherine nodded. She stared forward fixedly as though she were seeing the scene replayed before her eyes.

"I thought if I could get on the *Valkyrie,* I could radio a Mayday, lock him out of the cabin, hold him off until someone came. I was wearing leather-soled shoes and I fell on the dock. That gave him a chance to catch up. He caught me on the boat, before I could lock the cabin door."

Nic stood, transfixed, her blood pulsing, feeling as if she were living through it with Catherine. "What happened next, Catherine?"

"I fought. He fought. He pushed me back over the table. I groped around behind me for some kind of weapon, something, anything. Then I touched a filleting knife. When I pulled it out from behind me, he grabbed my hand, but his arm came close enough for me to bite." She laughed, and the sound chilled Nic. "He didn't expect that. It shocked him. He let go of my hand and I reached up and shoved that knife into his throat and pulled it across."

Her body heaved. Nic thought Catherine might vomit, but she recovered and went on, quietly.

"The rest of it was like the police said. I took the seiner away from the dock. While we were running in the bay, I washed and put on some old clothes I found in a locker. They were too big, but jeans and sweatshirts all look alike. I figured they'd do until I could change. Then I scuttled the boat. I aimed it out between the jetties, but I must not have been thinking very clearly. I either forgot to push the throttles up, or I misjudged how fast it would go down. I thought it had got out to sea before it sank. I *thought* it had. I took the skiff back in and left it way up Clark Creek, walked back to the house through the woods, changed into my own clothes from my pack, made sure the place didn't look like there had been a fight, drove out on an abandoned road back to the highway, and then took back roads to Salmon Bay and South Jetty Park."

"How did you know so much about the *Valkyrie?*" Nic asked.

"Where do you think he used to rape me? I was his little deck hand." Catherine's voice was bitter. "God, I was happy to see her go down."

"Why did you move the skiff?" That part hadn't made sense to Nic.

"It seemed like the best thing to do, once I found out I had a safer place to put it. It was important that it look like the *Valkyrie* went down at sea. Seiners don't go out to sea without their skiffs. They don't go *anywhere* without their skiffs. There wasn't much risk. People are always moving boats around, at all hours, even in foul weather. There are lots of Whalers, lots of skiffs. I didn't think anyone would be able to connect moving it with me. But if the skiff *had* turned up, they'd know something was wrong and start investigating, and I couldn't have that." Catherine smiled a tight, grim little smile as she went on.

"I'd worn oilskins, boots and gloves in the skiff. I left those at the house. If there were any traces of me on those or on the skiff itself, I thought I could explain those. But I was worried about the *Valkyrie.* There was so much blood! There might have been something they could trace to me in the wreck, even though I dumped my bloody clothes a long way off. I didn't want her found. I wanted her to stay lost at sea forever." Catherine looked up at Nic and added softly, "I wish she had." Then she continued her terrible recital.

"I thought I could hide the skiff here in the cavern until I moved out to the island and could sink it in the ocean. But the goddamned thing won't sink. It gets awash and stays that way. I thought about casting it loose when the rogue hit. After all this time, with all the junk that wave would wash up, I thought it might be safe." She shrugged. "The next morning, you were here, so I couldn't."

"I'm sorry." Nic knew that was inadequate. There was nothing she could say or do that would even begin to make up to Catherine for all that she had suffered.

"I'm not going to jail, Nic." Catherine said passionately. "I'd rather die than go through all of that again. And then they'd lock me up. I won't do it. Just go *away*. Let me go."

Nic knelt at the edge of the basin and examined the skiff. She sat back on her heels, then nodded. There was something she could do.

"You're not going to jail," Nic said firmly. "I can sink it."

∼ 32 ∼

"How?" Catherine seemed shocked. "I've tried a dozen times. The police — Henry — everybody says it's unsinkable."

Nic looked up at her and smiled grimly. "They mean unsinkable in ordinary use. It's a double hull with a lot of separate, watertight compartments. But it's made of aluminum, and that engine's heavy. Punch enough holes through enough of the compartments, and it'll go down." Nic stood up. "We'll need to tow it out behind *Wayward*. I'm going to need my tools."

Catherine remained sitting beside the console. She stared at Nic, puzzlement evident on her face. "Why?" she finally asked.

"You don't deserve what they'd do to you if they found the skiff. I don't know what they call it legally, but it seems to me what you did was justified."

Catherine shook her head. "Nic. Before you go any further, you need to understand. It was not an accident. I meant to kill him. And I deliberately, on purpose, cut his throat."

"I heard you the first time," Nic said. "Move over. Let me see if this thing starts."

Two hours later and twenty miles offshore, in the dark of the overcast night, they watched the skiff sink slowly beneath the ocean swells into water so deep *Wayward's* depth sounder showed only static.

"I don't believe it," Catherine said, relief evident in her voice. "There it goes."

Nic turned to her, clasping her arm urgently. "Yes. And Catherine, let it go. All of it. It's over. You don't have to live in the past anymore. Live now."

⚓

By the time the skiff was finally scuttled, *Wayward* was back at the dock, and the lighthouse's back door was repaired, it was well into Wednesday morning. Nic brought Catherine down to *Wayward* for breakfast and to await the arrival of the searchers.

Handing Catherine a cup of coffee, Nic saw her hands were shaking. "I heard Henry say they don't have a case against you without that skiff," she said encouragingly, setting the cup on the table.

Catherine took a deep breath and nodded. "So he says."

"But it's going to take a while for all the fuss to die down," Nic went on. Concern was written all over her face. And she was nervous. She wanted Catherine to know she didn't expect payment of any kind for what she'd done, but she still wanted a chance to see what she and Catherine could build together. "I expect you could use a change, maybe some peace and quiet. A chance to think about what you're going to do next, now that you don't have to stay out here to stand guard over that skiff."

Catherine shook her head. "I won't even be able to think about what's next until Henry says it's finished."

"Give some thought to this," Nic said urgently, moving to where Catherine would have to look at her. "Please. Take the summer off. Come to Alaska with me. You liked sailing when we took *Wayward* out. You'll learn more about it, we'll have some fun. See some different scenery. No pressure, no strings. The spare cabin's yours. Come fall, when it's time for me to head south for the winter, you'll have some distance on all of this. You might be ready to make some decisions."

Catherine twisted her braid. She had to tell Nic why it couldn't be. There was no future for her away from this island, no matter how much she, Catherine, wanted it, and no matter how much that wanting might have led Nic to believe something more was possible. At last, she reached out and squeezed Nic's hand. She looked the other woman full in the face.

"Nic, I don't know why you're doing this," Catherine said, "but it seems to me there's a lot of things that you don't understand. I *want* normal things, I'd *like* to have a normal life and somebody I could love. But I killed a human being. You act like I'm normal. But I'm not. I'm not out here by myself just because of the skiff. I'm out here because I'm frightened of myself, of what I was capable of doing. I can never trust myself again. And it terrifies me."

Nic regarded Catherine with fond exasperation and shook her head. "That was one specific situation, with one specific person who had hurt you terribly and was about to do it again." Nic struggled to present what she thought was a balanced view of what had happened to Catherine and to Glen Lowry. "I think you're perfectly normal. Why don't you give yourself a chance?"

Catherine shook her head. Before she could say anything more, Nic looked up, cocking an ear toward the harbor mouth. She glanced at her watch. "They're early," she said quietly.

~ 33 ~

Janet wore her flowing cloud-grey Anne Klein trench coat over black slacks and a grey sweater. The colors suited her mood...and the weather. A look at the sky told her the Wednesday-morning low clouds probably wouldn't burn off until after the search party returned from Seal Rock. Her face somber, she stood on the police dock in the Salmon Bay Boat Basin with Ed Nuñez, waiting for the rest of the search party to arrive.

"Are you sure you want to go through with this, Janet?" Ed asked.

"Yes." Janet thrust her hands into the pockets of her slacks. "I have to know the truth. We have to know the truth. Ruining my election bid isn't important next to that."

"I want you to know Daniels didn't get his opinions from us, Janet. At first, Mick and I wondered if you knew your own motives, but both of us trusted you to work it out."

She smiled at her friend. "Thanks, Ed. I had a few questions about that, myself. But the long and the short of it is, I couldn't live with myself if I didn't get this warrant."

"That wrapper we found on Junker's nightstand came from the cookie he bought at the bar," Ed said, buttoning his camel-hair topcoat against the rising breeze. "If I were guessing, I'd say Davis slipped the sleeping pills to Junker instead of headache pills. But we'll never prove it."

"I agree. Even if we could show where and when she bought the drug, which is doubtful if she got it over the counter in a Mexican resort, we still couldn't make a case. But I think I know *why* she might have done it."

"Are you going to share that with us, Janet? Good morning, Detective." Henry Charm, right on time, had come down the dock so quietly that neither Janet nor Ed heard him. He was followed by the uniformed officers who would form the search team. The officers boarded the boat.

Henry looked like his usual professional self this morning, Ed thought, in his standard brown suit, slightly rumpled, a yellow shirt, and a conservatively figured tie. His raincoat, a Burberry which looked like it had been slept on by a large dog, flapped open. Henry looked around vaguely and shivered. Setting his briefcase on the dock box, he opened it to pull out a pair of gloves.

"Let's get on board," Janet said, making a sudden decision. "I'll tell you about it on the way to the island."

The harbor patrol boat's crew cast off the lines. The massive engines reversed, backing the boat out of its slip.

"Come out on deck where we can be alone, Henry," Janet said.

On the afterdeck, out of the wind, Janet faced her colleague.

"I'm going to tell you what I think, Henry. It's not necessarily what I can prove. But I want you to understand why I'm going ahead with this warrant. I wouldn't tell you if I thought it would hurt our case or help yours if we find sufficient evidence to bring charges against your client. And I'd like to get your objective opinion."

"Objective, Janet?" Henry chided gently. "I can't be objective. I have a client."

"So do I." Janet took a deep breath. "I think she killed him, Henry. And given what he'd done to her, I think hearing about Lowry's abuse of the Davis girl sent her right over the edge." For some reason, she couldn't bring herself to say

Catherine's name. "I think she never left the house. Junker couldn't swear it was her car behind him. I think she went back into the house, and somehow — accident, self-defense, or pre-meditated first-degree murder — she killed him. She's been around fishing boats all her life. She'd be able to handle the *Valkyrie* well enough. She's an athletic, outdoorsy woman, strong enough to carry Lowry's body if she needed to. She'd know Clark Creek and the old road to the bridge."

Henry Charm listened intently. Suddenly, the police boat turned into the head-seas to cross the harbor bar. Both lawyers reached out automatically to grab handholds.

"So she scuttles the *Valkyrie*," Janet continued. "She comes back to Clark Creek in the skiff, walks back to the house along the creek bank below the tide line, cleans up any physical evidence left at the house, and uses the abandoned road through the woods to get her car back to the highway."

Henry's intelligent gaze searched Janet's face as she continued.

"She's bright and she's logical. She knows that if the skiff is found, the idea that Lowry was lost at sea won't fly. There'll be a homicide investigation, and she's bound to come under serious suspicion. When the lease to the island is terminated, and she has a better place to put the skiff, she moves it. As that old man, Spencer, said, rain gear's rain gear. The risk of being recognized was minimal. The benefit of moving it outweighed the risk."

"That would be true for anyone," Henry said mildly.

"I disagree. She's the only person with a specific connection to the Clark Creek location, in addition to the fact that it was by Lowry's house and the place where the *Valkyrie* was moored. She owns the place, she grew up there. She, much more than anyone else, is likely to know the creek and the trails through the woods. For her, and only for her, the risk of moving the skiff wouldn't outweigh the danger of leaving it there."

Henry shrugged and stepped back into the shelter of the cabin as the boat cleared the jetties. It turned into the ocean swells, and the wind began to whip around the cabin top. He buttoned his coat, and said, "But Catherine's also the only one with a legitimate explanation for any physical evidence — hair, fibers, prints — found at the house, on the skiff, or on the *Valkyrie.*"

"That's why she's in the best position to get rid of any other physical evidence, like a weapon, or bloodstains. Why not move into a waterfront house you own free and clear? She didn't. She cleared it out and got tenants in as quickly as she could manage it. Now, any physical evidence there might have been is long gone."

"I'm glad you recognize that. Go on, Janet. There's a certain surface plausibility about this that I'm finding very interesting," Henry added noncommittally.

Janet chose not to react to Henry's dig. "That's about all, as far as she's concerned," she concluded.

"What about the attack on Frank Vincent? I understand he says Junker did it, after Vincent wouldn't submit to blackmail. And what about Junker's death? Surely you can't be arguing that Catherine had anything to do with either of those incidents?"

Janet shook her head. "No. The rogue wave did two things, as far as she was concerned. It led to the discovery of the *Valkyrie,* and it put that sailor, Nic Cavanaugh, on her island. She couldn't take any further steps to cover up — like getting rid of the skiff — without Cavanaugh knowing about it." Janet smiled grimly. "You wouldn't have found out about the warrant until I served it on your client this morning if Cavanaugh hadn't been there."

"But what about Junker?"

"I reread the statement Sally Davis gave us. We left out an important question. She told us her mother came home at the usual time that Saturday night. But Sally didn't say whether or not Vicky went out again." Janet shrugged. "I doubt if that makes any difference. Whether Sally was asleep and doesn't know if Vicky left or absolutely knows she did, I think the best

we could hope for is a statement that she doesn't think Vicky
left, but she can't swear to it. Vicky's her mother, after all, and
she loves her. But I think Vicky did go out again; she was Jack
Simpson's 'blonde in the Pinto.'"

Janet took a deep breath before going on. This was the
most speculative part of her theory, one that was possible, but
hard even for her to accept.

"What if Junker told Davis he was trying to blackmail
Lowry with promises for silence about Lowry's assault on Sally?
Maybe Junker thought he was doing her a favor by letting her
know Lowry could be talked out of money. He was just the
kind of person to think of that as a favor. If Davis thought
Junker was going to get money out of Lowry's conduct, I believe she'd think she was entitled to something, too, and with
more cause."

The patrol boat's motion calmed as it set course for the
island. Henry stepped away from the cabin, and Janet released
her grip on the rail.

"I don't kno / what Vicky saw," Janet went on. "Maybe
it was just your client's car, maybe it was something more. My
guess is she hasn't spoken up because she'd just as soon have
Lowry's killer get away with it. Too, Vicky herself would come
under suspicion if she admitted she'd gone out there. She had
good reason to kill him herself.

"Vern Junker had tried to blackmail Lowry with promises of silence. He went to Vincent to get money to get out of
town. I think he had another ace in the hole. If Junker sent
Vicky Davis to see Lowry, he'd know she was the mystery
woman. I think that after Vincent wouldn't play, Junker went
to Davis."

"That works so far," Henry said judiciously. "Go with it."

"Vincent got hurt somehow when he and Junker were
together. Junker knew he was in trouble. I suggest that Vicky
told him she'd bring him money later, after the bar closed, probably from the cash receipts. Junker was still dressed when he
was found. I suggest she bought barbiturate sleeping pills over

the counter when she was in Mexico last winter. I suggest they were in her purse, and she made a quick decision to substitute a few of those for the headache pills Junker requested. She may not have been certain of the effect, but decided it was worth a try. She might even have figured it wasn't wrong, or not very, because she's around enough alcoholics to know that Junker was in the end stage of the disease, without very long to live anyway. I could see it myself, and the Medical Examiner confirms it."

"But her motive," Henry protested. "Surely it wasn't the money. She seems prosperous. Certainly Vincent is, and I understand he's been more than willing to help her out. He obviously loves the girl."

"I don't think it was the money." The island now loomed in front of them. "Vicky had two other motives. Mostly, she was protecting herself from suspicion in Lowry's death, but I also think she was protecting whoever killed Lowry."

"You believe she'd protect Lowry's killer?"

"She might. Especially if it was your client." Damn it, she still couldn't bring herself to say Catherine's name. "Vicky probably figured out that Lowry's stepdaughter might have been a victim herself. They're close in age and this is a small community. Vicky might have figured she owed her something for killing Lowry. And, as she said herself, good riddance."

Henry thought it over briefly, then nodded and said, "Protecting herself, returning a favor. For motive, it's plausible enough." He went on, repeating the lawyer's axiom, "One person's motive for murder is another person's minor annoyance."

At last they were in sight of Seal Rock Island. The patrol boat wallowed as it turned into the channel leading to the island's tiny harbor.

"What do you think, Henry?" Janet wanted to know.

Henry frowned thoughtfully. "As I said, it has a certain surface plausibility I find intriguing. It accounts for all the known facts, but it's hardly provable. Not against Catherine.

Certainly not against Vicky Davis. There's no evidence to get. Every fact you've given me has more than one possible explanation. As far as Catherine is concerned, you haven't got any facts at all. You're speculating. You don't have enough to charge her, much less convict her. Unless you find the skiff."

As the rock walls of the harbor entrance surrounded them, Janet felt her features harden into her courtroom poker player's mask; her stomach churned with the consciousness of the risk she was taking.

"I know," she said.

~ 34 ~

The cave below the lighthouse was cool and quiet. Janet stood beside Henry, looking about. She spied the mooring ring and stooped to touch it. The ring, smooth and shiny, told its own tale. Some boat, and she was sure it was the *Valkyrie's* missing skiff, had been tied up here for a long time, but it was gone now.

Their search of the lighthouse island had yielded nothing. The outer islets had so far proved innocent. Janet sighed deeply. She hadn't been wrong. The mooring ring told her that. But she had failed. Justice had lost out, she thought, and so had she. The publicity she had initially hoped would benefit her would boomerang against her.

"If it were anywhere on Seal Rock, it would be here," Henry said.

"I know," Janet replied flatly. "Let them finish up outside, and then we'll go."

Henry looked at Janet. Something Janet could only interpret as sympathy lurked behind the lawyer's impassive expression. "Come outside," Henry said. "I don't like it down here."

They went up to the bluff outside the lighthouse and looked west across the endless Pacific. The wind had risen from the north, scattering the clouds. Whitecaps dotted the blue-green sea. Janet leaned up against the lighthouse, crossed her ankles and thrust her hands into her trouser pockets. Henry stood a few feet distant, in a similar posture.

"Janet, you told me what you think happened. May I tell you my conclusions?"

Janet allowed one corner of her mouth to turn up. "Henry," she said, "I wish you would."

Henry nodded. "This is how I think it went." He began to pace, and Janet saw that he turned at precisely the length of a jury box. She knew she was about to see a demonstration of Henry's greatest skill, his ability to weave a tale so compelling that he vanished as an advocate, leaving only the carefully structured story in his wake.

"After Vern Junker left Lowry's place the first time," Henry began, "he went back to the Mermaid and got drunk. As the liquor began to affect him, he decided he wasn't going to wait for his meeting with Lowry. He wanted things settled immediately. Catherine was long gone, he knew. He'd seen her behind him when he returned to town, so Lowry would be alone."

Henry turned, facing Janet, and raised his hands in a gesture of futility. "I can't say what happened then, not with any certainty, but we know from the attack on Vincent that Junker was a scrapper. Perhaps they fought. Most boaters carry knives in their pockets. Junker and Lowry, both fishermen, probably carried them constantly. Lowry was bigger than Junker, so it was probably Junker who drew his knife first. He may have hoped to scare Lowry, or wound him, but whatever Junker's motives, Lowry wound up dead."

Henry resumed his pacing, stopping at the ends of his circuits to face his jury — Janet — to make eye contact and drive home his points.

"Junker knows the *Valkyrie* inside and out," Henry went on. "He's crewed on her. He knows exactly how to sink that boat. He can carry it out like the professional seaman he is, even though he's drunk. He knows the Salkum River harbor intimately. Finding Clark Creek is no problem for him. Of course he knows its relationship to Lowry's house.

"Maybe he saw the path through the woods from the creek bottom, or maybe he simply climbed up to the highway at the bridge and walked back to his car down the highway shoulder. It was the middle of the night, and no one was around." Henry turned to look west at the sparkling waves, then turned back to Janet.

"I know the house," he said. "I've been there often. If Junker parked his car beside the garage on that old road, it could have been missed even by someone who came down the drive, as long as he'd pulled it forward far enough. I agree that the woman in the Pinto was almost certainly Vicky Davis in her Mercury. The fact that Simpson said it might have been a turnaround shows she was backing out, and she would have backed out if she hadn't gone all the way down the drive. Maybe the lights were out. Maybe she lost her nerve. Maybe she knocked and got no answer. But I agree it was Vicky Davis. And you're right. No one will ever prove it."

Janet nodded. Coincidences happen, but not nearly as often as defendants allege, especially in homicide cases.

"So Lowry's reported lost at sea," Henry continued, "but Junker worries. He's afraid he might have left some trace of physical evidence in the skiff. There would have been a lot of blood. He was drunk. He can't be sure. He either knows or he finds out some way to get rid of it. They're double-hulled aluminum with watertight compartments, right?"

Janet nodded.

"It *could* be sunk, then," Henry went on, "or maybe cut up and destroyed if he could get his hands on a welding torch. My guess is he ran it up or down the coast and either sold it to someone who wouldn't talk or abandoned it where it would wash up on the rocks somewhere you can't get to by land." Henry waved a dismissive hand. "There are several possible explanations." He resumed his story. "So Vern borrows someone's Whaler, and you know they're a very popular make, and comes and gets the skiff. I simply don't believe Vern Junker, a professional seaman, couldn't somehow have gotten rid of that skiff."

Henry kept his tone soft, his voice persuasive, just loud enough to be heard above the waves crashing on the rocks below. He continued.

"Everything is fine, so far. Junker relaxes. He's safe. Lowry's lost at sea. But then the *Valkyrie's* found." Janet nodded, caught up in Henry's carefully crafted tale.

"He's questioned. You break his first story. Perhaps he can't remember exactly what he did. His health is gone; perhaps his memory went with it. He can't be sure he didn't leave traces. He alibis Catherine, hoping she can alibi him, but though she can say he left, she can't say he didn't come back.

"He's a haunted man. He's guilty and he knows it. He either has or gets some barbiturates. He feels you closing in. He knows you're looking for the skiff. All his original reasons for moving it still apply. If he sold it, he could be worried about your tracing the sale. The buyer might come forward if there was no question of prosecution."

"He goes to Vincent because he's scared?" Janet asked.

"Yes. He really does want to leave town. Lowry's attempted rape of Sally was good for blackmail once. Why not again? But Vincent stalls him. Junker tries to rob Vincent, but gets too little, and Vincent gets hurt. I think you're right, Junker did go to Vicky. But she's strong-minded. She has an ironclad alibi. She turns him down flat. Now all his avenues of escape are exhausted, except one. He gets acetaminophen capsules from her for his headache, then goes home and takes the barbiturates to ease the rest of his pains."

Henry turned to face Janet again. The lulling quality of his storyteller's voice vanished. In businesslike tones, he said, "I think that covers everything. That will make a very nice official version. Leaving Vicky's role out of it, of course."

Janet raised both her eyebrows in surprise. Henry was making her a present of this story. Implicit in the offer was a promise of support for her. Henry's offer meant most of the county's litigation lawyers intended to back her. The backing of her professional peers would overcome any objections Daniels might raise. It could swing the election in her favor, despite her failure on the island. She felt a glimmer of hope.

"Why did I get this search warrant, then?" Janet asked.

Henry shrugged. "That's simple. You're conscientious and thorough. With Junker dead, he couldn't be tried. Catherine would always come under some suspicion unless she was completely cleared. After all, she *did* inherit. Your warrant has exonerated her. It ties up the last loose end. She could actually be grateful that you completely eliminated her from any suspicion."

"Are you suggesting a press conference?" Janet raised an eyebrow. With this one additional move, Daniels would be completely blocked. There would be no objections for him to raise, no criticisms he could make.

"For you, yes. I'll release a written statement. With my client's permission, of course. It will be nice timing for you. You're going to announce your candidacy this Friday, aren't you?"

"You're being very generous, Henry." Henry would know that she saw the value of the exchange.

"No, I'm not." Henry's voice was firm. "This solution — and it's really the only possible one — is the right one for my client. That it also benefits us as lawyers is purely incidental. I want you elected Prosecutor. You and I don't always agree, but I always know where you stand, and you do what you say you'll do. That makes for a good working relationship."

Janet's mouth twisted into an involuntary half-smile. She had gambled, she had lost, and now, unexpectedly, her stake was pushed back across the table, doubled.

"I'd appreciate it a great deal if you had time to serve on my election committee," Janet said, willing to press her luck.

Henry nodded. "I could do that. I always planned to support you." Henry's gaze switched to a point over Janet's shoulder. She turned to see the detectives coming towards them.

"If you'll tell them," Henry said, "I'll go get Catherine's authority to release a statement."

Janet nodded. "I'll see you at the boat."

When Janet returned to the dock, Nic was sitting on the rocks above the harbor, her knees tucked under her chin and the collar of her grey fleece pullover pulled up around her ears. Janet couldn't see the expression on her face. Catherine was nowhere in sight. Henry emerged from the cabin of the sailboat as Janet started down the path. He was smiling. Nic immediately climbed down from the rocks and went aboard *Wayward*.

Henry nodded as soon as he caught Janet's gaze. They met on the ramp. "All set," Henry murmured. "We'll fix up the timing for our statements on the boat."

Catherine poked her head out *Wayward's* companionway as soon as the police boat pulled away from the dock and turned to head back to sea. As soon as the boat was out of sight, she went on deck. Nic followed.

She stood in the after portion of the cockpit, one hand on the wheel, facing Nic. *She looks so right there,* Nic thought. And then she had a flash of insight — Catherine was hers at heart, she realized, no matter how long it took to gently let Catherine become aware of it on her own.

"Henry says it's over," Catherine said hesitantly. "They're going to issue statements saying I'm completely cleared."

"Good," Nic said. "That boxes Janet. She can't ever come back after you again."

"That's what Henry said." Catherine twisted one hand around the wheel. Her braid fell over her shoulder. Unconsciously, she took it into her other hand. "I asked Henry if I could go away for a while. He said it was a good idea. Henry and the bank take care of almost everything anyway, so I wouldn't have to do a lot of arranging. Get a graduate student or somebody to live here and collect the data I need. That wouldn't be hard. There aren't too many summer jobs in this part of the world."

"Does that mean you're going with me?" Nic's heart leapt.

Catherine shook her hair away from her face and looked directly at Nic. Her face was radiant as she held out her hand and spoke. "Yes," she said. "I am."

※

Janet watched *Wayward* from the rail of the police boat. The crew started the engines and took in the lines. As the boat pulled away from the dock, she wondered if she'd ever see Catherine again. To her surprise, she found that it no longer mattered. She knew what had really happened between Catherine and Lowry now, and that told her all she needed to know about why Catherine had broken up with her.

As *Wayward* receded into the distance, Janet realized she was glad things had worked out in exactly this way. Though she knew in her heart her theory, not Henry's, was the truth, prosecuting a woman for killing her former abuser was a professional duty that Janet would have found a personal ordeal. Suddenly lighthearted, she turned away from the island and went forward to stand on the patrol boat's bow. It was time to look toward the future.

The End

More Fiction to Stir the Imagination from Rising Tide Press

RETURN TO ISIS
Jean Stewart
It is the year 2093, and Whit, a bold woman warrior from an Amazon nation, rescues Amelia from a dismal world where females are either breeders or drones. During their arduous journey back to the shining all-women's world of Artemis, they are unexpectedly drawn to each other. This engaging first book in the trilogy has it all—romance, mystery, and adventure.
Lambda Literary Award Finalist
ISBN 0-9628938-6-2; 192 Pages; $9.99

ISIS RISING
Jean Stewart
In this stirring romantic fantasy, the familiar cast of lovable characters begin to rebuild the colony of Isis, burned to the ground ten years earlier by the dread Regulators. But evil forces threaten to destroy their dream. A swashbuckling futuristic adventure and an endearing love story all rolled into one.
ISBN 0-9628938-8-9; 192 Pages; $11.99

WARRIORS OF ISIS
Jean Stewart
At last, the third lusty tale of high adventure and passionate romance among the Freeland Warriors. Arinna Sojourner, the evil product of genetic engineering, vows to destroy the fledgling colony of Isis with her incredible psychic powers. Whit, Kali, and other warriors battle to save their world, in this novel bursting with life, love, heroines and villains.
Lambda Literary Award Finalist
ISBN 1-883061-03-2; 256 Pages; $11.99

DEADLY RENDEZVOUS: A Toni Underwood Mystery
Diane Davidson
A string of brutal murders in the middle of the desert plunges Lieutenant Toni Underwood and her lover Megan into a high profile investigation which uncovers a world of drugs, corruption and murder, as well as the dark side of the human mind. An explosive, fast-paced, action-packed whodunit.
ISBN 1-883061-02-4; 224 pages; $9.99

PLAYING FOR KEEPS
Stevie Rios
In this sparkling tale of love and adventure, Lindsay West, an oboist, travels to Caracas, where she meets three people who change her life forever: Rob Heron a gay man, who becomes her dearest friend; Her lover Mercedes Luego, a lovely cellist, who takes Lindsay on a life-altering adventure down the Amazon; And the mysterious jungle-dwelling woman Arminta, who touches their souls. ISBN 1-883061-07-5; $10.99

ROMANCING THE DREAM
Heidi Johanna
A charming, erotic and imaginative love story which is also the tale of how women, together, have the power to make dreams happen. Set in the Pacific Northwest, it follows the lives of a group of visionary women who decide to take over their small town and create a lesbian haven. It will delight you with its gentle humor, beautiful love scenes, and fine writing. $8.95

DREAMCATCHER
Lori Byrd
This timeless story of love and friendship illuminates a year in the life of Sunny Calhoun, a college student, who falls in love with Eve Phillips, a literary agent. A richly woven narrative which captures the wonder and pain of love between a younger and an older woman—a woman facing AIDS with spirited courage and humor. ISBN 1-883061-06-7; 192 Pages: $9.99

LOVESPELL
Karen Williams
A deliciously erotic and humorous love story in which Kate Gallagher, a shy veterinarian, and Allegra, who has magic at her fingertips, fall in love. A masterful blend of fantasy and reality, this beautifully written story will warm your heart and delight your imagination.
ISBN 0-9628938-2-X; 192 Pages; $9.95

NIGHTSHADE
Karen Williams
After witnessing a fateful hit-and-run accident, Alex Spherris finds herself the new owner of a magical bell, which some people would kill for. She is ushered into a strange fantasy world and meets Orielle, who melts her frozen heart. Don't miss this delightfully imaginative romance spun in the best tradition of storytelling. ISBN 1-883061-08-3; $11.99

NO WITNESSES
Nancy Sanra

This cliff-hanger of a mystery set in San Francisco, introduces Detective Tally McGinnis, the brains and brawn behind the Phoenix Detective Agency. But Tally is no great sleuth at protecting her own heart. And so, when her ex-lover Pamela Tresdale is arrested for the grisly murder of a wealthy Texas heiress, Tally rushes to the rescue. Despite friends' warnings, Tally is drawn once again into Pamela's web of deception and betrayal, as she attempts to clear her and find the real killer. A gripping whodunit.
ISBN 1-883061-05-9; 192 Pages; $9.99

DANGER IN HIGH PLACES:
An Alix Nicholson Mystery
Sharon Gilligan

Set against the backdrop of Washington, D.C., this riveting mystery introduces freelance photographer and amateur sleuth, Alix Nicholson. Alix stumbles on a deadly scheme surrounding AIDS funding, and with the help of a lesbian congressional aide, unravels the mystery.
ISBN 0-9628938-7-0; 176 Pages, $9.99

DANGER! CROSS CURRENTS:
An Alix Nicholson Mystery
Sharon Gilligan

The exciting sequel to *Danger in High Places* brings freelance photographer Alix Nicholson face-to-face with an old love and a murder. When Alix's landlady, a real estate developer, turns up dead, and her much younger lover, Leah Claire, is the prime suspect, Alix launches a frantic campaign to find the real killer. ISBN 1-883061-01-6; 192 Pages; $9.99

HEARTSTONE AND SABER
Jacqui Singleton

You can almost hear the sabers clash in this rousing tale of good and evil, of passionate love, of warrior queens and white witches. Cydell, the imperious queen of Mauldar, and Elayna, the Fair Witch of Avoreed, join forces to combat the evil that menaces the empire, and in the course of doing that, find rapturous love.
ISBN 1-883061-00-8; 224 Pages; $10.99

CORNERS OF THE HEART
Leslie Grey
A captivating novel of love and suspense in which beautiful French-born Chris Benet and English professor Katya Michaels meet and fall in love. But their budding love is shadowed by a vicious killer, whom they must outwit. Your heart will pound as the story races to its heart-stopping conclusion. ISBN 0-9628938-3-8; 224 pages; $9.95

SHADOWS AFTER DARK
Ouida Crozier
When wings of death spread over Kyril's home world, she is sent to Earth on a mission—find a cure for the deadly disease. Once here she meets and falls in love with Kathryn, who is enthralled yet horrified to learn that her mysterious, darkly exotic lover is a vampire. This tender, beautifully written love story is the ultimate lesbian vampire novel! ISBN 1-883061-50-4; 224 Pages; $9.95

EDGE OF PASSION
Shelley Smith
This sizzling novel about an all-consuming love affair between a younger and an older woman is set in colorful Provincetown. A gripping love story, which is both fierce and tender, it will keep you breathless until the last page. ISBN 0-9628938-1-1; 192 Pages; $8.95

YOU LIGHT THE FIRE
Kristen Garrett
Here's a grown-up **Rubyfruit Jungle**—sexy, spicy, and sidesplittingly funny. Take a gorgeous, sexy, high school math teacher and put her together with a raunchy, commitment-shy, ex-rock singer, and you've got a hilarious, unforgettable love story. ISBN 0-9628938-5-4; $9.95

EMERALD CITY BLUES
Jean Stewart
When the comfortable yuppie world of Chris Olson and Jennifer Hart collides with the desperate lives of Reb and Flynn, two lesbian runaways struggling to survive on the streets of Seattle, the froecast is trouble. A warm-hearted, gritty, enormously readable novel of contemporary lesbigay life which raises real questions about the meaning of family and community, and about the walls we construct around our hearts. Finally, *Emerald City Blues* is a celebration of the healing powers of love. ISBN 1-883061-09-1; $11.99

HOW TO ORDER

TITLE	AUTHOR	PRICE
❑ Corners of the Heart-Leslie Grey		9.95
❑ Danger! Cross Currents-Sharon Gilligan		9.99
❑ Danger in High Places-Sharon Gilligan		9.95
❑ Deadly Rendezvous-Diane Davidson		9.99
❑ Dreamcatcher-Lori Byrd		9.99
❑ Edge of Passion-Shelley Smith		9.95
❑ Emerald City Blues-Jean Stewart		11.99
❑ Heartstone and Saber-Jacqui Singleton		10.99
❑ Isis Rising-Jean Stewart		11.99
❑ Love Spell-Karen Williams		9.99
❑ Nightshade-Karen Williams		11.99
❑ No Witnesses-Nancy Sanra		9.99
❑ Playing for Keeps-Stevie Rios		10.99
❑ Return to Isis-Jean Stewart		9.99
❑ Romancing the Dream-Heidi Johanna		8.95
❑ Rough Justice-Claire Youmans		10.99
❑ Shadows After Dark-Ouida Crozier		9.99
❑ Warriors of Isis-Jean Stewart		11.99
❑ You Light the Fire-Kristen Garrett		9.95

Please send me the books I have checked. I enclose a check or money order (not cash), plus $3 for the first book and $1 for each additional book to cover shipping and handling. Or bill my ❑Visa ❑Mastercard ❑Amer. Express.

Or call our Toll Free Number 1-800-648-5333 if using a credit card.

CARD # _____ EXP. DATE_____

SIGNATURE_____

NAME (PLEASE PRINT) _____

ADDRESS _____

CITY_____ STATE_____ZIP_____

❑ New York State residents add 8.5% tax to total.

RISING TIDE PRESS
5 KIVY ST., HUNTINGTON STATION, NY 11746